Iain Hollingshead studied Arabic and History at Cambridge
and writes a regular column in Saturday's *Guardian*,
called 'Loose Ends'. He has also written features for the
Daily Telegraph and the *Sunday Times*.

After graduating with a First in History, Iain worked for a year
in Westminster, including nine months on the successful 'Vote 2004' campaign.
During this time he found himself deported (somewhat unfairly)
from Brussels, interviewed on the *Today* programme and featured in
'The Sun Says'. In 2000 he was also deported from Ecuador
for having the wrong visa in his passport.

Iain is twenty-five years old and lives in London
with two long-suffering flatmates
You can find out a little more about |
www.iainhollingshead.co.uk

TWENTY SOMETHING

TWENTY SOMETHING

THE QUARTER-LIFE CRISIS
OF JACK LANCASTER

IAIN HOLLINGSHEAD

DUCKWORTH

First published in the UK in 2006 by
Gerald Duckworth & Co. Ltd.
90-93 Cowcross Street, London EC1M 6BF
Tel: 020 7490 7300
Fax: 020 7490 0080
inquiries@duckworth-publishers.co.uk
www.ducknet.co.uk

A catalogue record for this book is available
from the British Library

ISBN 0 7156 3557 3
EAN 9780715635575

Printed and bound in Great Britain by
Creative Print and Design, Ebbw Vale, Wales

To my parents, with much love and gratitude
(and apologies for the rude bits in what follows)

Soon we'll be out amid the cold world's strife.
Soon we'll be sliding down the razor blade of life.

(Tom Lehrer, Bright College Days)

.

PROLOGUE

'Fred, I was on the BBC website yesterday at work, and I started looking at their "On This Day" page. And do you know what I found out?'

'No, do tell,' said Flatmate Fred.

'Well, I discovered that, on this day, 30th December, in 1958, Fidel Castro's rebel guerrillas were engaged in hand-to-hand combat with government forces outside Santa Clara. I also learned that, on this day in 1971, 60,000 Iranians were deported by the Iraqis in freezing conditions at the border town of Ghassr Shirin.'

'That's very interesting,' said Flatmate Fred.

'It is. But then I suddenly realised that on this day, 30th December, today, I, Jack Lancaster, twenty-five years of age, heir to three million years of evolution and seventeen years of education, got up at 6.45am, showered, shat, shaved, put on Thursday's shirt and tie combination, read *Metro* on the tube, spent twelve hours staring into space at a highly paid job that I hate and then read the *Evening Standard* on the tube home again.'

'Yeah, it's not exactly *la vida loca*, is it?' said Flatmate Fred. 'It sounds a bit like you're having a quarter-life crisis.'

'What's that?' I asked.

'Like a midlife crisis, but worse,' said Flatmate Fred.

'But a quarter-life crisis can only be half as bad as a midlife crisis, surely.'

'Oh no, it's much worse,' said Flatmate Fred. 'It's twenty years premature. No one gives you any sympathy and you're too young and insignificant to buy a sports car and run off with your secretary. Believe me, you have all the symptoms.'

'Really? Well, maybe you're right.'

'Well, maybe you should do something about it, then,' said Flatmate Fred. Maybe.

JANUARY

Saturday 1st January

There's something really bothering Lucy, and I just can't put my finger on it. Neither can she. She's not happy, she feels useless, undervalued, blah, blah. She thinks she's looking fat (she *is* looking fat), she misses home, she hates her job, etc. I don't listen to her properly.

'Are you menstrual?' I ask, wisely, to show that I do listen.

Nope, she's bloody well not, she's mental. Lucy has her own unique cycle, which is the inverse of most women's — twenty-one days on, seven days off. I tell her this. She smacks me lovingly in the balls, and I come the closest I ever have to the male pain threshold. I tell her that the agony is worse than childbirth.

'No, it's not,' she says, quietly, in that scary way of hers. 'You just don't understand. I'm so unhappy.'

'Well, sod it,' I tell her. 'I'm not happy either and I was not happy first.' And with this Wildean parting shot, I storm out of her flat to go and not listen to her somewhere else.

'Tosspot,' she screams dementedly after me.

It's 2am on New Year's Day and I have just spent the last six hours arguing with my girlfriend of three years. If you can predict the next twelve months on the basis of your New Year's Eve, it's going to be a very bad year.

Sunday 2nd January

Am I a tosspot?

Today is Sunday, the day of rest, the calm before the storm of next year, and it appears a suitably restful question to think about.

I conclude that I possess all the external and surface elements of tosspottery: I still smell my farts under the duvet, I think it's cool to binge-drink every weekend until I pass out and I can't listen to a girl for more than five minutes without drifting off and imagining what she'd look like naked.

I work in a graduate job in the city, I wear a pinstripe during the week and chinos on dress-down Fridays and I live in a nice little flat with low rent because my Mum went to school with Flatmate Fred's mum (who once slept with my dad — though no one knows I know this) and so gives us a very generous rent settlement on their West London pad.

In many ways I am a smog-breathing, twentysomething, graduate arse of a stereotype.

But are there hidden depths beneath that surface? Who knows? When the woman in Prêt gives me too much change, I tell her so. When she gives me the right amount, I pop the coppers in the little metal charity tin that they hide underneath the chocolate bars. I cry at a good film, send my mum a card on Mothering Sunday and enjoy surprising Lucy. Underneath my cynical roving eye, I'm a soppy, slushy romantic at heart.

If I return home early from work I give my tube Travelcard to a friendly smackhead so he can continue to pump cheap drugs into his damaged veins. I work long hours and feel guilty about earning so much money. I'd like to do some good in the world and I'd very much like to pack it all in and spend some time travelling on the east coast of Australia.

Lucy's right: I'm a tosspot.

Monday 3rd January

Sitting in my flat contemplating the year ahead.

It's not a glorious prospect: my job stinks, my girlfriend hates me and I'm a pessimistic, ungrateful sod. I am Jack the Lad; Jack of no trades, master of absolutely nothing at all. Modern demographics will keep me working for another fifty years. Modern medicine might keep me alive for another eighty years. I am twenty-five years old and pissing my life away waiting for nostalgia.

On a more uplifting note, Flatmate Fred suggested at the end of last year that I start keeping a diary in the hope that it inspires me to do something worthwhile with my time.

'And how exactly does that work?' I asked.

'You can record your actions and see where you're going wrong,' he suggested. 'Write down your thoughts and then think your way out of your current crisis.'

'But only fat women, politicians and psychos keep diaries,' I protested.

'Well, call it a narrative account, then. Keep it lively. Update it when you feel like it.'

'But don't you remember that recent study which showed diarists to be the unhappiest and unhealthiest group in society?'

'Jack, you'll fit in perfectly.'

Flatmate Fred always wins. Middle-aged losers buy fast cars and start dressing like teenagers. I'm going to write a diary. Keeping in the spirit of things, here are my belated resolutions for the new year:

I will

- play my full part at work as a proactive team member
- be a self-starter when it comes to exploring alternative career plans
- think outside of the box regularly
- attempt to move the goalposts before the close of play
- drink less
- try to love Lucy more/break up with her in a mature and dignified manner
- explore my purpose in life
- read two chapters of the Bible every evening, thereby finishing it by the end of the year
- do the same with the Koran
- explore suitable remedies for premature hair loss before it is too late
- check my testicles regularly for lumps
- set up tax-deductible direct debits to worthy charities
- exercise every second day and turn my blancmange into a six-pack
- maintain a non-political, non-psycho, non-fat-woman narrative account of my year in diary format

I will not

- indulge in blue-sky thinking or run up any kites
- spend every weekend binge-drinking

- be so dismissive to my mum
- masturbate more than four times per week
- flirt with anyone at work
- be a tosspot
- wallow in a quarter-life crisis
- complain about working past 9pm
- read *Metro* on the tube when I could take a book instead
- be such a hypochondriac

And so to bed. Alone. With Adam and Eve.

Tuesday 4th January

Woke up to the sound of John Humphrys tearing slabs of raw flesh off a cabinet minister — this is another of my New Year's resolutions: listen to Radio 4 in the morning and not commercial radio — and briefly contemplated committing suicide.

Not Mr Humphrys' fault, but the prospect of going back to work today was almost too much to face. Felt marginally better after switching over to Magic FM and singing along to 'What's the Story, Morning Glory?' while indulging in some quality Jack-time. Congratulated myself on this little postmodern irony and made a mental note that I'm only allowed three more this week.

Yesterday was a bank holiday — but, the city being the shitty city, at least half of my colleagues had come into work. What a bunch of brown-nosers. Is it only bankers who work on bank holidays? I told Rupert (my bald line manager) that I'd been at home indulging in some downtime and thinking out of the box.

'Thinking about your girlfriend's box, more like,' he quipped.

Er, no.

But, while we're on the theme of boxes, let me tell you about investment banking. Essentially it involves putting large numbers of apparently meaningless figures into Microsoft Excel boxes. Any figures will do — one of my more entertaining colleagues once projected a blue chip's profit and loss column on the basis of his mates' telephone numbers. His team couldn't work out why so many of the forecasts started '207' and '208' (but mainly '207', as we don't like to have too many friends who live in Outer London). Once you've done this, you turn it into a 'model', which should be as opaque and needlessly complicated as possible. Then you make it all up into a presentation, which your boss will take credit for if the client likes it and blame you for if he doesn't.

One day, when you're thirty going on ninety-five and the concept of fun and a full head of hair is a distant memory, you'll marry a beautiful stupid woman who is madly in love with your wallet. Ten years later, she'll no longer be beautiful (but she'll still be stupid), and you'll have two kids with your looks and her brains whose names you have great difficulty remembering. Fortunately, you won't mind by then, as you're the boss and you get to sleep with your secretary in return for expensive presents to ensure that your once-beautiful, always-dumb excuse for a wife remains in the dark.

It's a wonderful career, and I'm very excited about it.

Wednesday 5th January

When I got home at 10pm last night, Flatmate Fred, a 'freelance' writer, was in a filthy mood, as I'd woken him with my morning sing-along. I tactfully suggested that if he got up before midday this would be less of a problem. Freelance Freeloading Flatmate Fred didn't like this lifestyle tip and stormed out of the room, still in his dressing gown from the weekend. Perhaps when your boss thinks you're slack and your girlfriend hates you, it's not a good idea to go and offend your only flatmate as well.

Talking of girlfriends, my domestic fun-bag rang at 11pm in search of a serious argument. When it became clear that I wasn't in the mood for chit-chat — what, did she expect me to apologise for calling her a vacuous, hormonal trollop? — she proposed a trial separation, and I agreed.

But after I'd injured my hand thumping down the phone, it occurred to me that there were all sorts of small points that we hadn't clarified. Just what the hell does 'trial separation' mean? When does the trial end? Who gets to give the guilty/not guilty verdict? How separate are we meant to be? Is texting allowed? Emails? Is it supposed to be a break which brings us back together, renewed and rejuvenated? Or is it a trial run for a much more permanent separation? Am I allowed to pull other people? As with many things, the devil is in the detail.

I try to ring Lucy back to clear up some of these troubling matters, but she's turned her phone off.

Devilish filly. I go to sleep fantasising about her sister by way of revenge.

Friday 7th January

Only three hours' sleep, as Flatmate Fred heard last night that he'd got an advance on his latest book idea (advance came from Daddy), so we went out to celebrate the greatest achievement of his life so far.

Turned up for work in odd socks.

Rupert (bald): 'It's dress-down Friday, not dress-like-a-tramp Friday.'

After that little vignette, however, the day got significantly better. Managed not only to leave at 6pm (a record), but also to fiddle my expense account so I could get a free taxi home (not usually allowed unless you work after 9pm).

While I'm cooking the books, Flatmate Fred is attempting to cook chicken for six of our friends. Flatmate Fred can't cook. You might have thought that, in three years of loafing around, the freeloading freelancer would have progressed beyond *Young, Broke and Hungry,* but he hasn't. When I enter the kitchen, the fire alarm's going off and he's running round the flat in his 'laundry day' Y-fronts, sweating like a pig and trying to smother the flames with the introduction to his third unpublished book. Not many people can set fire to roast chicken. Flatmate Fred can.

But, by 7.30pm, it's all sorted and our friends start arriving. Is it a supper party or is it a dinner party? Conundrum. We discuss this at some length and conclude that, while you take someone out for dinner, you have supper at home. And if that supper is a party? Then it's a dinner party, unless you're over thirty and it's a bring-the-kids-in-their-carrycots/leave-the-kids-at-home-with-the-babysitter-whom-Daddy's-shagging-type event, in which case it's a supper party. Simple.

But my friends are a good bunch really, despite their dubious conversational abilities: Flatmate Fred, the posing, pampered drop-out living in Daddy's flat; Rick, my ginger best mate, with his dad's looks and his mum's brains; and Jasper, who gave up a job in the city (which he was very good at) to become an actor (which he is very bad at).

There were girls there, too, of course — we needed someone to laugh at our jokes. I'd met them in alphabetical order. Claire and I used to play doctors and nurses together (as toddlers), I sent my first Valentine's card to Katie (aged twelve), my first kiss was with Mel (aged fourteen) and I lost my virginity to Susie at university aged nineteen (although I thought she was called Amanda at the time, which would have spoiled the alphabetical-order thing).

Katie is Rick's twin sister (Rick, but hairless in the right places), Jasper fancies Claire (I got there first aged two — back off), Claire fancies me (she's only human), Rick fancies anyone in a skirt, Katie fancies Jasper (which really annoys Rick) and Mel and Susie are both madly in love with Flatmate Fred, which is entirely wasted on him, as Flatmate Fred only fancies himself (and maybe Jasper, but this remains unsubstantiated conjecture).

It's so confusing that even we have forgotten the order and disorder of our little web. No matter. Considering that the evening had all the sexual explosive energy of a suicide bomber entering heaven to collect his seventy-two virgins, it was a most successful gathering.

And so to bed. Imagining a fivesome with Claire, Katie, Mel and Susie.

Saturday 8th January

Woke up with a herd of buffalo playing five-a-side football behind my eyes. Felt too rough to get up, so I lay in bed thinking about Lucy.

Sadly, it's horrifyingly simple in the cold, painful light of morning: we've reached the final stage of our natural relationship. We've done mad passionate shagging. We've done falling completely in love. And now we're completely done out. I know that she's not The One, whatever that might be. And when you've been together for three years and suddenly realise this, everything else falls away.

I used to enjoy her flirting with my friends. Now I get insanely jealous every time she talks to one of them. We used to have spontaneous sex in public places. Now she tells me every time she's faked an orgasm. I used to love the fact that she sounded so posh that she probably wore pashmina knickers. Now I shiver every time she opens her mouth. I hate her taste in music, I hate her friends and I hate the way she says, 'OK, then' at the end of every telephone conversation. I hate her clothes, I hate the decorations in her flat and I especially hate the way she drives her detestable little car.

There was a time when she could do no wrong. Now she can do no right. All her endearing eccentricities have become unbearably annoying faults. And I just can't cope pretending to like her any more.

I hate myself for hating her, and I hate myself for not being brave enough to do anything about it. We've been going out for three years, but if I'm honest about it, I've spent half that time inventing convenient internal excuses to delay breaking up: 'But I've already bought her a birthday present/it's only two months till Valentine's Day/what if she went off with any of my friends?/I might never have sex again' etc. etc.

In fact, I was trying so hard to think of something I did like about the two of us that the football-playing buffalo returned with a vengeance to put a stop to any further thought processes. I crawled to the sofa and watched TV. The most successful thing I did all day was take my dressing gown off (twelve hours after putting it on) and go back to bed.

Sunday 9th January

Home, sweet Home Counties, to visit my darling 'rentals – the street name I use to refer to Mummy and Daddy so my mates don't take the piss too badly. I always wanted to call them 'Mum 'n' Dad', but they're just not 'Mum' 'n' Dad' types. So it's stuck — Mummy and Daddy in the vocative; 'rentals in the third person.

Daddy (alpha male rental) meets me at the station.

'Who's your daddy?' he asks, climbing out of the battered Volvo.

'Er, you are, Daddy,' I reply, pushing the dog off the front seat and getting in beside him to give him a hug. No Public Displays of Affection for our family.

'Wicked,' he says, pulling away in third gear while trying to do the Ali G Westside sign.

Occasional excruciating references to outdated popular culture aside, my dad is the world's loveliest man. Mates who come to visit seem to spend as much time talking to him as they do to me. He is a retired headmaster, the same yesterday, today and for ever — a solid man mountain of integrity and bonhomie.

'Your mother's in a filthy mood,' the man mountain warns me on the way back in the car.

Never 'Mummy', never 'Amelia' — it's always 'your mother', as if he were somehow separated from any involvement in the process.

But he wasn't wrong about Mummy. She was in a tub-thumping, bottom-clenching howler of a grump. And, unsurprisingly, it was all my fault.

'How could you be so insensitive to Lucy?' she demands, refusing to kiss me as I walk through the kitchen door.

'What do you mean, "insensitive"?'

'I mean, breaking-up-with-her insensitive. That girl's the best thing that ever happened to you.'

'No, she's not. She's not even in the top ten of good things that have happened to me. And it's only a trial separation. And how did you know, anyway?'

Lucy, bless every little conniving cell in her beautiful body, is so bloody close to my mum that she'd rung her in floods of tears to indulge in a mutual oestrogen bonding, Jack bashing session.

My mum likes Lucy because she's just like her — vacuous, petty, pretty, snobby and attached to someone much better than her. Harsh — but there, I've said it.

Monday 10th January

It's now a week since I made my New Year's resolutions, and I've just flicked back through my diary to check on my progress.

Not good.

At work I'm treading water, spending most of the day entering obscure opinions under a variety of aliases in the 'Have your say' section of the BBC news website. I've drunk forty-two units in a week (the twenty-four of these on Friday night making me an official binge drinker — result). My Bible reading stalled on the sixth day (of creation, not of January) and I've just realised that I started at the wrong end of the Koran.

While I've updated my diary almost every day, I've only really used it to slag off my friends, my job and my mother. The only serious exercise I've undertaken is masturbation, and I've exceeded my limit of four for the week (by a factor of three, for which I blame Lucy's absence). I've given nothing to charity and I'm getting fatter by the second. On the plus side, I haven't flirted with anyone at work (because they're all male) and my testicles and hairline appear to be behaving themselves.

And I seem to have fulfilled my desire to 'love Lucy more/break up with her in a mature and dignified manner' by writing horrible things about her and brokering a trial separation with the luscious little frollop.

In a bid to remedy this, I phone her in the evening to try to talk things over.

'Why the fuck did you ring my mum to talk about us?' I ask in a conciliatory way.

'My mum,' she mimics. 'Little Jacksy's Mumsies-Wumsies. Mummy's not happy, is she?'

'Not as unhappy as Jack is.'

'Why are you referring to yourself in the third person?'

'Second sign of madness.'

'What's the first?'

'Deciding to go out with you.'

Click. Brrrrr. 15—0, Jack Lancaster.

Tuesday 11th January

Woke up this morning and counted at least thirty hairs on my pillow while listening to *Thought for the Day* on Radio 4 (Bishop of Liverpool talking about spiritual implications of the Congestion Charge).

Realised after a while that four of these were Lucy's (I haven't washed the sheets for two weeks), but it's still a worrying statistic. Five more came out in the shower and I swept my hair back to examine the view in the mirror. Aaaargh, spamhead! It's retreating in all directions like a brigade of Italian war heroes. Upwards, sideways, diagonally. This isn't meant to happen until your fifties. This is the end of my youth. Baldness goes hand in hand with arthritis, impotence and senility. It is the first sign of my mortality. I will never pull randomly again unless I'm at a cowboy party and wearing a hat.

Spent so long considering these unpleasant implications that I turned up late for work.

Rupert (bald): 'Why are you late for work?'

'Because my hair started falling out in the shower. I'm going to have a bald patch.'

'That's not a bald patch — that's the solar panel for your sex machine.'

It would take more than energy-harnessing sunshine to sort out my current excuse for a love life.

Wednesday 12th January

Not many things can make a hundred city bankers in an open-plan office stop what they're doing and simultaneously look in the same direction. The last time it happened was when the managing director's jilted wife evaded security and came up to the fourth floor to have a cat fight with his secretary. Apart from that, it would require news of an anthrax attack at Bank station — or maybe an announcement that we were going to IPO and could all retire early — to raise our collective noses from the grindstone.

The girl who arrived at work today, however, succeeded. She was a walking vision of everyone's perfect girl. Petite without being fragile, slim but curvy, blonde but natural, and a sweet angelic face which said, 'I'm the loveliest person in the world but if you were ever lucky enough to get me into bed I would go like *The Flying Scotsman*.' I caught the gaze of at least twenty guilty pairs of eyes belonging to twenty dirty minds who all, like me, had been imagining what it would be like to spend five minutes alone with her in the stationery cupboard. The death of gentlemanly capitalism? Rubbish.

I watch her as she moves about the room being introduced to her new colleagues by her 'buddy' — ironically, an American called Buddy who looks like the cat who's just frotted itself in the cream. Nervous, geeky analysts, who haven't spoken to anyone outside their team for years, wipe their messy Prêt hands on their polyester suits and shuffle to their feet to greet her. Confident M&A bankers swagger over to introduce themselves. Managing directors and vice presidents hitch up their red braces as if girding their loins for action and try to hold in their paunches. The secretaries all eye her warily.

But she never makes it as far as my corner of the room, settling instead in the Financial Institutes Group, the Basingstoke of the banking world. I watch as she makes herself comfortable, shuffling and shifting in her chair, her dark trouser suit pressed against the leather folds. Oh to be a £500 swivel chair now that January is here.

'Pssst.' I grab Buddy as he returns from his lap of honour. 'What's the fittie's name?'

'Leila — and don't even think about it, Jack. She's fifteen leagues out of your league.'

Leila. Lovely little Leila. There are a number of names which guarantee attractiveness — Lucys, Amys, Sarahs, Nikkys and Amelias are nearly always fine-looking fillies. But 'Leila' has an ethereal etymological beauty in a league of its own. It soars with the iambic Greek gods, it dances on Mount Olympus, it erupts with Mount Vesuvius. (Jack, you're talking crap.)

Tomorrow I'll find out her surname, look her up on the email database and send her some witty banter. In a month's time I'll give her a Valentine's card, pull her on 20th February, sleep with her on the 24th and go out with her by 3rd March.

In Arabic, *Leila* means 'night'; in English, it means 'Jack's'. I am delightedly, desperately, dribblingly in love-lust.

After all, I'm on a trial separation, aren't I? And I've been with Lucy for three years — I must be due a loyalty scheme upgrade by now.

Thursday 13th January

I've just Googled Leila. She was a wing defence for her school's under-16 netball team (no photos, unfortunately), spent a year doing charity work in South America and once proposed a motion at her university's union (Newcastle) in favour of more varieties of chocolate in the vending machines. Put it another way: she combines sufficient intelligence, compassion, sporting ability and endearing girliness to be crowned Jack's Number One Target. Google never lies.

More worryingly, her surname is Sidebottom. Her dad should be in The Hague on a war crimes trial for passing on that name to someone as beautiful as her. Leila Sidebottom. *Voilà la chute du sublime au ridicule.* I'd like to know which pig-arse idiot of an ancestor came up with that name.

'Can you tell me where I can barter my mule for some chariot wheels?'

'Ah yes, you want to go and see old Harold. He lives on the bottom side of the creek.'

'Ah, Harold Sidebottom — of course.'

I have to marry her to save her from herself.

Friday 14th January

Lads' night out.

At 7pm Buddy and I headed straight out after work for a couple of rounds and then met up with Flatmate Fred, Jasper and Rick in a pub in Fulham. We were an unlikely combination — two bankers, one freeloading freelancer, an actor and Rick, who never stays in a job long enough to have a job title. His current contribution to civilisation is to perform the ultra-quick voiceovers at the end of radio adverts   the gabbled disclaimers that end with 'terms and conditions apply'. This amuses just about everyone apart from Rick's dad, who is a QC and therefore has a proper job.

By the time we left the pub, we were completely slaughtered. Jasper suggested going somewhere to sweat off our alcohol intake and we all piled into a taxi.

'Drive on, James,' cried Flatmate Fred, banging the roof of the cab, 'and don't spare the horses.'

'Where are the horses?' asked Buddy.

I made a mental note that I was going to have no difficulty outshining him in front of Leila next week.

We pulled up in front of Mad Barry's and Buddy took charge. This was his domain. No clever little quips. This was business. He marched up to the bouncer and demanded that he let us all straight in.

'No, I won't. You'll go to the back of queue like everyone else.'

'But you don't understand. We're not everyone else. We have significantly more money than everyone else.'

'If you carry on like that, you're not coming in at all.'

'It's a simple economic choice. We have superior purchasing power to the rest of the people in this queue. If you let us in now, you'll be maximising shareholder value.'

Jasper at this point wisely intervened and led Buddy to the back of a queue, which only consisted of a few fifteen-year-olds, in any case. They all glowered at him with as much intimidation as four public schoolboys in pink shirts with upturned collars could muster.

Flatmate Fred, less wise, used this diversion to try and leap over the cord and walk in without paying. About six paces in, a Neanderthal hand descended on his shoulder.

'And what do you think you're doing?'

'Er, I don't know.'

'You're a dickhead, aren't you?'

'Er, yes.'

'Say it.'

'What?'

'Tell me that you're a dickhead.'

'Er, I'm a dickhead. I think I'll go home now.'

'No, you won't. You're coming in, and you're paying double.'

At which point the brute of a bouncer marched Flatmate Fred up to the vapid Sloane behind the counter and forced him to hand over £3 instead of £1.50. All of which shenanigans meant that it took us twenty minutes to get from queue to girls, instead of five.

Unfortunately, the path from queue to girls rarely runs smooth and we had no joy on the dance floor. By 2am we were all alone in an exhausted, sweaty, blokes-only circle, loving angels instead. We decided to head back to my place.

'Drive on, Sam, and don't keep the horses,' yelled Buddy with fire (and four bottles of champagne) in his belly.

'Buddy... Oh, never mind.'

The taxi dropped us several streets away, as Flatmate Fred was too drunk to remember whether we lived in a place, a street or a mews.

On the short walk home we passed a beautiful winter-flowering cherry tree in one of the private residents' gardens near our flat. The only sensible thing seemed to be to take it back with us. We were five drunk guys who hadn't scored. If we couldn't get a trophy pull, we could at least take a beer trophy home with us.

'Can't we just snap off a branch?' said Jasper.

'Bollocks to that,' I said, flushed with the scent of victory. 'We're taking the whole thing.'

Flatmate Fred was dispatched inside and came back with a saw. Feeling a bit like Hugh Grant (minus Julia Roberts, but plus metal blade) I climbed into the garden with the weapon of choice and did the dirty work on the trunk. Fifty panting minutes later we were sitting triumphantly in our kitchen with a sixty-kilo, two-metre mass of foliage. Buddy laid his weary head down in its soft leaves and passed out.

Saturday 15th January

'There's fucking stolen property in our goddamn fucking kitchen,' Flatmate Fred croaks as he walks into my room at ten the next morning.

'Huh?' The footballing buffalo are back in my head.

'There's a dense mass of fucking foliage in our motherfucking flat and I want to know how the fuck it got there.'

I feel like I'm in a Tarantino film. Next Flatmate Fred will be calling in Mr Big to help us get rid of the 'body' without trace.

I tell Flatmate Fred that it got there because he couldn't remember where we lived, caught sight of a *Prunus subhirtella* (aka winter-flowing cherry) on the walk home and then dashed inside to get a saw to help cut it down. He denies everything.

We go through to the kitchen to examine the damage and find Buddy surfacing from his soily slumbers. We take a photo so that we can frame him if things get nasty.

'Oh, hey, you guys,' he drawls, a flower lodged behind his left ear. 'I've just realised why the doorman didn't buy my line about maximising shareholder value. Mad Barry's isn't publicly listed; it's a limited company. I'm such a jerk.'

Buddy is indeed a jerk, but if I were compiling the top ten reasons as to why he is a jerk (which I might just do at work on Monday), his ignorance of Mad Barry's' corporate governance structure wouldn't feature highly.

By the time hangover TV drew to a close at 3pm, everyone had decided that the tree theft was someone else's fault. Buddy claimed exoneration on some obscure point of international law as he had used the tree as a pillow. Flatmate Fred, whose memory loss had evaporated, argued that he was using the episode as a research project for his book (Rick: 'Which book now? *101 Greatest Horticultural Thefts?*') and Jasper kindly pointed out in dramatic thespy tones that I had wielded the saw and was therefore the ringleader. At which point Rick added in the moronically slow voice he uses when he's not doing radio ads that the final buck lay with Flatmate Fred and me as the stolen property had come to rest in our flat. The others swiftly agreed and sidled off home.

Bastards.

Thursday 20th January

Came back from work to find Flatmate Fred waving a piece of paper excitedly in my face.

'What are you doing, you mad freak? And why are you wearing my dressing gown at eight in the evening?'

'Because mine's in the wash. But listen, Jack, I've cracked it. I've worked out how to save ourselves from going to prison.'

'Why would we be going to prison?'

'For stealing the *Prunus subhirtella*. They'd bang us up, and then we'd get banged up the bum by big black men called Ron.'

I briefly wonder whether Flatmate Fred might quite enjoy meeting big black Ron. He'd just have to remember not to pick up the soap in the shower — given his current hygiene regime, it wouldn't be too much of a problem.

'No, seriously,' he continued. 'Read this: it's an anonymous letter to the local residents' association. It will put us in the clear.'

Here is Flatmate Fred's epistle in full:

Dear Flower People,

In a moment of madness last Friday evening, we cut down one of the winter-flowering cherries in the private garden in Onslow Mews. Like the forbidden fruit, it is an item of great beauty. We should have left it well alone.

In a spirit of utter remorse and shame, we now return the item to you. While it may have temporarily brightened our lives, it has blackened our souls for ever.

To ease this process, we are enclosing some money. We shall also be donating a small sum to a suitable charity. Alcoholics Anonymous would seem an appropriate choice under the circumstances.

Yours sincerely,
Stupid White Men

'Fred,' I said, after rereading the *chef-d'oeuvre* that has taken him four days to compose, 'that's lovely. But we're not at school any more. You can't just write an apology note to Matron and hope it's all going to be OK. And how exactly do you intend to hand over the *Prunus subhirtella* and the cash anonymously?'

'It's simple. What comes down goes up. Swings and roundabouts. Circle of life. We'll take it back down to the gate and leave an envelope full of cash.'

'Like bollocks we will. It weighs a ton and some tramp will nick the cash.'

'Some South Kensington tramp?'

'Yep, or a bunch of filthy-rich yuppies on their way home from a night out.'

It's staying in our kitchen and that's that. Sod the flower people. There are better anonymous gestures than a mouldy tree and a lump of cash. I think I'll pluck some of the rose-pink flowers and leave them on Leila's desk.

Friday 21st January

Felt like a prize plonker stepping on to the underground in the morning with a bunch of stolen flowers tucked under my suit. I think the person sitting opposite was sniggering at me over his copy of *Metro*.

He would have sniggered even more if he'd known what was going to happen later. By some nasty quirk of fate I walk into the lift at exactly the same time as Leila. There are just the three of us: Leila, me and the drooping *Prunus subhirtella*.

'Are you going down?' she asks.

Don't say, 'Only if you press the right buttons.' Don't say, 'Only if you press the right buttons. Don't say, 'Only if you press the right buttons.'

'Only if you press the right buttons.'

'I'm sorry?'

'Sorry?'

'I didn't hear what you said.' Her voice is a Galaxy bar advert of pure silk. She genuinely didn't hear.

'Erm … Yep, free breakfast in the basement for me, too.'

Free breakfast. Pure bloody Noël Coward.

She smiles. It's like someone has turned up a wattage dial in her back. She glows. I'm glowing, too — with sweat. I try to smile back, wrinkling up my forehead so she can't see the beginnings of my receding hairline.

'Flowers for the canteen ladies?' She motions to the dripping bunch, which is forming a small puddle between us on the lift floor, a little love loch of my awkwardness.

'Oh, ha! No. They're for my granny. It's her birthday.'

My confidence hits the basement about the same time as the lift.

'See you, then,' she says.

I doubt it. I'm a cack-handed, flower-stealing arse of a Casanova. I put the flowers in the shredder. Which broke.

Saturday 22nd January

Lucy rang to request a meeting for tomorrow. 'Somewhere cheap and cheerful.' A pity that she's so expensive and miserable.

'What am I?' I raged. 'Some sort of awkward fixture that has to be keyed into your little Outlook diary? Private appointment, out of the office, highlighted in pink, set reminder fifteen minutes beforehand.'

'It's green for private appointments,' she said calmly. 'Magenta pink is for vital appointments that absolutely can't be moved. And you're not one of those.'

Cow. What kind of colour is magenta pink, anyway? Magenta pink cow.

Before Lucy rang, my mind had been on other things such as Excel spreadsheets, stolen trees and Leila. But her call made me realise how much I'd been bottling up my thoughts again. I know I've written some horrible things about her, but my mind is all jumbled up. I'm scared by commitment, but I'm equally frightened at the prospect of losing her for ever. I don't want her myself, but I don't want anyone else going within five paces of her, either.

Maybe all relationships go through this 'I hate everything about you' stage and then you come out the other side and get a mortgage and get married.

Then again, maybe I should develop a spine at some point.

Sunday 23rd January

My spine and I went along after lunch today with the intention of having a brief chat about our trial separation and proposing a lengthy adjournment before making a final decision.

I hadn't counted on her looking stunning. She'd stuck to the first rule of meeting up with your exes/trial exes: Make it look like you're coping very well without them.

Unfortunately, she really was coping very well without with me.

'Jack, I kissed someone last night.'

I felt like my entire world had caved in. I wanted to be sick — preferably on her. How dare she? I was not happy first. No wonder she hadn't replied to my text requesting further information on the rules regarding pulling during our trial separation. She had been too busy getting on with it herself.

But I was determined to be big about it. Rule two of meeting exes/trial exes: Never let them realise that they can hurt you. After all, hadn't I almost given a bunch of stolen flowers to a colleague who didn't know my name in a lift? 15—15.

'Who?'

'I'd rather not say.'

'Is it someone I know?'

'Yes.'

'Then, who the hell is it? Whose dirty little tonsils have you been playing hockey with?'

She paused, and then, with a flash of triumph in her eyes, dealt the deathblow: 'Rick's.'

I didn't know whether to laugh or cry. So I cried. Right there in an alfresco bar in Covent Garden, I, Jack Lancaster, wept my bloody eyes out for the first time since my hamster died when I was thirteen. But it was easier back then. At least Frisky had just died. He hadn't been playing tonsil hockey with my best mate.

For some reason, the whole twenty-first century man thing went down quite well with Lucy.

'Oh, Jack,' she simpered. 'I'm so sorry. It was a silly drunken thing. I didn't know it would cause so much emotion in you.'

Not so much... so much emotion; more like, so *many* emotions. Part of me wanted to kill her. The other wanted to run my hand up her little skirt and take her there and then. In some weird way, that would solve everything. Cock my leg. Reclaim my territory.

Lucy, however, wasn't a lamppost and didn't want to be peed on. She wanted to talk. I didn't. If she wanted a conversation, there was only one way it was going to end.

'Lucy Poett, this is not a mutual breakup; I am dumping you. Be mine no more. Go forth and multiply in dark corners in dank little clubs. Live long and weep. Never again will I go shopping with you on Oxford Street in mid-August. Never again will I stroke your hair while you puke up your four JD and Cokes. The Jack 'n' Lucy roadshow has come to an end. Kaput, *finito*, over and out. Sod off out of my life.'

It wasn't that fluent, of course. But it did the trick and made her cry, too. 30—30.

And with that I turned on my heel and sodded off out of Covent Garden, tears streaming down my face, heading towards Leicester Square for no particular reason, occasionally pausing to practise my monologue of rage with a passing shop window. Like bollocks, she didn't know it would hurt me. She'd done it on purpose. Hit me at my weakest point.

And, as for Rick, what a ginger dickhead. No wonder he didn't want to come round and play FIFA on the Xbox with me and Flatmate Fred last night. He was too busy trying to get into my ex's box. I hate the little carroty bastard.

I ring him up to share my thoughts, but he has the good grace to put me straight on to answer machine. So I share my feelings with the mechanised Orange woman. 'If you want to re-record your message, press one at any time.' Why, thank you. So I re-record my message about ten times in an attempt to get the right combination of invective and bile.

It's a hollow victory. I go to bed a broken excuse for a man.

Monday 24th January

Pulled a sickie at work. Just couldn't cope with heading in today and facing an email barrage of emotional blackmail from Lucy. I've got a fairly croaky voice in any case in the morning, so I thought I'd find it pretty easy to hoodwink my line manager over the phone. What I hadn't counted on was the company's new policy of transferring all sickie-takers through to the corporate nurse.

'What exactly is wrong with you?' she asked.

'Er, I think my thyroid is swollen and my left ventricle is playing up again. I've been vomiting all weekend.'

Arse, I wasn't prepared for this.

'I'm sorry?'

'So am I. My ulna and my nephrons are in absolute agony. I think I've got food poisoning.'

She wasn't convinced.

'Look, OK, I'm faking. But my heart was broken yesterday and I need some time off.'

'We'll see about that.'

She could see about it by herself. I hung up, feeling genuinely ill by this point.

The best thing about pulling a sickie when you're sharing with Flatmate Fred is that you can count on him to be free during the day.

'Any important meetings today, Fred? Any conference calls with the

Washington office? Any quarterly appraisals? No? Right, get out of your dressing gown, put on some clean clothes and we're going to the pub.'

And so we did. Looking like two well-heeled alcoholics (which, I guess, is exactly what we were), we went to our local at 11am and drank until closing time. Interesting landmarks along the way included:

11.30   Lucy texts to ask why I'm not replying to her emails.

12.14   Lucy texts to ask why I'm not replying to her texts.

14.52   Rupert (bald) rings to ask how I'm feeling. 'Fucking fantashtic,' I reply, which in retrospect was probably a poor answer.

15.30   Flatmate Fred declares that he loves me.

15.35   After due consideration (this is no light matter), I declare that I love Flatmate Fred.

16.47   Buddy rings from work to tell me that I'm, like, in big fucking shit, man.

18.01   Lucy rings and leaves a message on my voicemail asking why I'm not answering my phone.

19.23   Lucy texts to ask why I'm not listening to my voicemail messages.

19.24   Flatmate Fred comes back from the loo with lucky-dip, curry-flavoured condoms. 'I was hoping for glow-in-the-dark ones,' he mourns. 'Only way they'd find your cock,' I suggest. 'That's harsh, but I still love you.'

22.35   Rick rings to say that we really need to talk. No we don't. We really need to fight. Flatmate Fred wrestles the phone from me and hangs up on Rick. He hates Rick, too. I love Flatmate Fred.

22.44   Pretty barmaid suggests that we've had enough and might want to leave.

22.45   I ask pretty barmaid whether she'd like to leave with us.

23.30   We leave. By ourselves.

23.50   Flatmate Fred and I carry the *Prunus subhirtella* (minus five flowers) back to the scene of the crime and leave it there with the letter and some money (£1.25 — our collective change from the £50 we both took out in the morning).

00.45   Blissfully innocent and comatose sleep.

Wednesday 26th January

This is agony. No one at work has mentioned anything about my little sickie misdemeanours on Monday. I feel like they're playing mind games with me. Am I meant to come forward and confess? I'd rather just have a bollocking and get on with things as normal.

Only Buddy can be relied on for continuing moral support.

'Oh. Still here, are we, mate?' he asks every time he walks past my desk. Buddy calling me 'mate' causes almost as much distress as seeing his emails with the words 'color' and 'thru' in them.

'Yes, Buddy, old buddy, I'm still here. Milk, two sugars, there's a good boy. Make one for yourself while you're there.'

Friday 28th January

There was a generic email to the entire company awaiting us this morning asking everyone to be at their desks for a short announcement at 2pm. The rest of the morning rushed past in a flurry of nerves and excitement. Internal email speculation pinged backwards and forwards.

Buddy: 'This is it, Jacko, boy. They're announcing your promotion to everyone.'

At 2pm exactly, the plummy tones of the chief executive came over the Tannoy.

'I am delighted to announce that, due to market conditions, there will be an element of restructuring at Citicorp. This is part of our commitment to providing a 360-degree approach to client-oriented relationships in the twenty-first century. Our greatest asset is our people. The following assets, in alphabetical order, will no longer be required.'

I couldn't believe it. The wanker of a banker was planning on sacking half the workforce over a loudspeaker.

'Ahmadi, Alexander, Atkinson, Babbington, Baker-Wilbraham...' *Actually, I'd sack someone with a name like that.* '...Holloway, Holston, Laird...' I look up at my computer screen. The log-in is no longer working. Sod a dog backwards, I'm going to be next. But no, Laird is followed by Robson who is followed by Waterman. People with surnames in the early part of the alphabet must be worse at their jobs.

So I'm safe in the career that I hate more than life itself. The only consolation is that Leila Sidebottom is safe, too. Buddy Wilton-Steer had a rather long and nervous wait, but he also made the cut.

I rang my dad to tell him the bad news.

'Don't worry, Jack. You'll get out of there one day,' he laughed. 'In the meantime, your job still gives your mother something to boast about at dinner parties.'

Oh, good.

Sunday 30th January

Rick finally rang, after waiting six days and playing me like a girl.

'DonthangupJackIvereallygottoexplain,' he says in his best radio advert voice.

'OK, you ginger scrot-face, but terms and conditions apply. This better be good.'

And so I go round to his flat in Angel.

'Did it happen here?' I ask plaintively, nervously examining his bed for signs of Lucy's existence.

'No, you fool, if you'd just shuddup and listen, innit.'

For all the benefits of his outrageously expensive education, Rick remains incapable of constructing a full English sentence without a nod to street vernacular. Rick's dad QC talks like Prince Charles. Rick is Prince of Estuary. He maintains this is natural, whereas the rest of us argue that he picked it up to avoid getting beaten up at the university formerly known as the Anglia Polytechnic.

Eventually, Rick manages to explain that he didn't pull Lucy at all. She'd launched at him in a club on Saturday night and he'd jumped backwards to avoid her.

'So why the hell did she tell me that she'd pulled you?'

'Easy, Jack. Get with it. She was just trying to make you jealous, izzit. Win you back for herself. Drive a wedge between you and your best mate.'

Oh God, I feel awful. I start crying for the second time in a week. What a loser.

'Did your lips touch?' I ask, between shuddering sobs.

But Rick doesn't hear, as my face is muffled into his shoulder and he's thumping me on the back in a manly, syncopated way. We're bestest mates again and all is right with the world.

FEBRUARY

Tuesday 1st February

Found out at work why they didn't sack me — apparently I'm too expensive. Now that I've been here for four years, they'd have to give me a hefty payoff, which I'd probably spend on an expensive car and a backpacking trip before picking up a better-paid job in a rival bank. It's reassuring to know that I'm such a valuable asset to the company — too crap to be promoted, too good to be sacked. My sly sickie last week seems to have been overlooked in the general excitement of firing everyone else.

As it is, ninety per cent of the 'assets' whose services are no longer required are from the new graduate intake. Leila seems to have sneaked through the net, which is probably because she's only just arrived and the bosses would rather get in the sack with her than sack her. For the first time in my glittering career, I find myself applauding the result, if not the motive, of one of their decisions.

Friday 4th February

I'm in heaven

Corporate restructuring has led to Leila 'netball wing defence' Sidebottom moving to the same desk as me. Admittedly, we're at opposite diagonals and there's a sizeable partition blocking our view, but if I sit up straight in my chair I can just make out a perfect rectangle of forehead and blonde hair. As long as I keep below her eye line I can watch her all day. I feel like Camus's prisoner who's content to stare at his fragment of sky through the bars. I also feel like a pathetic old pervert.

Mid-afternoon, and I'm disturbed from my pleasant revelries by Leila herself. She's standing over me, wearing a short business-suit skirt. Her breasts are pushing against her white shirt. I have to slide my chair further under my desk so that she can't see the bulge in my trousers.

'Hi, Jack,' she says.

How did she know my name? I must have registered surprise, because she motions to the name plaque on my monitor.

'It says so there. I'm Leila.'

As if I had to be told. Leila, light of my life, fruit of my loins. *Lay me on my knees, Leila.* Hadn't I written a panegyric to that very name?

'We met in the lift,' she adds, somewhat unnecessarily.

Oh bollocks, she remembered.

'How's your granny? Did she like her flowers?'

'Oh, yes. She loved them.'

This is one of the longest personal conversations I've ever had with a colleague at my desk. People are starting to look at us weirdly. Perhaps we're endangering the wellbeing of the FTSE with our lightning banter.

'I'm making coffee,' she continues. 'Would you like some?'

Would I like some? God, would I like some.

'Yes, please. Really milky.'

'Sugar?'

Don't say, 'I'm sweet enough already.' Don't say, 'I'm sweet enough already.'

'I'm sweet enough already.'

Oh, Lancaster, you blundering arse. Again.

Sunday 6th February

In these dark, private confines, I would like to write something in my diary about masturbation.

Two things, in particular, strike me as extraordinary about the topic of self-gratification. The first is that it still happens at all. In the twenty-first century we can perform uniquely wonderful feats such as sending astronauts to the moon. But successful, attached, attractive men still tug themselves off on a regular basis. I know very little about the animal kingdom, but I'm pretty certain that elephants don't pleasure themselves with their trunks. I know our family dog Buzz certainly doesn't — although he does like a good chair leg.

The other thing that amuses me about onanism is the way in which people broach it. Guys adopt a boorishly laddish approach to the subject. It's something to joke about in games of 'I have never...'. Four times in one day? Well, I never. Caught by every single member of your family? Unbelievable. Are you a once-a-day man? Yep — me, too. Legend.

Girls, on the other hand — or, at least, the demure little things that I seem to hang around with — appear to be shocked by the subject. Never believe a girl who claims never to have had a fiddle in the basement. This is like having a brand-new Ferrari in the garage and never taking it for a test drive. Get to know them better — Claire, Susie, Katie and Mel are all cases in point — and you'll elicit fuller confessions.

Enough beating about the bush. the really tricky bit as a home-movie director is deciding whom to cast opposite you in the role of leading lady. It's fine when you stick to celebrities or random encounters whom you're never going to come across again. It crosses the borderline into awkwardness when friends and colleagues start playing cameo roles. It becomes even more awkward if this recollection suddenly hits you during a conversation. Part of the reason for my appalling conversation with Leila on Friday afternoon was that she'd been bouncing on my lap in a full-length feature movie only eighteen hours previously.

In fact, I can pretty much divide my female acquaintances into girls I've fantasised about and girls I haven't. I always wonder what they would make of this if I told them. Probably nothing. When they're not being so demure (i.e. untruthful), they'd probably admit to entertaining similar fantasies themselves. Except that theirs have a plot involving conversation and flowers, and we cut straight to Act V.

And with these enlightening thoughts on the human condition, I retire to bed, wondering if I'm missing Lucy more than I've admitted to myself.

Monday 7th February

I've never been an Olympic athlete, but I'm normally capable of walking the whole way up the fast lane on the Underground escalator without a pit stop. Today I had to pull over, panting, to let a pensioner overtake.

Concerned, I checked my BMI with the doctor at work, who confirmed that I am now officially an overweight, balding, single banker. I complained about this to Buddy.

'Hey, be a man about it,' he advised kindly. 'Take it on the chins.'

Later I tried to keep my chins up by popping into Boots to sort out my other imperfections. But incredibly, they had nothing to prevent premature balding. There were entire sections devoted to bladder weakness and hair removal products but nothing to keep my precious remaining follicles on my head.

It reminds me of a group of Parisian students who formed the Suicide Club in the 1850s. Their manifesto declared that all members should kill themselves before the age of thirty, or before they went bald — whichever came first. If I had drawn the last ticket in the lottery of life — born 150 years ago in France with suicidal bohemian tendencies — I fear I would have been one of the first to go.

Tuesday 8th February

After re-reading my little masturbation monologue entry from the weekend, I began to worry that I was a slightly unpleasant person. Not to mention shallow, perverted, sly, verbose, vindictive, competitive, inept, jealous and lonely. I mentioned this to Flatmate Fred on Monday and he decided that I had overdosed on male company and was in need of some counterbalancing feminine input. So we decided to invite some girls around for pancakes this evening, Shrove Tuesday.

Katie was away with Rick for their parents' wedding anniversary party, so it was just Claire (doctors 'n' nurses), Mel (first kiss) and Susie (first shag). Mel and Susie were caught up in their usual battle for the attention of Flatmate Fred who was at his metrosexual best tossing pancakes in the kitchen. So I had a bit of time to spend with doctors 'n' nurses. Ironically, Claire is now a doctor and going out with a male nurse. It's funny how these things change. When we were toddlers, I was always in charge of the stethoscope.

'Claire,' I ask. 'You've known me ever since I was an itch in my alpha male 'rental's pants. Why am I so unhappy at the moment?'

'Well, let's see. You hate your job, you've just left your girlfriend in an ugly scene involving your best mate, you're getting fat, you're hopelessly in lust with a colleague who's twenty miles out of your league and you're beginning to lose your hair.'

'I'm what?'

'Your hair, darling, your former hair. You're going bald. Your hairline is retreating like a polar icecap.'

'What, five metres per year?'

Claire's the first person to point this out to me. It's official now.

'But why don't you do something about it all?' she asks.

'About the hair? There's nothing to be done about the hair. I'm not having transplants. It costs a bomb and it looks lame.'

'No, dummy, the hair's fine. Balding men are sexy. Testosterone-packed. I mean the rest of your wretched life. Why don't you take some affirmative action to sort it out?'

This is quite a revelation. She's right. I, Jack Lancaster, can sort this all out myself. I am not some piece of flotsam at the mercy of the waves of fate. I have a mind of my own. I can do anything I want. I am in the driving seat of my life.

I am still smiling about this abstract thought when we're all sitting down later and discussing what to give up for Lent.

Predictably, the three girls are all renouncing chocolate for forty days. I wonder what student chocolate activist Leila would make of this. None of them is overweight, so they're not doing it for cosmetic reasons. Apparently, it's about self-denial, an appreciation of life's essentials.

'Oh toss,' I protest. 'It's the gastronomic version of tantric sex — delayed pleasure. Waiting a few weeks allows you to enjoy stuffing your face on Easter Day without feeling guilty. And in the meantime you feel empowered and feminine. "Oooh, what are you giving up for Lent? Chocolate? Oh you're *so* brave."'

'I am brave,' sniffs Mel. 'You can't understand how chocolate makes us feel. If there were no men in the world, the planet would be full of happy, fat women eating Mars bars. It's so much better than sex.'

Women have no idea how inadequate that makes us feel.

'Masturbation is often better than sex, as well,' I say. 'And we don't go on about it.'

'Why don't you give it up for Lent then, Jack?' asks Claire.

'Yes,' chorus first kiss and first shag. 'I dare you.'

'I double-dare you,' adds Flatmate Fred. Mel and Susie titter at his witticism.

OK, then, I think. I am in the driving seat of my life, and I will. If the son of God managed to resist the temptation to turn stones into bread in the desert, I'm sure that I can keep away from my trouser snake for six weeks.

'OK, then,' I tell my four disciples. 'I will. And what are the terms of the bet?'

The girls look at each other and giggle.

'You get what you've always wanted,' says first kiss.

'A medal?'

'A foursome with all of us.'

Oh. My. God.

Wednesday 9th February

Spent all day thinking about Mel's offer last night. She can't really have meant it. Surely. It must have been a sly little ploy to frustrate me. How can I possibly abstain for six weeks when that image is constantly in my mind? It's devious psychological warfare: the reward is the torture itself.

But hey, we all need challenges in our lives. Some people row across the Atlantic and climb Everest. I'm going to have simultaneous sex with three of my best friends.

Friday 11th February

Remembering the doctor's diagnosis at the beginning of the week that I am, indeed, a fat, balding bastard, I decided to go the gym this morning. It was surprisingly fun. The padded exercise bikes can be quite comfortable for watching *Sky News* as long as you don't move around too much. The weights are OK, too, on the condition that you put the key on the easiest level and keep to five repetitions. And I positively loved falling off the ergo machine onto a sweaty patch of unprotected metal below.

But what is it with communal changing rooms? I saw Rupert (bald) standing on a bench and blow-drying his pubic hair while whistling an out-of-tune Marseillaise. Well-endowed men trotted around naked ('No towel is big enough to cover it,' they seem to imply), as if they were expecting a round of applause whenever they walked into the shower. We less blessed mortals scurried around nervously trying to wash, dry and dress in under seven seconds.

'Do you want to work on your abs or your pecs first?' asked the personal trainer.

Stupid man. I just want to look good naked.

'That could take a little while,' he replied.

Monday 14th February

Valentine's Day. The day of commercialism, despair, desperation and love.

There was the usual card from my dad, which he's sent every year since I was twelve. When I was at school he used to write 'love from Daddy' on a Post-it note so I could tear it out and pretend I had a secret admirer. There was also a card signed jointly by Claire, Mel and Susie. Now they're really playing me.

Today, however, I had other things on my mind. Today I was going to make a tentative move on Leila. Stepping into the driving seat of my life (can you step into a seat?), I started to compose an email.

To: Leila Sidebottom (*yeuch*)
From: Jack Lancaster
Subject: No subject (*what subject could I give it? 'Re: trying to pull you'?*)
Monday 14th February 14.35

Hey Leila, how you doing?! (*why the exclamation mark?*) How are things on the Westside of the desk (*what kind of joke is that?*)?! A bunch of us are going out for a few drinks after work today. Do you fancy coming along?

J *(pretty cool, eh?)*

My mouse hovered over the 'send' button. I hesitated. I paused. And then I thought, *I am not flotsam, I am going to send this email.* And so I did.

I heard a little chuckle from the 'Westside' of the desk. Brilliant, she loved it. And then ping, straight back, I had mail.

To: Jack Lancaster
From: Leila Sidebottom (*yeuch, I really have to marry her*)
Subject: Drink (*the girl calls a spade a spade — excellent*)
Monday 14th February 14.36

Ayeee, all's well on da Westside. Finding work kind of boring today (*wow — kindred spirit*). Would have loved to come along (*ouch, that's an ominous tense*), but I'm already going on a girly night out (*she's single, she must be single*). Maybe another time (*she didn't say never*).

Leila

X (*she put a kiss, a capital-letter kiss no less*)

But my sense of triumph over the electronic kiss was short-lived and I soon felt like a thoroughbred loser again. Of course she wouldn't have a boyfriend. She's too perfect to have a boyfriend. No one could put up with the jealousy that a girl that beautiful would arouse. You'd lose all your genuine mates instantly. Other blokes would just hang around with the two of you so they could catch her when you screwed up and she moved on.

And so I suddenly felt lower than I had done for ages. There Leila was in all her perfection, holding out for Mr Perfect and I was moping around on Valentine's Day feeling like a lonely loser. And perhaps the worst thing about feeling like a lonely loser is that you soon start acting like a lonely loser. It's a self-fulfilling vicious circle.

I reached for my mobile and composed a lonely-loser text to Lucy: 'Missing you so much today. Thinking of you even more than usual'. It wasn't strictly speaking a lie. I'd thought about Lucy very little recently, and today I was thinking about her a little more than a little. But the sentiment was false and the motives were self-pity and loneliness. I filled the remaining ninety-seven characters of the text with kisses — 2.5 for every day since I'd last kissed her. Options, send, search, scroll — she was the fourth name under L in my phone book after Laura, Lois and London Transport.

Which is pretty much where she ranks in my affections at the moment. Marginally below the Underground helpline, marginally above Ludlow Thompson, the house-letting agency.

Thursday 17th February

Lucy is three years older and wiser than Leila and so far too practised in the rules of the game to text me back straight away. She also knows my excitability too well to reply instantly and get my hopes up. In fact, she practically wrote the rules of the game herself.

So the cunning little character didn't get in touch until this afternoon. And her text sounded all the right notes with such accuracy that I reckon she took half an hour composing it straight away on Monday, saved it and sent it with only a few edits today.

'I missed you too big boy', it said. 'Didn't really compare to last year's v day, did it?! Why don't you come round tonight and I'll cook for you? Wld be good to catch up.'

And in those four simple sentences you have irrefutable evidence that women are a more evolved species than men. 'Big boy' — makes me feel special and sexy. Reminder of last year's Valentine's Day — I surprised her with a candlelit London Eye trip, after which we stayed up all night making the beast with two backs and a funny-shaped middle. Cooking — she's a wonderful cook. Motive of visit — catching up only, which arouses my hunter-gatherer instinct. It's a mini masterpiece.

I press options, reply, include original text — she had two characters left and didn't even include a kiss. She's never done that before.

But when I go round to her flat after work, I know that this is going to be the least of my worries. She's wearing a short, floaty skirt that's more suited to July than February. She leans forward to peck me on the cheek, which feels weird, as she's never kissed me on the cheek before. We'd kissed properly the first time we'd met. And that was over three years ago.

But the peck on the cheek turns into a quick peck on the lips. She hugs me tight. I can feel her breasts against my chest. I cup my hands around her face and start to kiss her properly. She slides one of her slender legs in between mine. *Oh Jack*, she was moaning now, her curves pushed up against me, her crotch taut against my bulging trousers, her hands gripping fistfuls of my hair. She reaches for my belt. I groan too. In expectation.

And then I'm inside her, and everything is pure white as we're lost in a commotion of grunts and squeaks, flashing unconnected images and explosions of a million little particles.

And the very worst thing was that, the moment we'd finished, I felt absolutely nothing. It was the most intense physical experience of my life; it was the least emotional. It wasn't making love, it was shagging. It was animalistic. It was bloody good. But I've felt more emotional connection shaking a friend's hand than I did in those brief moments of sweaty frotting. She had gone from being an unobtainable object of desire to an object of possession. And by repossessing her, I had nothing left in myself.

I stayed the night — she begged me to — when all I really wanted was to leave and go home and wash the smell of her away. And as she lay there cradled in my arms in our favourite spoons position, I knew that I was cuddling the past and not the future. She made me breakfast the next day. I kissed her on the forehead. And when she said, 'Goodbye', I think she meant it. And when I said, 'See you around', I'm pretty sure I didn't want to.

Friday 18th February

I had to go into work via Marks and Spencer's to buy a clean shirt. I didn't want to look like the kind of dirty stopout who had spent the previous evening with his ex-girlfriend after acting on a lonely-loser text message.

There was a card shop next to M&S so I popped in and had an idle browse through the reduced Valentine's merchandise. I realised with a jolt that this was the first year that I hadn't sent any cards at all since I was thirteen and sent one to myself at school (which doesn't really count). I bought one I thought Leila might like.

'Saving up for next year?' asked the smiley cashier.

'Er, no. Have just been a bit disorganised,' I mumbled.

'Ah. In trouble with the lady, are we?'

'You could say that.'

I tuck it into my jacket and get into a mercifully empty lift at work. *This time I'm not going to screw it up, this time I'm not going to screw it up* — I repeat my mantra to myself. Round one: Shredded flowers and a little love loch of awkwardness. Round two: Piss-poor coffee conversation. Round three: A clumsily botched email seduction on Valentine's Day. Round four: Knockout.

Leila's away from her desk, so I pluck out the embarrassingly large red envelope, hide it under my copy of the *Financial Times* (with which it clashes hideously) and open up a document on my computer so that I can have several goes at writing and editing the perfect droll message. After ten minutes or so, I've got it pretty much sussed. I open the card to transcribe it and, bugger me if the little bastard doesn't start playing a song. 'I believe in miracles, since you came along, you sexy thing', etc.

I slam the card shut, but it's already too late. Not only are half the office looking in my direction, but Leila has returned from her meeting and is looking over my shoulder sniggering. Buddy is looking over her shoulder in fits of hysterics. I just have sufficient presence of mind to minimise the document on my screen before Buddy launches into prosecutor mode.

'Nice shirt, Jacko, boy. You've ironed it in such a strange way that it looks like it's come straight out of a packet this morning.'

'Very good, Buddy. It did come out of a packet this morning.'

'Dirty stopout. Who's the lucky lady?'

Was it my imagination, or did I see Leila wince at this point?

'Rick was the lucky lady. I kipped over at his.'

'And is the card for Rick, as well?' He delivers his killer line.

A little titter goes up around our section of the room. Twenty of the capital's premier bankers laughing at a gay joke.

Leila: 'No, it's for his granny. It's a follow-up to the flowers.'

The little cow of a crowd-pleasing sheep (if that makes any biological sense). Only she and I really understand the significance of her jibe, but it stings like someone's rubbed citrus-flavoured excrement in my eyes. The crowd roars. Mingers have to crack funny jokes. Pretty girls only have to make an approximate stab at humour.

I sink lower into my seat as Buddy twirls Leila around to the polyphonic tones of Hot Chocolate's hit. I don't believe in miracles. Water into wine? A magician could do that. But I could certainly do with a few conjuring tricks in my current excuse for a life.

Monday 21st February

Came back from work to find Flatmate Fred hopping around with another letter in his hands. It went like this:

Dear Mr Hardy,

Thank you for your 'ashamed and remorseful' letter. How considerate of you to lighten the workload of the Royal Mail and deliver it by hand. I must apologise for the delay in replying; it took us a few weeks to wipe away the soil.

Thank you also for the kind donation of £1.25. Although this is approximately 0.5% of the value of the stolen winter-flowering cherry, it did allow me to buy a small *café latte* on the way home from work.

You mention the forbidden fruit. I'm sure I don't have to remind you what happened to Adam and Eve after eating the apple. If you don't want to be sent forth from the Garden of Eden that is Onslow Mews, to till the ground whence you were taken, I suggest you come up with a more weighty sum of money in the very near future.

Otherwise I would recommend that you ask Alcoholics Anonymous for your money back and donate it to a more suitable charity, such as Legal Aid.

Kind regards,

Bertrand Rogers MBE

(aka Flower Person)

'Oh buggeroonies. We're doomed,' says Flatmate Fred when I've finished reading the letter. 'Shotgun, Big Black Ron takes you up the bum first in jail.'

'No, we're not,' I reply calmly. 'All we have to do is find a bit of extra cash and Mr Rogers will leave us alone.'

'But he's threatening us. He's going to prosecute us.'

'No, he's not. He's just playing Billy Big-Bollocks. We'll pay him and then he'll leave us alone.'

I can see Flatmate Fred is still unconvinced. But then I look at the letter again and realise that it was addressed to him directly with the correct address.

'Fred, how the hell did Mr Rogers know your name and address when you wrote him an anonymous letter signed "Stupid White Men"?'

'Er, because I wrote it on headed notepaper.'

'You silly, silly tit. You can find the money yourself.'

Tuesday 22nd February

My fitness obsession has got so bad that, as well as having my corporate membership, I've now joined a local gym.

I don't know why I bother. I mean, it's hellish: the overweight women who look like they were poured into their Lycra and forgot to say when; the work-shy layabouts spending their dole money on Lucozade; the bored housewives who drive to the gym, walk on a treadmill while watching MTV, eat a Mars bar to celebrate the successful completion of their exercise routine, and then drive home again. Not to mention the middle-aged losers attempting to pull (the only time they'll hear heavy breathing is on the running machine); the city traders trying to out-stomach-crunch the intern; or the Nuremberg workout classes with rows of people slavishly aping the hectoring instructions of the short, moustachioed person at the front.

On the plus side, I now look a little better naked... as long as I take a big breath and hold it in for several minutes.

Wednesday 23rd February

Leila's intended Valentine Card followed Leila's intended flowers into the shredder at work today, playing the little electronic ditty as it went. The final requiem of mangled miracles.

I had thought of presenting it to her anyway — a grand, sweeping, comedic gesture — but she had annoyed me so much with her 'Granny' jibe that she was still in the doghouse as far as I was concerned. But when I got back from the shredder room, there was an email waiting for me.

To: Jack Lancaster
From: Leila Sidebottom
Subject: Sorry
Wednesday 23rd February 10.28

Hey Jack, I just wanted to apologise for my joke about the card on Friday! I felt like a complete cow as soon as I said it!! Poor you, you looked so embarrassed! I hope you weren't offended. It looked like a really sweet card, and I'm sure the lucky girl who received it was very touched. Can I buy you a drink some time to apologise properly?!?

L
xx

OK, rather too many exclamation marks, but a five-star email regardless. Two kisses at the end — admittedly not capital ones — but two kisses nonetheless. And she signed it 'L' — L for Lucky Leila, L for love, lust and longing.

Play it cool, Jack, I thought. *Leave her to stew a little. Make her feel really guilty. Feign an aura of aloof mystique.*

I emailed her back three minutes later with four kisses. We're going for a drink on Monday. And then I went to the gym to work on my abs a little more.

L for Lancaster. L for loser.

Friday 25th February

This is hell at work. Now that Leila is sitting so close to me, I can't concentrate on anything at all. She has to walk past me to get a coffee or to go to the loo, and I spend half the day trying to catch her eye and elicit a glass-shattering smile. I'm finding my Lent fast a little tougher than I thought.

Returned home to find Flatmate Fred dressed in a suit.

'Are you going out?' I ask.

Most people get up in the morning and put on a suit to go to work. Then they come home and change into jeans before going out in the evening. Flatmate Fred gets up in the afternoon and stays in his dressing gown until 6pm. Then he gets changed into a suit to go out on the town.

'No,' he says morosely. 'I've just had an interview.'

I thought I'd misheard him. Flatmate Fred never uses the 'I' word. An interview is the first step towards having a job, and that's a fate worse than death.

'What for?'

'Data entry.'

I snigger.

'It's not bloody funny. I've got no transferable marketplace skills and I need to pay Mr Rogers £300 hush money so they don't set Big Black Ron on me.'

I think this is just about as bloody funny as you can get.

'Why don't you get your dad to help you out?'

'Cos he's a blinking accountant and he makes me produce spreadsheets every month on how I spend my allowance. You know how he's subsidising my writing career. This is his way of keeping tabs on me. I can't put down "Miscellaneous — one stolen *Prunus subhirtella*". He'd kill me.'

I reflect that, if I were a financial whiz of a father and had a son like Flatmate Fred, I'd probably kill him anyway.

But Flatmate Fred is adamant. He's going to install broadband internet at home and do the first week of honest work in his life. And then he's going to pay the Flower People to keep the bum-police at bay. I almost offered to bail him out myself, but he seems so energised by his new sense of purpose that I leave him be.

Monday 28th February

Donned my lucky boxer shorts, applied some of the aftershave that Lucy gave me for Christmas and went for a drink with Leila straight after work.

It started off so well. Did she want a double? Of course she did — that more than doubled the chances of her sleeping with me. We talked about everything and anything. I delivered my top five anecdotes with exquisite timing. I laughed when she laughed, smiled when she smiled, and listened for over twenty minutes before drifting off and imagining what she would look like naked.

We didn't mention the *Prunus subhirtella* or the Valentine's card or my granny. Leila's endearingly oblivious to the effect she has on men. She's sweet and funny and modest. It was fantastic.

But then, at 10.30, she dropped the bombshell.

'Jack, I've got something I need to tell you.'

Check me out. Three double G&Ts and the most beautiful girl in the world is about to say that she likes me.

'OK.' I smile my most boyish, charming smile. 'You can tell me anything you want.'

'I fancy Buddy.'

She could tell me anything she wanted apart from that.

'As in Buddy Wilton-Steer Buddy?'

'Yep, I just think he's so cute. He's so direct, so confident, so lacking in British cynicism.'

'Right.'

No Jack, not right: wrong, wrong, wrong.

'I mean, I know you're mates with him. I was wondering if you could perhaps find out subtly for me. In whatever way you blokes do that kind of thing. Just don't embarrass me — I couldn't carry on at work if I messed something up.'

And just how does she expect me to carry on at work knowing this?

'Sure,' I say, just about holding myself together. 'I can do some research. But you should know that he's already got a girlfriend that he cheats on regularly.'

Was that the right thing to say? I muse, as I walk home. If she's the kind of girl I'd like her to be, then that would put her right off. If she's not, then it might just stoke the fire. Either way, I'm in trouble. Buddy is as single and as desperate as I am, and she prefers him to me.

Round five: Failure.

Bugger.

MARCH

Wednesday 2nd March

Buddy swings by my desk at work.

'Jacko, my son,' he appears to be adopting a more British vernacular. 'How about a coffee?'

Leila looks up expectantly from the other side of our desk. She gives me the tiniest of nods.

'Sure, Buddy. Let's go.'

Buddy's idea of a coffee is four espresso shots and five lumps of sugar. I wonder idly whether he might die of a heart attack before he finds out that Leila likes him. He did ninety hours in the office last week. His hands are already shaking.

'Jackie, my boy, I really like that Leila chick.'

'You like her, or just want to screw her?'

'Don't be a jerk, Jacko. Of course I just want to screw her. You had a drink with her last Monday. Did she say anything?'

I meet Buddy's gaze.

'No, mate. Nothing at all, I'm afraid.'

'Are you sure? You can tell me.'

'Well, actually mate,' I put on my best doctor-breaking-bad-news face, 'I did ask her if she fancied anyone at work, and she said no. Sorry.'

As I walk back to my desk, Leila raises her eyebrows and I give her a sympathetic little shake of my head. There's already a one-word email waiting for me from her: 'So?' No kiss this time.

So I explain that Buddy is very much in love with his current girlfriend and wants to remain faithful to her. I also write that he doesn't fancy anyone at work.

Leila emails back: 'You're a star, Jack. Feel much better now that I know. Always better to get these things sorted out, don't you think? I loved our drink on Monday. Let's have lunch tomorrow.'

Am I a star? I feel more like a shitbag. I console myself with the thought that I was trying to protect her from Buddy's predatory one-track mind. But I know deep down that I was motivated by rancid jealousy, and that they're both going to find me out.

Thursday 3rd March

Talking of finding people out, I came home slightly early from work today to find a flushed Flatmate Fred desperately trying to close all the windows on his computer. It was his first day of broadband internet access and his first day of work.

'Aha! Welcome to the world of work. How goes the data entry?' I ask, craning my head forward to look at his screen.

'Oh, good. Yeah — tiring,' he blushes traffic-light red.

A pop-up page flashes on to the screen: 'Free tits here', it screams.

'Oh yes,' mumbles Flatmate Fred. 'One or two teething virus problems with the broadband connection.'

I look closer and discover exactly why he is so tired by the world of work. He has at least ten pages open that have something to do with sex. Lolitas, uniform, teens, lesbians, facials, anal, threesomes, toys. The deviant list is seemingly endless.

'Who's the data entry actually *for*?' I ask. 'Hugh Hefner?'

'Er, no. I was doing some research for my book.'

'I thought you'd given up writing for Lent.'

Poor Flatmate Fred. Well and truly stumped, he ran out for a much-needed shower.

But it got me thinking. The internet is for porn. Everyone knows that. Sure, it might be useful every now and again to pay a bill online or book cheap flights, but essentially it's a convenient way of looking at naked girls without the old-fashioned embarrassment of walking into a newsagent's and trying to reach the top shelf. Even the shortest of short-arses can access a mouse.

I'm always struck by the hypocrisy of anyone who uses the internet in this way. Broadband service providers write a great deal of guff in their contracts about using the internet in a non-offensive way. But they know perfectly well that the biggest selling point of a broadband connection is the fact that you can access porn much faster. No one cares if it takes a little while to book your cinema tickets. It does bother you if a porn clip keeps stalling halfway through because your dial-up connection is too rubbish to deal with it.

Access someone's computer and it will tell you more than you ever wanted to know about them. Which keywords have they typed into Google? How many times a week have they whacked off while watching two people they don't know have sex?

My parents' generation, and the generation before them, is always going on about the lax moral standards of today's youth. But it was much easier to be moral back then. You had to go out looking for temptation. Nowadays it's only a right click, left click, double click away.

Friday 4th March

Second lunch in a row with Leila and people are beginning to gossip in the office. Most people here don't socialise together. It hurts more if you get promoted and have to sack a friend.

But let them gossip. All the little details that normally bore me about someone are fascinating when it comes to her. I'm genuinely interested to hear about her dad's army career, her love of Damien Rice, her phobia about stickers and the adventures of her first pet — a half-blind guinea pig called Nelson. It's mundane, but she's so fit, fun and amusing that I could listen to her all day. I don't even mind that she was born in Yorkshire.

'I went to the north once,' I told her, 'when I missed my tube stop at Moorgate.'

And she even laughed at that. I spent two hours in the gym to celebrate.

Saturday 5th March

I was carrying out my monthly check in the shower this morning when I chanced upon a lump in my left testicle. I'm going to die a slow and horrible death, unloved and unmourned.

I tell this to Flatmate Fred.

'Jack, you're the biggest hypochondriac in the world.'

'No, I'm not.'

'Yes, you are.'

'No, I'm not.'

Aren't we a little old for this?

'No, seriously, Jack. What do you do every time you have a headache?'

'I put my chin on my chest to check if I've got meningitis.'

Hmm, maybe he has a point.

Sunday 6th March

Mothering Sunday, and it was back home to see my 'vacuous, petty, pretty and snobby' mother. Whom I love dearly.

I gave her a bunch of flowers, which delighted her, even if they were the wrong colour for the time of year. How was I meant to know that there was a March colour? I'm reminded of Lucy's comments about magenta pink.

Speaking of Lucy, that's exactly what Mummy did, all day long. But it was Mothering Sunday so I let her practise her mothering as she laid into me about the huge mistake I was making. I let it wash over me. I mean, what could I say to placate her? *Don't worry, Mummy, on Thursday 17th February I bent Lucy over her kitchen table and made her come within thirty seconds, so it's all going to be OK.* I may have spent nine months inside her womb, but there are many topics parents and their offspring should keep to themselves.

Brother Ben also came home, which was nice, as I hadn't seen him since Christmas. Ben is better-looking than me, younger than me, more intelligent than me and generally nicer than me, but he wears his effortless superiority with such good-natured charm that I love him almost as much as I hate him. He's a medical student, so I asked him about the little lump in my bollock. He didn't have a clue — he's only done the kidney and the right leg so far.

'Your father and I are off skiing next week,' announced Mummy as she was clearing away the pudding.

'But you've never been skiing before,' said Brother Ben.

'Oh no, not real skiing,' replied Mummy. 'I mean SKI-ing. Spending the Kids' Inheritance. It's all the rage these days. We're going on a five-star safari in Tanzania.'

And parents think it's traumatic watching their children grow up? It's far worse the other way round.

After we'd all had enough of Mummy, Ben, Daddy and I escaped in the afternoon for the golf course — a blessedly girlfriend-/Mother-free zone. I lost seven balls and went round in 118.

Not a good day.

Monday 7th March

The lump has gone. Hallelujah — I'm not going to die.

Another nineteen days of my Lent fast, and my flawless testicle and I will be sleeping with Claire, Mel and Susie.

Tuesday 8th March

I've been helping out with graduate recruitment a little bit this year — that unrivalled process which puts the likes of Rupert (bald), Buddy, Leila and me together in the same office.

We finished the first round of interviews a couple of weeks ago and it was my job to send out the rejection letters. I rather liked this riposte, which came back from a student at Oxford today:

Dear Milkround Company,

I did enjoy jeopardising my degree to meet with you on multiple occasions during December, January and February. However, despite the large quantities of expensive alcohol, food and hotel rooms you forced upon me, I have decided not to extend you an offer this time.

I know this news will come as a disappointment to you, but I must stress that I have an unprecedented number of better things to do with my life. The competition was harder than ever this year. You should focus on the positives. I'm sure you will have plenty of other debt-ridden eager beavers clamouring to take you on.

I am collating some feedback on your performance, which should be with you just after it can be of any use for other applications. In the meantime, however, I think you need to work on the standard of your employees' chit-chat at post-presentation mingles. I did enjoy meeting Buddy, and hearing his views on the excellent work–life balance that your company offers, but frankly his chat stank. Also, the impact of his message was somewhat diluted by his colleagues' glazed eyes and the continual muttering of 'Need sleep, need sleep' before an HR woman (remarkably fit, I give you) rushed over to wind up the cogs in their backs.

You see, my experience with you has been remarkably like a bad relationship. I'd heard good things about you; I'd admired you from afar. Your exes sang your praises. We met and plied each other with alcohol in the hope that we would get along. We were on our most charming, courting behaviour. I only knew about your good points. True, I was two-timing you (eight-timing, to be exact), but you were the one I really wanted, the one I was holding out for. And now, just as we were on the verge of real commitment, I find myself brutally dumped. No consoling words, no regrets of what might have been, just a telephone call midway through my evening in the pub. Well, the feeling's mutual. I was going to dump you, too. You just got in there first.

But I'd like to emphasise again how much I enjoyed meeting you. I hope you will not be put off bombarding me again with inane brochures and yo yos embossed with your delightful logo. I wish you all the best for your banal, soulless future.

Best wishes,
Nigel O. T. Bitter, Esq.

PS I was wondering what your policy would be on my reapplying next year?

Mr Bitter is definitely one to watch, in my opinion. I gave the letter to Leila and it's now pinned up on her desk.

Wednesday 9th March

Flatmate Fred is sinking into a deeper and deeper depression. He's bored by his data entry and doesn't want to write his books any more. He doesn't fancy any of the girls who like him, and he hasn't met anyone he likes for ages.

I suggest that he gets dressed like everyone else in the morning and goes out and interacts with people while the sun is still up. He could copy Rick's example of using offices like a dating agency. Rick stays in a job just long enough to fall for a hopelessly unsuitable colleague before moving on and beginning the cycle all over again. He's a collegiate whore, a workplace slapper.

Talking of Rick, we have decided to repeat our boys' night out on Friday. I'm a little apprehensive. Buddy will soon have every reason to hate me, Rick is acting oddly around me and Flatmate Fred and Jasper are flirting more outrageously than ever before. It could be interesting.

Friday 11th March

It *was* interesting. It was also one of the worst nights of my life.

It started off so well — economy pizza and beers on the balcony while we discussed Important Things such as politics and whether girls had ever put their fingers up our bums during sex.

Then some fool (I think it was me) suggested playing a game of 'I have never...' to get us drunk quickly. It's a stupid game, but it can work well when you're in a mixed group of people who know each other well and others who don't.

Buddy thought he'd kick off in a suitably light-hearted way: 'I have never slept with Lucy.' Good lad — he'd picked up on the rules quickly.

Everyone looked at me, and I guffawed and took a hearty swig out of my can. *Yep, that's right, I've slept with her more than a hundred times.* Legend, me.

And then Rick took a little surreptitious sip of his beer.

'Richard Fielding,' intoned Jasper, 'I do hope that was an "I'm thirsty" sip of your beer, and not an "Oh, yes, I too have carnal knowledge of Lucy Poett"-type sip.'

It was the latter. I am not a violent man, but the next thing I knew I had pushed Rick to the floor and was kicking twenty hues of crap out of him. It was the first time in my life that I had hit anyone. I think it probably hurt me more than it hurt Rick.

Buddy, who is even bigger than me, hauled me off and I strained like a Rottweiler on a leash, yapping a torrent of invective at Rick.

Girls in a similar situation would want to know why. How could they hurt someone who was a friend? Were there emotions involved? But all I wanted were the facts. All of them — when, how, and how many times?

But facts don't help in a situation like this. You want to know them all, but each little detail hurts a little bit more than the one before. There are a thousand questions, but each answer twists the knife a little deeper.

Yet there was one 'why' I did want to know. Why had he lied to me so successfully when I went round to his flat to confront him, and then confessed in this extraordinary way during a stupid drinking game six weeks later?

'I didn't lie, Jack,' he whimpers. 'I hadn't slept with her at that point, innit. I really did back away from her in the club. And then she texted me on Valentine's Day, and I was so low and lonely that I popped round for a quick drink.'

So there you go. Valentine's Day — the day of commercialism, despair, desperation, love and sleeping with your ex-boyfriend's best mate before replying to his lonely-loser text and sleeping with him, as well.

'Get out of my flat before I fucking kill you,' I say, marvelling at the dangerously low volume of my own voice. Jasper the thespian nods approvingly. I sound like I mean it. I think I probably do.

After Rick has cleared off, Flatmate Fred says, 'That was a bit harsh, Jack. At least he owned up to it. That's the beauty of "I have never..." – the drink never lies. The opportunity to show off in a self-consciously coy way always wins through.'

'Right, you can get out of my flat before I fucking kill you, too,' I scream dementedly.

'Jack, you tit, it's my flat. And having just witnessed your little performance,

I'm not convinced that you could "fucking kill" a fly. I am not a fly, ergo I'm staying.'

How do you argue against such classically erudite logic?

And so to bed. Thumping the pillow and imagining it's Rick's face.

Saturday 12th March

Made up with Flatmate Fred over a very long and boozy pub lunch.

Afterwards, I came back to the flat and started thinking about last night's news again. Would I have done the same if I were Rick? After all, Lucy is very attractive, and they'd always got along very well together while we were going out? Had he actually done anything wrong?

Of course, he knew from my anger over her invented snog how much this would hurt me. Some things in life are meant to be off limits. It's one of a few simple, unwritten rules. You don't mock your mates' parents openly, and you don't sleep with their ex-girlfriends.

But then I'm just as angry with myself. It's a curiously powerful emotion, jealousy. I just can't put my finger on the aspect that bothers me the most. Is it the pure physical act? Am I worried that he was better than me? Is he bigger? Did he last longer?

Or is it the emotional theft that it was Valentine's Day and he was going through the motions of making love to the former love of my life? Did they lie around and chat afterwards? Was there pillow talk? Did they mention my name? Had she been thinking about him while we were going out? Had she fantasised about him during sex with me? Did they share all our private little jokes together? Did she tell him our pet name for my penis? And how could she sleep with a ginger?

These thoughts were all spiralling out of control in my head. They were gut-wrenching in the extreme. That's the problem with being the dumper as opposed to the dumpee. You get all the pain of the loss and none of the sympathy. It's all your fault.

Flatmate Fred had tried to listen, but I needed solutions not empathy. I had to talk to someone who would really understand. I rang my dad and told him everything.

'Jack, you'll go mad if you carry on thinking about the little details. You've got to look at the bigger picture.'

'Which is?'

'Well, were you happy with her? Do you ultimately want to be with her? Was she the right woman for you to spend the rest of your life with?'

'No.'

'Well, that's your answer, then. You've got to hold on to that. The rest will sort itself out.'

He was right. Bless the wise old bugger, he was absolutely right. I resolved not to think about it any more. I'd dumped Lucy, I'd foolishly slept with her again (*after* him — so I still win that one) and they were both free to run their lives as they saw fit. If two lonely people wanted to liven up their drab existence with a couple of hours of meaningless grunting, that was their business. And, with these generous thoughts, I headed out for a night on the tiles with Flatmate Fred and Jasper.

Sunday 13th March

I often wonder how different individual lives in Britain would be if alcohol had never been invented. Just imagine all the couples who would never have got together without a little encouragement. All those unsent text messages and undeclared intentions. Can you imagine dancing, let alone pulling, in a sober club? And just picture all the hair-brained moneymaking schemes and madcap adventures which would never have happened if ethanol hadn't pickled the sensible connectors in our brains. Not to mention all the unfulfilled resolutions to sort our lives out as the wrath of grapes takes hold the morning after.

Yesterday evening, for example, would have been a great deal less embarrassing for me if I'd decided to curl up on the sofa with a good book and a cup of hot cocoa. As it was, I came home on the night bus at 2.30am and decided to ring Lucy.

This in itself was a stupid idea. All my generous feelings from my earlier conversation with my dad had evaporated. A two-day hangover was starting to kick in, and I wanted to have it out with her about Rick.

What I'd forgotten was that I'd added Leila into the 'L's in my mobile, thereby distorting the order in my phone book. This unforeseen hiccup, plus the fact that I had just drunk the recommended monthly units of alcohol in a single weekend, meant that I rang Lucy's parents by mistake.

For some extraordinary reason I'd set my phone to record our conversation. Perhaps I wanted to use it in evidence later — I cannot fathom the drunken workings of my mind. And so, thanks to the wonders of modern technology, I can now transcribe the exchange.

'Archie Poett speaking,' says a tired voice.

'Luscy. Ish that you, Luscy?'

'This is Salisbury 755750. What do you want?'

'Who the bloody duck face are you? Where's Luscy? Hand the mobile over to her. I demand to shpeak to her. And I demand to shpeak to her now.'

'This is Lucy's father. Who is this? Why are you ringing at this time? Is something wrong?'

'Luscy's father, my blubbering bollocksh. You're her new boyfriend. You're sleeping with her, aren't you? I bet you've got a tiny, flacshid, little penish. I know she's there. Let me shpeak to her.'

'Is that Jack?'

'Yesh, it's Jack.' I think the mention of my name must have sobered me up slightly. There is a sudden note of fear in my voice.

'Jack, you've rung Lucy's parents' house by mistake. Put the phone down, have a cold shower and go to bed.'

'Yesh, Mr Poett. Oh, my God. I'm very sorry, Mr Poett.'

'And Jack?'

'Yesh, Mr Poett.'

'You won't remember this, but I just wanted to say that you could have been a son to me. I'm very disappointed.'

'Mr Poett?'

'Yes, Jack.'

'Go fuck yourself, Mr Poett.'

Tuesday 15th March

Flatmate Fred's finally done sufficient internet 'research' to raise the money for the stolen winter-flowering cherry. He's also been offered a full-time job doing data entry in a real office with real people. He was data enterer of the month. March must have been a bad month without precedent in the www.crapjobs.com community.

However, the 'ghastliness' of his brief contact with the working world has convinced him to give his writing career a serious shot again. Anything is better than waking up at a regular time each day, getting dressed and commuting to an office job, he maintains. As he puts it, PJs versus P45s — simple choice.

Wednesday 16th March

Lucy wrote me a very long and very touching letter today (I haven't received a handwritten letter since school) outlining all the fun times we'd had together. It was uplifting and sad at the same time. It dripped with nostalgia but it wasn't expectant. I think she was trying to wrap up everything that we'd had into a neat bundle, compartmentalise it, celebrate it and move on. It made me cry — things had been so crap in the last few months that I'd blanked out all the happy times. But it was also a weight off my shoulders. 'Closure', I think the word is. It's a good word.

I also had some apologising to do. Mr Poett is a nice man and doesn't deserve to be rung up at two-thirty in the morning to be told to go and copulate with himself. So I wrote him one of the most awkward letters of my life.

And it's here that I feel there is a gap in all our educations. Instead of teaching us stupid role plays in foreign languages — 'You're in charge of a broken-down minibus of schoolchildren in Dieppe; explain to the garage mechanic that the carburettor is leaking' — our schools should have stuck to situations closer to home. Perhaps GCSE English could include a letter-writing module: 'Whilst inebriated, you telephoned your ex-girlfriend's father in the early hours to complain about her sleeping with your best friend.

In no more than 200 words, write an apology note to the father. Remember to write on alternate lines and leave sufficient time to read over your answer.'

And then there was Rick, who had left a series of long answering-machine messages trying to explain himself. I had begun to feel like a dick for my reaction last Friday. And so I went round to his flat for our second make-up session in two months.

'I'm so sorry, mate.' Thump on back. 'Let's never let something like this come between us again.' Double thump on back, pause, another thump, stifled sob, etc., etc.

And then I went home and texted his twin sister, Katie, to see if she'd like a drink sometime. Revenge is a dish best served cold.

Thursday 17th March

I walked in on a conversation between Buddy and Rupert (bald) after lunch today. It went something like this:

Buddy: 'The problem with girls in the city is that they are valuable, overpriced commodities. Even the fattest and ugliest are heavily bid up, like private equity deals in the Middle East.'

Rupert (bald): 'Yeah, mate, you're so right. All the best girls are highly leveraged (and they know it). And then there's the exit strategies to worry about. Very few of them are keen on trade sales.'

Buddy: 'Haw, haw. These days I like to play the international markets with a diverse portfolio stretching across different jurisdictions and time zones. The Thai market has long been strong on liquidity, and Vietnam is catching up fast in depth.'

Rupert (bald): 'I agree. I used to like the US market, but it started getting too litigious.'

Buddy: 'Haw, haw. Emerging markets are often better than more mature markets in my experience, despite the difficulties in securing deal flow.'

Rupert (bald): 'That's the great thing about the listed sector: you can dump your holdings overnight if you need to. Leave the last ten per cent to the next man — that's what I say.'

Buddy: 'Haw, haw.'

It's official. I work with absolute arseholes.

Friday 18th March

Perhaps I should qualify my last entry: only ninety-eight per cent of the people I work with are arseholes. Leila 'spokesperson for the rights of student chocoholics' Sidebottom has just permanently established herself in the two percent minority with the invention of a new game at work: business-card Top Trumps.

It works like normal Top Trumps, except that you play with the various business cards of contacts you've made during your career — a bit like a sane version of *American Psycho*. The choice of category is completely up to you: longest email address, most embossed text, job title seniority, number of colours, most judicious use of fonts, widest variety of contact details, etc.

I established an early lead with Rupert's (bald) use of Helvetica 12 embossed in cyan. Leila struck back with an Andrew Billington from BNP Paribas who gave three mobile numbers, two faxes, two emails and a PO box for his secretary (everything, in fact, apart from a carrier pigeon number). I countered with <*geoffrey.blundell-radomir-blundell@uk.lowsoncommunications.com*> (easily beat her <*bob.hall@gs.com*)>

But then she had me: Sheikh Abdul Al-Rahman, most expansive use of Arabic on a business card. I was stumped.

Top Trumps; top girl. What is she doing in a place like this?

Sunday 20th March

Only a week until my foursome. My balls are the size of melons.

Tuesday 22nd March

I am starting to really hate my job. And I don't mean the vague, unsubstantiated way in which everyone dislikes what they do for a living. I really, really, hate my job.

It was exciting in the early days when I suddenly found myself unspeakably rich after university. The suit, the Blackberry, the free taxis, the Christmas bonuses, the corporate entertainment — it was a heady mix. And even when this wore off, it was still bearable when I had Lucy to look forward to in the evenings. I enjoyed taking her out and buying her expensive presents. She worked in PR. I was the flash city boy. We felt like the perfect London couple. I could have been someone; I could have been a contender.

But now that I'm not with Lucy any more, I realise how fake those little baubles were. I hate the lifestyle I've grown to accept as normal. I hate the fact that I can go out and spend £20 on a Caesar salad at lunchtime and think nothing of it. I hate the fact that girls perk up when they realise how much money I earn.

And the work itself? Well, it's beyond useless. I don't even understand what I'm doing. I've got absolutely no idea how I've benefited anyone in any way. The words on my tombstone will be, 'He never failed to maximise shareholder value'. I remember my father's retirement party and the hoards of happy teachers and former pupils who would never forget the impact he had made on their lives. And then I compare it to my situation. Even if I could, I wouldn't want to go to the top. I remember reading an interview last week about a marketing guru who was coming up to retirement. And I just thought, *Well done, you've sold lots of shampoo really well.*

We spent the entire time at school and university being told that we could do anything we liked. We played sport, joined societies, learned instruments and travelled… and then we totted up all our experiences into CV points so that we could get a job in a bank. I got drunk at a careers fair and scribbled on the wrong dotted line. It's completely nonsensical. We are a spineless generation that signs up to graduate schemes and pension plans in our early twenties. We treat blue chips like well-paid dating agencies to meet the right kind of person.

Well, I've met Leila, and I'm pretty sure she's the right kind of person. At first I thought it was just a rebound thing. But now it's become so much more. Normally the girls I find fun are absolute moose-bags. And the girls I find physically attractive are hideously boring. But Leila is different.

I can't describe it without resorting to clichés, but she's been a ray of sunshine in this rank, putrid tunnel of corporate hell. We've had lunch together almost every day this month. We've kept business-card Top Trumps as our own exclusive game. We talk about another world beyond these glass lifts and plastic trees. She livens up every bleak moment I've spent in this dank hole.

But now that she appears to like Buddy and he likes her, the scales have fallen from my eyes. I've realised just how crap my job is. Chasing a new colleague only temporarily diverted my attention away from how much I hate the whole caboodle. Do you work to live or live to work? Recently, I've just been working myself to death.

I can't stand introducing myself to new people as a banker. I don't want to blue-sky think, or move the goalposts, or network (networking is for paedophiles). I have to start looking elsewhere.

Friday 25th March

Very Good Friday Indeed. Katie texted midweek, which cheered up the old misery guts I've turned into.

We were just having a drink together this evening when Rick rang halfway through.

'Sorry, mate, can't talk now. I'm on a date.'

'Who with, you cheeky slag?'

'Oh, you know her quite well. I'm with Katie.'

At which point protective twin Rick hung up on me.

15—15.

The victory was only soured by Katie slapping me just as I put the phone down.

'You didn't tell me this was a date date. I thought it was just a date.'

'Oh no, don't worry, Katie. I was just using you to get back at Rick.'

At which point she slapped me again.

'Why have you slapped me twice?' I said, grinning.

She slapped me again.

'Thrice. One for the date, one for the date date, one just for fun.'

Not convinced I'm going to make the Fielding family Christmas card list this year.

Sunday 27th March

Hallelujah, I thought, as I woke up on this glorious Easter Sunday. After forty days and forty nights of torment, tempted still yet undefiled, I get to have simultaneous sex with three of my female friends. Tonight I become a real man, the ultimate champion of 'I have never...', the doyen of internet purity tests.

It's not been easy, I can tell you. Every time Leila turned up to work in a new outfit I almost screamed in internal frustration. Sexy advertising aroused me on the Underground. Bumpy buses caused embarrassing bumps in my trousers. And coming home to see Flatmate Fred chomping over his computer was almost the final straw. I even took to changing TV channels whenever a romantic scene started in a film.

After breakfast today, I went out to the local shop to buy four bottles of cheap wine and a bumper packet of condoms. Pure class. The newsagent gave me a wink which said, 'You absolute hero.' I might have imagined it, but I could have sworn that the old lady in the queue patted me on the bum.

I was just walking back to the flat when my mobile rang. It was Claire.

'Happy Easter, Jack. Congratulations. Your Lent fast is over.'

'Thanks, I feel very pure spiritually. So what time are you guys coming round?'

'Ha ha. You're a funny one, Jack. You didn't honestly believe us, did you?'

'No, er, of course not. Ha ha. Don't be silly. Happy Easter to you, too. Enjoy the chocolate.'

I returned home and went into the kitchen, where Flatmate Fred was making coffee in my dressing gown.

'That's a lot of wine for two of us, Jack... Oh my God, that's a lot of condoms for two of us, as well.'

'You know me, Fred. Just stocking up on supplies.'

We had a drunken Easter lunch together in celebration of our saviour's resurrection. And then I went off to my room for some quality Jack-time, acutely aware of a burning emptiness in what I used to call my soul.

APRIL

Friday 1st April

We're a quarter of the way through the year and I can't get rid of the niggling feeling that I haven't done a huge amount with my time. April is the cruellest month:

One *Prunus subhirtella* — stolen, returned and paid for
One ex-girlfriend — slept with and returned; paid for a million times over
One best mate — almost lost, but returned semi-intact
One beautiful colleague — complete mess; will pay for my lies
One ugly American colleague — see above
One left testicle — still slightly painful
One flatmate — data enterer of the month
One foursome — don't even go there

In fact, about the only thing I've achieved is my Lent fast, which isn't the kind of thing to shout about from the rooftops. And a fat lot of good it did me, too.

To cheer me up at work, I decided to play a little April Fools' joke. Leila had slipped away from her desk for a meeting at around 11am and forgotten to lock her computer. Ah, the sweet innocence of the youthful new recruit. The less innocent old-timer (me) slipped into her chair and accessed her email account.

I opened up a new message.

To: Buddy Wilton-Steer
From: Leila Sidebottom
Subject: No subject
Friday 1st April 11.06

Hey sexy! Any plans for the weekend?

Leila
xxxx

Buddy replied straight away (keen Yank) and the exchange continued like this:

'Hello there my favourite little tutee fruitee, how are things? Going out with a few friends on Saturday — fancy coming? B x'

'Oh please, big boy. I always fancy coming. What are you wearing? L xxxx'

'Now or then? B x'

'What are you wearing now, my great big Buddy. Tell little Leila what Buddy's wearing right now, on 1st April, before midday. L xxxxxxxxxxxxxx'

'Leila? X'

'No, you fat cunt, it's Jack.'

I am a genius. Absolutely raw, undiluted genius. I could just make out Buddy going red with rage in the distant corner of the office. I deleted the emails from Leila's inbox and returned smugly to my desk.

Monday 4th April

I am a fool. A raw, undiluted, smug dick of a fool. The poo has hit the fan. It's one big tits-up, pear-shaped cock-up.

Leila emailed me at around 7pm to ask if I wanted to pop out for a quick bite to eat. *Brilliant*, I thought. We'd done lunch (twenty-four times). We'd done coffee. We'd even done drinks. But we'd never done an evening meal. This was surely a positive sign. Perhaps she'd got over her little infatuation with Buddy and was going to declare her undying love for me. Perhaps she was tired of waiting for me to summon up the courage to say something.

But Leila didn't seem to be in a loving mood as we stood in an awkwardly silent lift together.

'Not the canteen,' she muttered, as I moved to press the button for the basement. 'Somewhere outside the office.'

Aha, romantic, I thought. *She's feeling embarrassed and doesn't want our first kiss to be over a plastic container of ravioli.*

But she insisted on Starbucks when I wanted to take her somewhere a bit nicer. We sat at the table where I'd told Buddy over a month ago that Leila didn't fancy him.

'Explain yourself,' Leila said sternly. I'd never seen this side of her before. The giggly girl had gone. She was steely and determined. She looked even better than ever.

'Er, sorry, I'm not sure what I've done.' I had the *FT* on my lap and I could feel it rising above the bulge in my trousers. An upward trend in the Dow Jones — sponsored by Jack's willy.

'Perhaps I can jog your short-term memory. What were you doing on my computer last Friday?'

'Oh, there was that presentation we were working on. I couldn't find my Excel slides, so I had to check the spreadsheets on your H-drive. Sorry.'

God, how I would love to spread her over my sheets.

'So you weren't using my computer to send ridiculous emails to Buddy, then?'

Arse, that's exactly what I was using her computer for. Although I'd cunningly deleted the emails from Leila's inbox, I'd completely forgotten to delete them from her 'sent items' as well. Arse, arse and more arse. I was busted. I couldn't think of anything to say to her, so I opted for a statesman-esque silence. But Leila wanted a statement, not a statesman.

'Well, did you? Yes or no?'

'Yep,' I mumbled.

'Why couldn't you just own up straight away? And you know you've got me into trouble with your last line — the "No, you fat *unmentionable word*, it's Jack" bit? You know that words like that flash up on the IT department's radar if you spell them out in full.'

I did know that. Sh*t. What a silly bl**dy d*ck I am for forgetting.

'I'm so sorry.'

But it wasn't the use of the 'c' word which really angered Leila, although I had clearly dropped at least twenty brownie points merely for knowing the word existed. What is it with girls and the c-word? It's just a word. Cunt, cunt, cunty cunt. There you go — it's really not that bad. It's got the same number of 'c's as the word 'dick'. Same *Countdown* structure: consonant, vowel, consonant, consonant. It's merely an anagram of a Viking king.

But I digress. What really bothered Leila was that she wanted to know why. 'Why, Jack?'

'It was just a silly joke, Leila. I'm sorry. A dumb-arsed April Fools' gag. I didn't mean to get you into trouble or embarrass you.'

'No, not that. Why did you lie to me and Buddy? Why did you gain both our confidences and then lie to us both about how the other felt? I thought you were my friend. I've really grown to like you over the last month.'

Oh god. Buddy's email exchange must have made the two of them talk a few things over.

This is it, I thought. *Don't screw it up, Lancaster.* Carpe *the bloody* diem. *Tell her that you've liked her since you first saw her. Tell her that she makes you feel like no one else has ever done. Tell her that she makes you want to be a better person. Tell her that she's beautiful in every way that a mortal human being can be beautiful.*

'I dunno, Leila. I guess I'm just a bit of a dick.'

I'd seized the day with all the dexterity of a dead hamster. Leila got up and stormed out — 'Jack, for the first time, I agree with you' — and I was left by myself.

I was lower than the low. A quick caffeine fix at the counter didn't do much to lift the spirits, either. When you've just had a row in an American-owned coffee house in Britain and then have to order an Indian-made tea from a Spanish waiter who makes you give your desired size in mock-Italian ('A venti darjeeling to go — smashing'), you begin to wonder whether life is worth living.

Work is never going to be the same again. I have to leave.

Wednesday 6th April

As if my life didn't suck enough already, I am ninety per cent certain that I have testicular cancer. All the symptoms are there; I've looked them up on the internet. They went away for a bit, but now they're back and I can't keep on pretending that they're not.

I have a painful left testis and a general feeling of heaviness in the scrotum.

My man-breasts are slightly enlarged and I have a dull ache in the groin. The risk of contracting the cancer is higher for boys born with their testicles in the lower abdomen (I had to have an operation on mine aged eleven to bring them down — my first public erection) and for those with a history of injury to the scrotal area (viz New Year's Eve).

Now, I'm aware that there are a number of different ways of dealing with such a set of circumstances. The most logical course of action would be to book a doctor's appointment straight away. The GP would probably tell me to stop being a hypochondriac and go home. Or, worst-case scenario, he'd carry out a series of tests, diagnose me with testicular cancer and send me in for an inguinal orchidectomy (aka chopping off the offending bollock). If that didn't work, he'd zap me with a spot of radiotherapy followed by chemo, which would at least give me an excuse for going bald. It might be a long, drawn-out battle but I would almost certainly survive. Testicular cancer is nearly always curable if found early.

The other course of action would be to ignore all the symptoms in the hope that they'll go away again.

I choose the second option.

Friday 8th April

The final straw to break Jack's back.

Buddy and Leila came round to my desk together and asked me out for lunch. I'd been studiously ignoring them both since Monday. This looked ominous.

But Leila looked radiantly happy; she had that luminescent beautiful air which girls only have when they're in love.

'Jack,' gushed Leila, 'I thought you should be the first to know that Buddy and I have got together. Thank you so much.'

Smash all the clocks. Piss on the pianos. Shoot the bloody dog with his bone.

'Wow. That's, er, great. But why are you thanking me? I thought you were annoyed with me.'

'Oh, not at all, Jacko, boy,' said Buddy. There was a look of pity in his eyes as he took me in. 'Much better for us to have found out for ourselves.'

'Yes,' chipped in Leila. 'And if it hadn't been for your April Fools' joke, it could have taken us ages to find out how the other one felt.'

The illogical little filly. If I'd really wanted to help out, I wouldn't have lied to them both when entrusted with my Cupid mission. Women really are a conundrum. But unlike 'Jimmy the barber shaves all the men on Anglesey, except for those who shave themselves. Who shaves Jimmy?', women are at least a conundrum with breasts.

Office love, it would seem, forgives all.

Buddy's hand was on Leila's thigh. *How bloody dare he.* That was private property. No trespassing. I love her as much as I hate Buddy. There is no doubt about it: I *have* to leave this office now.

Sunday 10th April

'Fred, I was on the BBC website again at work yesterday, and I started looking at their "On This Day" page. And you know what I found out this time?'

'No, do tell.'

'Well, on 9th April 2003 Saddam Hussein's statue was toppled in Iraq. On 9th April 1999 the President of Niger, a certain Ibrahim Bare Mainassara, was shot dead in a coup attempt. And I suddenly realised that, yet again, yesterday, I, Jack Lancaster, got up at 6.45am on a Saturday to go to work, showered, shat, shaved, read my book on the tube and spent twelve hours staring into space at a highly paid job that I hate.'

'Yeah, not much has changed, has it?' said Fred.

He paused before adding, 'Although you aren't having as much sex as you used to.'

'Thanks. I mean, for many of the five billion human beings with whom we share this little in-joke of existence, Saturday 9th April will have been a memorable day. Thousands will have got married, had their first child or paid off their mortgages. Others will have won the lottery, visited long-lost friends or run over the cat. Relationships will have stopped and started, grandchildren born, dogs died, wars waged, deals struck, enemies made, friends lost, parents divorced. Someone, somewhere, has just this second had their first unforgettable orgasm.'

I paused, waiting for Flatmate Fred to grasp the significance of what I was saying.

'Jack, you really are having a midlife crisis.'

'Can we call it a quarter-life crisis at least?' I protested.

'Sure,' he continued. 'But crisis away. Get it out of your system. You're young and liberated. Do young and liberated things before you're too embarrassingly old to do them any more. Make love to two women at once. Nose-hoover Peruvian narcotics off an ice ledge. Run naked through flowered fields. Stand in the middle of a chapel and scream. Live the dream.'

'Right.'

'I mean, there's nothing sadder than a middle-aged man with a sports car and a comb-over, combing the streets for his lost youth.'

'Indeed. But what exactly do you have in mind? Specifically, I mean.'

'In your case, I'd recommend trying to get sacked from work, followed by a few weeks of heavy, debauched partying, followed by an attempt to work out what your purpose in life is.'

Flatmate Fred's a genius. That's exactly what I'll do.

Monday 11th April

Day one of trying to lose my job. Of course, I could do this the boring way and hand in a resignation letter like everyone else. But where's the fun in that? Or I could do one outrageous act — such as getting naked on my desk and dancing the Macarena with my pants over my head — which would lead to instant dismissal. But that's far too easy.

So I plan on waging a long-term war of attrition. Stage by stage I will wear the bastards down. My trench is dug and I'm coming over the top.

I started my campaign by sending an email to Buddy with every swear word I could think of spelled out in full. I'd rather not repeat the torrent of bile and invective in my diary, but the essential gist was as follows:

'Dear Buddy (you canine copulator), I think you're a bit of a wally. Perhaps you'd like to go back to the States at some point and leave us all in peace. Jack.'

Except that, in the course of the email I managed to use thirty-five of the forty-two words which are banned by our IT department. I always wished I'd been at the meeting where that list was drawn up:

'Derek?'

'Yes, Martin.'

'Can you close the door, please. This is a bit of a sensitive topic, I'm afraid.'

'Oh sure, Derek. All very hush-hush, need-to-know basis.'

'Exactly. Right, Trevor. Why don't you blue-sky-think this one.'

'Sure, Martin. So far I've got "shit", "cock", "twat", "nob", "dick"....'

Nervous cough.

'Yes, Richard. Do you have something to say?'

'Well, yes, Martin. It's just that if we ban the word "dick", some of my emails aren't going to get through. A lot of my friends call me Dick.'

'Good point, Richard. I can see we're going to have to think out of the box on this one.'

Etc., etc.

My email to Buddy pinged straight back, which means he never got to read it. IT have reported me to my managing director and I am in big sh*t. Excellent. The fact that I'm dying from a lump in my bollock aside, I haven't felt this good for ages.

Wednesday 13th April

Big sh*t.

Rupert (bald) asked me to step into his office just after lunch.

'Wotcha, Jack.' He punched me playfully on the arm. 'I see your hair's still receding.'

'Yes, Rupert, it is. One day, if the gods continue to smile on me, I'm going to be as handsome as you.'

'Maybe, Jack, maybe. God knows, you've already got a pretty handsome vocabulary. What was going through your mind when you sent that email?'

I could have handled a dressing-down from Rupert (bald). He's early thirties, unmarried and a bit of a prat. He talks incessantly about girls but never has one. He thinks he's still twenty-three. He's a warning to us all of how we might turn out. But he means well.

But I hadn't counted on Mr Cox joining our little discussion. I'm not sure that Mr Cox has a Christian name. He's just Mr Cox. His wife probably calls him Mr Cox. He's mid-fifties, the overall managing director for both Rupert (bald) and me, and one of the top five scariest people in the world. He came into the office, shut the door behind him and eased his pince-nez down his beak of a nose.

I'm ashamed to say I had to lock my knees together to stop them shaking.

'Jack Lancaster, through sins of both omission and commission, it has been a little while since I, open brackets, your managing director, close brackets, have had a *tête-à-tête*, that is to say a head-to-head, with you.'

'Yes, Mr Cox.'

Mr Cox hitched up his red braces and smoothed down his shiny parting.

'And, PS, Jack, *post scriptum,* it would be untruthful of me, in my capacity as your professional and moral mentor, to pretend that this is not a bad state of affairs. PPS, to put it more simply, I am not unconcerned by your recent behaviour — *id est*, I am rather concerned.'

'Yes, Mr Cox?'

'*Exempli gratia, inter alia*, your electronic communication with young Mr Wilton-Steer. Pray, which unusual cognitive processes led you to conclude that this might not be an unreasonable course of action?'

I couldn't think of any reasonable answer to give this walking Cicero. So I was scared into telling the truth.

'Love, Mr Cox, love.'

'Love, Jack, love? Would it not be incorrect for me to conclude *a priori* that you are emotionally attached to Mr Wilton-Steer? The love that dare not speak its name?'

How do you disagree with a double negative?

'Yes, Mr Cox. I mean, no, Mr Cox. I'm in love with Leila. Buddy stole her off me.'

'*O tempora, o mores!* Leila Sid-day-bot-tome?'

I stifled a giggle.

'Yes, Leila Sidebottom.'

Mr Cox glared at me down his pince-nez.

'Young man, I will not be corrected on my pronunciation by someone with a vocabulary as vulgar as yours. This is your final warning. You are not here to fall in love. You are not here to embark on courtships *in situ*. I do not pay you for your abusive electronic communications. I pay you to maximise value for our shareholders. Be so good as to leave my presence and do that now. *Mutatis mutandis*, you might make a respectable banker one day.'

'Yes, Mr Cox. I do hope so.'

Cunnus maximus.

Saturday 16th April

First boys' night out in over a month. Buddy wasn't invited (for obvious reasons), but it was the first time that the core four of us had been together since the disastrous game of 'I have never...'.

Rick and Jasper joined Flatmate Fred and me, and we drank ten beers each before getting changed and going to School Disco at the Hammersmith Palais. I've never felt that easy about the whole schoolgirl erotica thing. It strikes me as slightly odd that a society that is so vigilant about paedophilia can actively promote school uniform as saucy attire.

Slightly odd. But who cares? Twentysomethings look great in short pleated skirts and white shirts. Hell, when you're wearing your ten-pint beer goggles, fortysomethings look great in short skirts.

Which is lucky, because the Palais (and what a palace it is) was full of middle-aged secretaries on hen nights. It's enough to make you feel proud to be British. Ageing Italians don't dress up like slags and go on the pull. Arab women don't behave in such a debauched fashion.

Fortunately, we found a corner with some younger-looking slags and we were soon gyrating away merrily to S Club 7. I felt a hand on my trousers and a tongue in my ear.

'Take me back to yours.'

She was fit, or at least she acted fit. It would have been rude not to. Jasper and Flatmate Fred, who were dancing either side of another girl, gave me a big thumbs-up. Rick waved from the bar where he was ordering Smirnoff Ices and chatting up the cross-dressing barmaid.

So I did the honourable thing, took her back to mine and took her to heaven and back five times before sunrise. It was even better than sex with Lucy, because there was no gulf between what it was supposed to mean and what it actually meant. It was raw and it was inevitable and it was very, very good.

I recall one particular highlight when she put a finger up my bum.

'Don't touch me there... Oh touch me there... Touch me there.'

Spring is in the air, and I am one frolicking, randy ram.

Sunday 17th April

I am no expert at one-night stands — in fact, this was my first since university — so I had no idea of the etiquette the next morning. Was I meant to wake her up and sleep with her again? Did she expect a cuddle? Did she want breakfast? Could I walk around my own room naked? Were we meant to go to a Sunday-morning church service together? And why was my school tie knotted around the bedpost?

So many meaningless questions and only one really counted: what the hell was she called?

She was still asleep, so I had a rummage in her handbag, which was lying by my bed. I fished out a credit card — 'Miss P. M. Gilmour'. *Oh shit-sticks.* Was it Polly? I was pretty sure she was a Polly. She looked like a Polly. Definitely not a Penelope. Or was she Pam? What if she was called by her second initial? Mandy, Marian, Mary? She was hardly the virgin Mary. Miss P. M. Gilmour. I couldn't call her Miss Gilmour.

'What are you doing in my handbag?'

Polly/Marian had woken up and wasn't looking very happy.

'Oh. Sorry. I was just being nosy,' I stammered.

'You can't remember my name, can you, Jack Lancaster?'

'No, don't be silly. Of course I can remember your name.'

'Well, what is it then, Jack Lancaster?'

'Er, Miss Gilmour?'

At which point Rick, Flatmate Fred and Jasper all charged into my room singing 'Build Me Up Buttercup' and tried to give me a wedgie.

Miss P. M. Gilmour gathered up her tattered dignity and her school uniform and ran outside.

'Polly, Polly, I'm sorry. come back.' I ran after her.

Miss P. M. Gilmour put her head round the corner and said in a voice loud enough for everyone to hear, 'Jack, it's Prudence. And, by the way, you've got a small cock and you're crap in bed.'

Yeuch. Prudence — lucky escape. I was also consoled by the fact that she had to do the walk of shame in her schoolgirl outfit the entire way back to Clapham.

Friday 22nd April

A very boring week at work. My continuing campaign to undermine the system from within is the only thing that's kept me going.

The attrition war is mounting. On Monday I put my bin on my desk and fastened the word 'In-tray' to it with sticky-backed plastic. No one batted an eyelid. On Wednesday I changed my voicemail to 'Please leave a message for me to ignore'. No one rang me. On Thursday I changed my email footer. It now reads:

Jack Lancaster
Managing Director
Tantric Love Ltd
0898 69 69 69

No one commented.

Today I brought in a postcard from home and glued it to my monitor. It was a free card handed out by the Unison trade union: 'Work me to the bone, pay me a pittance, never let me go home.'

Mr Cox swung by my desk.

'Jack, *salve*. Not to mention greetings. Are you quite well? You're quite well, I trust.'

'Yes, Mr Cox, I am very well indeed.'

'That is not unpleasing to hear, Jack — far from unpleasing at all. So you are quite *compos mentis*, then? It's just that the picture postcard that you are displaying on your monitor might suggest otherwise.'

'Oh really, Mr Cox? I'm merely identifying with the struggle of the proletariat. The workers of the world are uniting. We have nothing to lose but our network log-ins.'

'No, Jack. That's a *non sequitur*. The workers of the world are revolting, and you are more revolting than most. Now take that postcard down and put it in your "In-tray".'

'Yes, Mr Cox.'

Mr Cox will be the first against the wall when the revolution comes.

Monday 25th April

On the plus side, I have now given up on going to the gym — that temple to inadequacy and despair, vain aggression and directionless virility. I am bored of competing subconsciously with people twice my size (almost certain to lose) or against the machines themselves (absolutely certain to lose). The treadmill's power supply will always last longer than mine. The step machine might not be able to carry on stepping without my help, but at least it won't be lying on the floor retching its guts out.

Gym-philes have two illusions: one, that they will get more action in the bedroom; two, that physical prowess will translate into wider success. These fantasies aren't helped by the fitness fanatics currently occupying some of the most powerful positions in international politics.

Well, I'm under neither of these illusions. Welcome back, my lovely beer keg. All is forgiven.

Wednesday 27th April

The irony of the little Buddy 'n' Leila sideshow is that Leila and I have made up and become really good friends again. Now that I'm no longer seen as a sexual threat, she's even more open with me than before. And now that she's no longer on my direct target list, I am much more at ease around her. Our lunches have started again. And Buddy works such long hours that Leila and I have regularly gone drinking *à deux* in the evenings. She even knows that I'm having a quarter-life crisis and am trying to get sacked (although I've kept the testicle bit to myself — cancer isn't much of a turn-on, I'm told).

We might have turned into genuine friends, but I still like the fact that I can see beyond her obvious charms. Others might think she's fit; I think she's beautiful. And somehow she manages to be bubbly and shy, giggly and serious, compassionate and ironic, modern and old-fashioned, ambitious and homely, in all the right measures.

And, as for her, I think she looks up to me in a bemused — if depressingly asexual — sort of way. I might not be Buddy with his cocksure American ambition, but I do at least make her laugh. I think she admires my silly give-a-damn attitude. She is straight out of university. This job is a dream come true for her. She lacks my cynical nature.

'I'm not a cynic,' I tell her. 'I'm just a lapsed idealist.'

'Same difference,' she giggles. 'Now just tell me again why my favourite lapsed idealist would like to leave a job with such lovely colleagues and a six-figure salary.'

That's the problem. Some of the colleagues are just that little bit too lovely; the rest are subhuman/shagging the lovely ones.

In some ways I've grown to see her in a new light. She's no longer a very fit girl who happens to be a nice person. She's now a very good friend who just happens to be attractive.

Well done, me. But it doesn't mean that I've stopped fantasising about her. She ticks every box and I'm madly in love with her.

Saturday 30th April

Lucy rang up to say that she was pregnant.

MAY

Sunday 1st May

Lucy refused to give any more details on the phone yesterday, arranging only to meet up on the Bank Holiday tomorrow to talk properly. Until then I am left in a living hell of unanswerable questions. Is she sure she's pregnant? Isn't she on the pill? Is she going to terminate it? And who the hell is the father — Rick, me or someone else?

I try to take my mind off this by buying a newspaper, but the advert on the front page is for baby bonds — 'investing in your child's future'. A glance at the TV guide tells me that there is a documentary in the evening on unwanted pregnancies. I turn on the TV in the morning and there is a nappies advert. I try to escape the flat and the first thing I see on the Underground is a three-metre poster for pregnancy-test kits. I go into Boots to buy some painkillers for my pounding headache and the girl in front of me is crying and asking for the morning-after pill.

My own subconscious is stalking me and there's nothing I can do about it. Why the fuck did she ring and hang up like that? I try to phone her back, but her phone diverts straight to answering machine.

I don't even know what I want her to say. I think I'll make a great father one day, but not now. *Now* it would ruin my life. My parents would kill me. I'd probably end up marrying Lucy out of a perverse sense of guilt. My mum's delight that the two of us were back together would be outweighed by her anguish at having a semi-bastard grandchild.

But could I face Rick having a baby with my ex-girlfriend of three years? I'm not sure I could. Especially if it's ginger…

Monday 2nd May

Blur sang about bank holidays. It was a happy song about barbecues and six-packs of beer. It didn't mention anything about discussing pregnancies with your ex-girlfriend.

We met up in the same bar in Covent Garden where Lucy had made up the news about pulling Rick back in January. I think the barman recognised me as the madman who'd stormed out crying.

'So?' I said.

Poor Lucy, she looked tired and withdrawn.

'So. Here we are.'

'Yes, here we are.'

'Did you know that today is our anniversary?' she asked, somewhat surprisingly.

Of course I didn't know. I've never quite understood anniversaries. Do you start counting from when you first meet? Or when you first pull? Or when you first introduce them as your girlfriend to someone?

'Oh yes,' I mumbled, correctly guessing that now wasn't the time to share these thoughts.

'Jack,' she said, cutting to the chase, 'I am a hundred and ten per cent sure that I am pregnant.'

I winced at the maths. You don't have to be a banker to understand that that's pretty certain.

'I wasn't sure at first,' she went on. 'I took the pill for over three years while going out with you, and I stopped it recently to give my body a rest. As you know, the pill regulates your periods.'

Lucy Poett, BSc Biology.

'So when I missed my first period at the end of February I didn't worry too much. Then I missed my second period and then my third. I did my own pregnancy test and it was positive. I went to the doctor on Saturday and she confirmed it.'

'And are you going to keep it?'

'Well, at first I didn't want to. But I'm now eleven weeks pregnant.'

Eleven weeks? It's exactly eleven weeks since Rick slept with her on Valentine's Day. Ten weeks and four days since I bent her over the kitchen table.

'You can use an abortion pill up to nine weeks, but after that they have to do a vacuum aspiration. I just can't face hoovering up our baby.'

'Our baby?' I was trying to be gentle with her, but I must have shouted the words. People started looking at me weirdly.

'Yes, baby. Our baby,' she said in a soothing voice. 'Who else's is it going to be?'

'Well, you slept with Rick three days before me, didn't you? Isn't it just conceivable (bad choice of word) that his sperm had a head start on mine? They can't swim that slowly.'

'I'm sure his sperm are Olympian athletes. But they couldn't get very far inside a condom, could they?'

'Rick used a condom?'

'Yes.'

'And you slept with me without a condom after you'd stopped taking the pill.'

'Yes.'

'Why? You didn't tell me that you'd stopped taking the pill.'

'Because I love you, Jack. Because you're The One. Because I'll never stop loving you. And I know that you feel the same way about me. You're just too scared to admit it. You're too afraid of commitment.'

'You love me so much that you'd trick me into making you pregnant? You'd make a fool out of me to dupe me into coming back to you?'

She gave me a long and emotional answer which boiled down to one word: yes. Women never use one word when a thousand will do just as well.

'I can't handle this. I need time to think,' I said.

I got out enough money to cover our drinks and left calmly, too numb to show any emotion. I didn't walk back to the tube. I stood still and the road moved in slow motion under me like a movie. Happy extras floated past me. I was the star in my own tragicomedy. This was the kind of thing that happened to other people. Not to me.

And now that I've thought about it long and hard, I cannot imagine a worse situation.

I wanted to ring Leila to explain everything to her, but I was worried that she'd take a pretty dim view of me sleeping with my ex-girlfriend. So I rang my dad and he was a sympathetic listener, but there wasn't much he could say to help.

I'm going to have to sort it out for myself, but I just don't know what to do. I don't want this. I don't want her, I don't want a baby and I certainly don't want a baby with *her*. This is a living nightmare and I have absolutely no idea what to do about it.

I try to lay my thoughts out logically:

(1) Babies

Babies are good things. They chuckle and call you 'Dada', and one day you can teach them to play football for England and they'll buy you a nice big house in Cheshire. It's good for the human race to procreate. I have above-average genes and I'd like to see them passed on. More than anything else, I want to be a good father one day. Being a family man would make me very happy.

But babies are also bad things. They cry and they stink, and they cost a lot of money. They require a great deal of attention. They deserve a responsible father, and not someone who's too scared to go to the GP about his testicular lump/steals trees/shags random slags dressed as schoolgirls/wants to get sacked from work.

I don't want a baby.

(2) Lucy

Lucy is a nice girl. She makes me laugh. She's also very attractive. We have good sex together, especially when we're not actually together. Having a baby with Lucy might jolt me into sorting out the rest of my life. It might teach me to put others first and to stop being such a whingeing hypochondriac.

Lucy, on the other hand, is vain, petty and snobby. She's also a freak. She tried to pull my best friend to make me jealous. Then she slept with him on Valentine's Day. Then she tricked me into having unprotected sex with her three days later. Her lovely closure letter on 16th March was merely a pack of lies while she waited to see if she'd trapped me into becoming a father. Hell, I trust her so little that I can't even be sure if her pregnancy story is true. There is no way I am going back to her.

I don't want Lucy.

(3) Abortions

I don't like the idea of abortions. I don't like the idea of killing anything. And how could I kill my own son/daughter? A quick bit of research on Google tells me that an unborn baby's heart begins to beat between the eighteenth and the twenty-fifth day. Electrical brain waves have been recorded as early as forty days. Lucy has been pregnant for at least seventy-three days.

But then I don't think it's fair to bring an unwanted child into this world to satisfy the whim of a mad girl who's trying to lure her boyfriend back.

I want an abortion.

And so I plan to call Lucy's bluff. If she wants to go ahead and have the baby anyway, I'll work it out as it comes. And I also *really* have to talk to Rick — who's chosen a very bad time to go away on holiday.

Tuesday 3rd May

Mr Cox dragged me into the office again.

'Jack, I could not help noticing, that is to say I did notice, as I walked past your desk yesterday, that you were not there, that is to say you were *in absentia*. Perhaps you would not mind explaining why.'

'Mr Cox, yesterday was a bank holiday.'

'Yes, Jack, I am not unaware of that fact. That fact is, in fact, irrefutable. But what possible relevance do you imagine that irrefutable fact has on your position here?'

'I'm not sure I understand, Mr Cox.'

'OK, dear boy. Let's start *ab initio*. What do you do for a living, Jack?'

'I'm not sure, sir.'

'No, Jack, neither am I. *Nil desperandum*. Back to first principles. Where do you work?'

'In a bank, Mr Cox.'

'Very good, Jack. And in what kind of bank do you work?'

'An investment bank, Mr Cox.'

' 'Excellent. A *Proxime accessit* answer, if not a First Class one. And what kind of banks close on a bank holiday?'

'A high-street bank, Mr Cox?'

'Eureka, young Lancaster. *Quod erat demonstrandum*. So why weren't you here yesterday?'

'Personal problems, Mr Cox.'

'*Plus ça change*. Pray, who was the lucky recipient of your youthful affections this time? Ms Sid-day-bot-tome?'

'No, Mr Cox, a former girlfriend.'

'Jack, what do I pay you for?'

Friday 6th May

It has not been an amusing week. I sent Lucy a very long email on Tuesday outlining a toned-down version of my thoughts from 2nd May. She still hasn't replied and time is running out for her to have a safe and effective abortion. I'm hanging on for Rick's return next Monday.

More depressing still, they appear to have given up censuring me at my work. Even my comic attempt at dress-down Friday today — ripped jeans, trainers and a T-shirt which said 'Fcuk the system' — raised nothing more than a wry eyebrow from Mr Cox.

Bad things come in threes, I mused, as I went to bed with no plans for the weekend. First, Leila and Buddy. Second, a lumpy testicle. Third, a pregnant ex-girlfriend.

It's all plain sailing from here.

Wednesday 11th May

Or maybe it's *not* plain sailing.

'No plans for the weekend' turned into a very long weekend with Flatmate Fred in Amsterdam. I smell, I'm tired and I've got horrendous memory loss. Even if I do decide to go in tomorrow, I'm not sure if I can remember where I work. I've been AWOL for three days.

It all started when we woke up at lunchtime on Saturday.

Flatmate Fred: 'What shall we do this weekend?'

'I rather thought I'd read the papers until mid-afternoon, shower, get dressed, go out, drink eight pints, get into a sissy fight and then crash and burn with half the female population of our great capital.'

'Isn't that what we do every weekend?'

'It's what I do every weekend. You do it every weekday, too.'

'Ha, very funny. I just find that every week in London merges into the next one. I can't think of a single weekend that's really stood out. Why don't we do something properly different this weekend?'

'Like what?'

'I don't know.'

We sat in contemplative silence for a while.

'We could go to a museum.'

'Five minutes' sustained thought and you've come up with that brainwave. You're a crazy party-pooper, Fred.'

Another longer silence.

'Jack, do you have a passport?'

'Yes.'

'Right, line your stomach. We're going to Amsterdam.'

And so we did.

Amsterdam is truly the armpit of Europe (and it's an unshaven smelly one, too). I'm told there are nice parts, but we stuck to the fun areas with entire streets of small windows lined with semi-clad women. It was like the Hammersmith Palais, but more honest (and probably marginally cheaper). The eldest, fattest women were placed at the end. Flatmate Fred coined the term 'last-window girl'.

We tried to assimilate ourselves slowly into the culture by having a Coca-Cola in an English pub. It seemed a safe bet — we hadn't banked on the barman making us clarify what we meant by 'coke'.

So we decided to go and get stoned. I'm sure the coffee-shop tenders could spot the novices a mile off. We were the ones sidling up to the bar and mumbling, 'I'd like a, y'know [*cough*], joint, if that's OK.' 'Which joint do you want?' 'Shh, not so loud — there might be teachers around,' etc., etc.

But, once we'd convinced ourselves that we weren't going to be writing out lines in detention, we were the happiest people in the world. Flatmate Fred was spouting lines of pure golden comedy. 'Last-window girl — rahahahahaahaha.' My left testicle stopped aching, I stopped worrying about Lucy and I had a warm, glowing feeling that I was going to end up with Leila.

I still had this warm, glowing feeling on Sunday evening, so we decided to stay a little while longer. Work and Mr Cox could take a running leap. The next two days passed in a contented blur. Some events stand out clearly; I remember the 'only gay pancake shop in Amsterdam' very vividly. (How do you have a gay pancake shop? It's like having heterosexual recycling bins.) Other events merged into a confused collage. Others still, flowed past, unrecognised and forgotten. The whole experience felt like a few minutes. It also lasted an eternity.

It was all perfect until this morning, when Flatmate Fred decided it would be a good idea to try a hash cake. I ate one and it had no effect. So I ate another. And then a third. No one told me that it takes a little while to get into your system. I smoked another joint to ease the process along.

Forty minutes later, I passed out in the loo. Flatmate Fred had to help me back to the hostel dormitory, where I spent three hours lying on my bed convinced that the slumbering backpacker opposite was going to axe me if I took my eye off him for a second. Paranoia spread all over me. I was pulling the whitie of the century. I could feel panic rising up my legs. It reached my waist. I had to stop it getting up to my vital organs or it would kill me. I had to concentrate. The walls were flying in at me, laughing at me, mocking me, crushing me.

I couldn't hold on to a thought for more than a split second. They rushed madly through my brain; wild dislocated connectors. Leila — Buddy — American — New York — apple — Garden of Eden — sex — Rick — baby — Lucy — abortion — sin — Bible — school — Daddy — Mummy — New Year's resolutions — tosspot — Buddy — Leila, etc., etc., all in half a second. I couldn't slow them down. It was like an internalised game of Timmy Mallett's Mallet on speed.

I started to sing softly to take my mind off impending death.

'Baa, baa, black sheep, have you any hash?'

'Sleepen or fuck off,' gargled the axe murderer.

I couldn't sleepen. It was time to fuck off. Pulling myself together, I found Flatmate Fred and bought a very expensive ticket back to London to face the music of pregnant ex-girlfriends and irate bosses.

Friday 13th May

Not the most auspicious date of the year — I decided it would be bad luck to go into work today. Actually, I decided it would be bad luck to go into work yesterday as well, but that's beside the point.

I'd deliberately left my mobile behind when I went to Amsterdam. When I came back, there were over twenty texts and voicemail messages waiting — one friendly text from Claire (doctors 'n' nurses) arranging a drink, one from Katie (first Valentine's card and Rick's twin) asking me to the theatre (she must have forgiven me), one from Daddy asking about the Lucy situation, four from Leila showing an increasing level of concern about my absence, one mocking voice message from Buddy, three irate from Rupert (bald), five whingeing from Lucy and one and a half from Mr Cox.

New message, received Wednesday, 12th May, at 10.52am:

> '*Salve*, Jack. *Deo volente*, this is Jack. My message was prefaced by a somewhat mechanised-sounding lady. Pray, are you courting her as well? What a busy life you lead. Too busy, it would appear, to come into the office... This is Mr Cox... Rupert Boscawen, who, as you no doubt will not be unaware, is your line manager, has informed me that you have not turned up for three days. Are you dead? Are you *in rigor mortis*? Might we dare to expect a resurrection at some point in the...'

Beep. End of message.

New message, received Wednesday, 12th May, at 10.56am:

> 'Lancaster, this is Mr Cox again. That bloody woman cut me off. Contact me as soon as you get this. You're in a mountain full of excreta.'

Charming.

There was also a text from Rick.

'Easy mate, Rick here, innit. Where the hell are you? We really need to talk, izzit. R.'

Rick was right. We really did need to talk — me in English; him in Rick-speak. Right away.

I couldn't face the forced jocularity of the Friday-night crowds: the wretched office workers who'd been waiting for their weekly chance to hit expensively themed bars and forget that they hated their colleagues almost as much as the jobs they were bitching about with them.

So I went over to Rick's flat in Angel. I gave him the summary of what Lucy had told me. And I told him how I felt about it.

'Izzit. That's exactly why I had to talk to you, Jack. That baby could equally well be mine.'

'But she told me you guys used a condom.'

'We did. A lemon-flavoured one, in fact.'

The vague notion of my best mate sleeping with my ex-girlfriend was just about OK. The specifics were far from OK.

I soldiered on.

'So what happened?'

'It broke, innit.'

Not only did Rick sleep with Lucy; his cock is so big that it shatters johnnies. How inadequate do I feel?

'And you didn't tell her?'

'No, I assumed she was on the pill. Thought she made me wear the johnny in case I caught any nasty diseases off you.'

'Cheers, Rick.'

'So what are we going to do?'

'Fuck knows.'

If only 'Fuck' did know.

Deciding that Friday 13th was no day to go about making life-changing decisions, we played five hours of FIFA football on the Xbox instead.

Am not convinced that either of us is sufficiently mature to be a father.

Wednesday 18th May

Still haven't been into work post-Amsterdam. I think I have hit upon the perfect way to get sacked — don't turn up. This is a great deal easier than showing my face and performing elaborate ruses with email footers and trade union postcards. The only irony is that I can't be sacked without a written warning, and they don't have my home address to give me one. I find this incredibly amusing.

Leila finds it less amusing. Because she's supremely fit, I'm always willing to give her the benefit of the doubt.

She came round for a drink this evening.

'Jack. Oh Jack, Jack.'

I love it when she says my name.

'Jack, I thought something serious had happened to you. What on earth is going on?'

'I'm so sorry, Leila. I should have told you everything.'

So I told her everything. Everything about Lucy and Rick and Amsterdam, at least. The bit about wanting to wrap her up into a cute little bundle of perfection because I like her so much — that I left out.

'That's awful. Oh, God — poor you. But you can't let Lucy ruin your life and your career. You've got to come back to work. You don't really want to leave, do you?'

'Leila, we've had this discussion a thousand times. You know how much I hate working there. You know I have to move on.'

'I'm sure if you apologised now, they would forgive and forget.'

'Forgive and forget? Mr Cox? Now come, Leila Sid-day-bot-tome, I don't think it would be amiss of me to suggest that the man has neither forgotten nor forgiven anything in his life. *Mea culpa* is not his favourite Latin expression.'

'Oh Jack, you're so funny.'

Yes, I am rather, aren't I?

'Please come back to work and entertain me.'

'You don't need me, Leila. You've got Buddy. Three's a crowd. Too many bankers spoil the broth, etc.'

'Too many bankers spoil everything, Jack. And Buddy? Well, if you'd deigned to pop into the office at some point during the last ten days, you'd know that we've split up.'

Oh Frabjous day. I'm chortling in inner joy.

'Oh, Leila, I'm so sorry to hear that. That's awful. Poor you.'

Can I give her a hug? Of course, I can — it would be rude not to.

I can feel her breasts against my chest. It feels very nice. Very nice indeed. Hmmm, have to break away now.

'Yep, the office is hell,' she sniffs. 'Everyone knows about it. All he wanted was sex, and now he's bad-mouthing me to everyone.'

'I'm so sorry. What are you going to do?'

Now is the time, Lancaster. Now is the bloody time. Tell her how you feel, you arse.

'I'm going to tough it out. I've done nothing wrong. And I'm also going to be celibate for a very long time. Men are crap.'

She's not wrong. None of us deserves her.

'Sure, most of us are.'

'Not you, Jack. You're different. You're a good friend. Well, if you do have to leave, can't you just go quietly? Hand in your notice like everyone else?'

'I think it's a little too late for that, Leila. I plan to enjoy myself along the way.'

'You're a funny one,' she says. 'I guess that's why I like you.'

She reaches up and kisses me very delicately on the cheek and then skips out.

Sunday 22nd May

Spent the weekend composing my resignation letter. I know there's no possible way that they're not going to sack me, but I'd like to nip in there so I can say I dumped them first.

I'm rather pleased with it. It goes like this:

Dear Mr Cox,

I'm delighted to be able to inform you that I am handing in my notice.

I trust that this news is neither surprising nor unwelcome. I hope that this letter makes up for that.

You are a fat tart, an *Arschgeige*, a *gilipollas*, a *manyak*, an *espèce de salaud* and a nob-jockey of the premier rung. You are a pitiful excuse for a human being. You were the last to be picked in the playground. Your mother — if, indeed, you have one — swims out to troop ships.

However, I would like to thank you for giving me the unique opportunity to start my career with Citicorp. I have learned many things. I have learned how to lie, how to deceive and how to flatter. I am au fait with hypocrisy, fraud and selfishness. You have taught me greed, envy and boredom. I am skilled in meaningless apologies, time-wasting and email banter.

Most of all, I have learned that I want to be nothing like you in forty years time.

I believe that my official notice period is one month. However, if you expect me to spend another second in this dreary shithole that I have learned to call hell, you can think again.

I wish you all the best for what remains of your soulless, humourless life. In the hope that the fleas of a thousand camels infest your armpits, I now end our acquaintance.

Hugs,
Jack Lancaster

Monday 23rd May

Another day mooching around at home.

'She can't really want to be celibate, can she?' I ask Flatmate Fred.

'If you're her only option, then, yes, probably.'

'But it's sacrilege for someone as beautiful as her to be celibate. It's one big torment for all of mankind. It's a tragic waste.'

'Jack, I'm trying to work.'

The irony of hard-working Flatmate Fred trying to shush Jack the slacker. He's perked up remarkably recently, giving himself six months to have a proper stab at his screenplay. He's waking up before 9.30am every day, washing regularly and not allowing himself to watch any daytime TV. He seems at peace with himself.

'But, mate, maybe I've got it all wrong. Maybe I should go back into work, make my apologies, get on with everyone and get it on with Leila. It won't be so unbearable now that Buddy's out of the picture.'

'For bollocks' sake, Lancaster.' Flatmate Fred flings down his Biro in anguish. There are ink stains on his forehead. 'Either you're having a quarter-life crisis or you're not. Make your sodding mind up. Even if they don't sack you — which will take a miracle — the job's still going to stink as much as it ever did. Get out now while you still can. It might be easier to say something to Leila once you're no longer working with her.'

He's right. Of course he is. But it's hard leaving a routine, even one you hate. I've been utterly miserable loafing around at home doing nothing for the last ten days. I'm like a hostage who's grown affectionate towards his captors. All I've done on the outside is watch *Neighbours* twice a day in case I've missed anything in the plot the first time. Sometimes I long for my golden handcuffs and the pearly whips of the city slave galley. (*OK, let's not get carried away here.*)

Tomorrow is D-day. Tomorrow I walk through the door into a glorious future.

Tuesday 24th May

Slept through my alarm and didn't wake up until *The World at One* came on the radio. Decided that it was too late to start my glorious future today.

Watched *Neighbours*. Twice. And then bugged Flatmate Fred.

'Fred, I've just realised that I've got a few days' paid holiday left this year. Perhaps I should take them first and then hand in my resignation.'

'Listen up, arse-for-brains. How many messages have you had on your mobile from work in the last ten days?'

'Er, about twenty.'

'And how many of those have been pleasant, friendly ones offering you bonuses and promotions?'

'Er, about none.'

'And what did your last quarterly report say about you?'

'That I'm undermotivated, lazy, idle, obnoxious, stubborn and almost certain to be made redundant before the end of the year.'

'Isn't that enough for you?'

'Well, Churchill and Thatcher had some pretty useless reports when they were at school.'

'Yep, but so did Hitler. Face it. It's over. It's what you wanted. Hand in your notice, and we'll go and do something fun afterwards to celebrate.'

He's right. Tomorrow I walk through the door into a glorious future.

Wednesday 25th May

Glorious future D-day.

Turned up at work just before 9am dressed smartly with my resignation letter in hand. I was going to do this properly.

Suddenly realised I was far too scared to do it properly, so I opened the champagne which I'd brought along with me for afterwards. The tramp outside the office raised his bottle of meths to me in a friendly gesture.

'Celebrating something?' he slurred, in a remarkably posh accent.

'Kind of,' I mumbled. 'Kind of celebrating being too scared to hand in my notice sober, in fact.'

'Ah, my dear young chestnut. Come sit with me and we shall resound our gongs and clang our cymbals and speak in the tongues of men and of angels.'

I'm not sure I wanted his gong anywhere near mine. Or his cymbal either, for that matter. But I sat with him anyway — me in my pinstripes, him in his rags. It turned out that he used to be a stockbroker until he was made redundant two years previously. He had lost his wife, his kids, his house, his car and his gym membership along with his job.

But Tramp — we shall call him Tramp because I have forgotten his name — had lost none of his mental faculties.

'Don't think for one minute that you're not doing the right thing,' said Tramp. 'Don't let those bestial bastards grind you down. Snipe them before they snipe you. 5.45pm, you're the last man in, eighteen to make off the final over. Matron's arms are tightly folded under her heaving bosoms on the boundary. Father's come down to watch for the day. Play up, my boy, and play the game. Front foot forward. Jolly well give them what-for.'

I slugged the last drops of my jeroboam of champagne. It was time. It was 11.17am, in fact. It was now. I was padded up and ready for battle.

'Thanks, Tramp,' I slur, although I think I could still remember his name at this stage.

'Don't mention it, my boy. Don't mention it. Just do more with your freedom than I did with mine.'

He struggles to his feet and stands stock still like an umpire at the crease, left arm raised at right angles to his body. He brings it down to his side.

'Right arm over. PLAY,' he booms.

I take a running leap at the security barrier while Tramp diverts the guard. The barrier is ten metres away. Seven sprinting strides and I take off, my left arm angled forwards towards my outstretched left leg, my right leg tucked underneath me. I am Sally Gunnell. I am an Olympic athlete.

Thwack! I am a nob.

But I roll out of my crash-landing and I'm in the lift heading up to my floor — the fifth.

The lift doors open and I stand there in front of an open-plan office, my arms and legs akimbo, my head raised heavenwards. I am like a *deus ex machina* in the final part of a play who's been slowly elevated on to the stage to save the day.

The room is quiet. I spring into action.

'You're all fuckers,' I intone in a deep Shakespearean bass. 'Collectively and individually, morally and spiritually, personally and socially, you all have first-class degrees in fuckdom.'

Everyone — that's almost fifty people — is looking at me. I am so drunk that I'm on the verge of passing out, but I still have a vague notion of how ridiculous I must look to everyone else. I carry on regardless.

'Ladies and gentlemen of the pissing jury, I present to you exhibit A for my fuckdom thesis — David. Negative equity going through the floor, hasn't pulled for months, hasn't shagged for even longer. Spends his evenings in Boujis trying to impress girls on their gap years by buying them crap champagne. Exhibit B – Geoffrey. Married for fifteen years, his wife is cheating on him with her personal trainer. Both his kids are being bullied at school and he still can't get his golf handicap below nineteen.'

I move around the office picking on other hapless and innocent individuals. People are laughing — some of them are even laughing with me.

I end up near my own desk. Leila is looking at me in absolute astonishment. A rapid calculation of her look says: shock (70 per cent), amusement (20 per cent, embarrassment (5 per cent), pity (3 per cent), love (2 per cent). It's a poor ratio.

I jump on my desk for the grand finale.

'In conclusion, my beloved former colleagues, we are gathered here today to bid farewell to Jack Lancaster. He advises that you all find a mirror and have a word. He would like to close with a song.'

I'm just fumbling with my shirt buttons and launching into the first verse of 'You Can Keep Your Hat On' when Rupert (bald) and two security guards pull my legs from under me and restrain my hands behind my back.

'All wight, all wight, Wupert. You can keep your hair on.'

Another titter goes up round the office. I don't think they've had this much fun for years. Buddy tries to start a chorus of 'Go, Jackie! Go, Jackie!' No one joins in. He gives me the thumbs-up and I reward him with a grin.

At which juncture, Mr Cox slides across the floor from his corner office.

'*Quo vadis,* Mr Lancaster? Your appearance, like foie gras, is a rare and exquisite pleasure. Pray, what brings you here? And what do you have between your grubby paws? A letter, if I'm not mistaken.'

'Piss off, you crapulent old fart.'

'Oh Jack, how vulgar. Vulgar and erroneous. I work here; you do not. I am *in situ*; you are *ex officio*. I am the managing director; you are nobody. Ergo, I suggest that *I* remain and you "piss off".'

Faultless logic. I look down at my desk and notice that all my belongings have been swept into a single black bin liner. The bilious remains of four years of my life.

'Right you are, Mr Cox, you flatulent segment of lower intestine. Here is my resignation letter, ergo I'm resigning.'

Mr Cox opens the letter with a small silver knife. His brow furrows as he reaches the second paragraph.

'What's an *Arschgeige*, Jack?'

'That's you, Mr Cox. German for "arse-fiddler".'

'And *gilipollas*?'

'Spanish for "dickhead". Also you.'

The whole office is still listening and tittering.

'My goodness, what a talented linguist you are. *Manyak*?'

'Arabic for "wanker".'

He reads on, tutting about a misplaced comma in the third paragraph.

But then his good humour appears to desert him. Turning to the security guards, he says in a dangerously quiet voice, 'Get this little turd out of my sight.'

I am man-handled — foot-dragging, expletive-hurling — towards the lift by the two brutes. I wriggle free just long enough for a parting *Braveheart* moment.

'Freeeeeeeeeeeeeeeeeeedom.'

The windows shake. Leila runs up to me.

'Jack, go quietly, please. And ring me when you've sobered up.'

'Leila, I love you. I fucking love you.'

She reddens. I can't tell why.

'No, you don't, Jack. Just go.'

She turns away.

'Who is coming with me?' I yell, as the guards grab hold of me again.

No one is coming with me. I'm not as good-looking as Jerry Maguire.

'They can take your P45s, but they can't take your freeeeeeeeeeeeedom.'

I am bundled into the lift and then into a waiting taxi. I hold tightly on to my bin liner, my head seemingly unattached to my neck as it nods backwards and forwards. As the taxi draws away, I see Tramp struggle to his feet and salute me. I salute him back and he grins from ear to ear.

I wind down the window and I can just make out his ringing plummy tones.

'That's the over. And stumps.'

Indeed, I think it is.

Sunday 29th May

Daddy, the solid man-mountain of integrity and bonhomie, came up to visit me in London. We went out for dinner in a quiet restaurant in St James's. I love it when it's just the two of us together.

'Your mother's well. She sends her love.'

'That's great. Send it back.'

Daddy frowns.

'No, I don't mean it like that. I mean, send her my love, too.'

'Ah, I will. So, how's work?'

'Hmm, there's something I've been meaning to tell you.'

He listens patiently while I give him an edited version of the last three weeks. I expect him to hit the roof, but he's smiling. When I get to the bit about Tramp, he breaks into a broad grin.

'Jack, I'm the proudest father in the world.'

'You're not utterly ashamed of me?'

'No, I'm the proudest father in the world. You were so excited when you first got that job in the bank, but I always had misgivings about it. I didn't want to watch my eldest son grow into a city boy. It just wasn't you. The people there weren't your people. You're so much better than that.'

Am I? I'd like to be.

He continues: 'So, what are you going to do now?'

'I have absolutely no idea. I'm thinking about going travelling for a bit. Maybe do a bit of work experience somewhere. Find out what I really want to do. Find my purpose in life — you know, that kind of thing.'

He's smiling at me benevolently. I'm painfully aware of how immature I must sound to him.

'Give it time. You'll work it out. But let's keep this from Mummy for a bit, shall we? You know what she's like. She loves telling the Gauges how much money you're... Hold on, Jack, what's wrong?'

He's aware that I'm hurting before I am. Something in my face must have twitched. I can't keep it bottled up any longer.

'Daddy, I think I've got a lump in my testicle.'

'How long have you had that?'

'Well, I've been aware of it since March, but I've been trying to ignore it.'

'Jack, you can't do that. You've got to go and see someone. You have to nip these things in the bud. It's my biggest regret that... Hang on; isn't that Rick Fielding over there?'

I look over there. It certainly is Rick. There's no mistaking that ginger bob.

'And isn't that Lucy he's with?'

It is.

'Hmm, that's interesting,' says Daddy.

It certainly is. Rick's holding her hand and kissing her delicately on the nose across a plate of oysters. She's looking sufficiently aroused not to require the aphrodisiac.

Daddy, bless him: 'Shall we leave?'

We left.

JUNE

Wednesday 1st June

The first day of the rest of my life. I have escaped the bank for ever and I'm not going to die.

On Daddy's advice, I finally went to see Dr Singh yesterday.

'Hello, Dr Singh, I've got testicular cancer. I think I'm going to die.'

I looked across at my computerised notes as Dr Singh fiddled down below. 'Perennial hypochondriac', he had written. 'Regular patient. Receding hairline. Overweight. Moderate alcohol abuse.'

'No you're not,' said Dr Singh, after he'd resurfaced from the depths of my crotch. 'You have mistaken your epididymis for a suspicious lump. And you've touched it so much that it's become inflamed.'

I feel almost as stupid as I do relieved. I am alive. I have a new lease of life. Nothing else matters.

Thursday 2nd June

Summer is in the air, and I'm loving it.

Summer is about one thing — girls. Girls in short, floaty skirts looking incredibly attractive. Girls giggling in the bronzing sun. It notches up their desirability by at least three points. It's like being permanently a little bit tipsy.

When I was at university, we used to call it 'exam term goggles', as anything looked sexy when you'd spent ten hours in a library cramming Latin grammar. Now I can see that it's really the sun that transforms everything. It brings hope, health, happiness and the vague possibility that you might get laid before the nights start drawing in again.

And summer is particularly good when you don't have to spend it in sweaty tube trains and air-conditioned offices.

Summer is in fact made for the unemployed, I mused, as I meandered contentedly through Hyde Park this afternoon. Kites flew, children played, couples strolled, tourists pointed, pedalos pedalled. Here I was enjoying this little Eden while thousands of office workers drafted crap PowerPoint presentations and checked the BBC weather website to see if it was still going to be sunny at the weekend. (It's not; I've already looked. Ha!)

I also like walking through the park, as it gives you time to think in a way you can't in a busy street or a claustrophobic flat.

(1) Lucy and Rick

Don't want to dwell on this too much, but I've found it almost impossible to get the image of them in the restaurant together out of my head. Hearing that they'd slept together was one thing. Learning the precise condom details from Rick was another. But actually seeing the two of them together, schmoozing over oysters while the ginger toss-rag kissed her on the nose was something else altogether.

I know I dumped her. I'm aware that they're both free agents. I do want her to be happy. But I'd slightly prefer it if she spent the next five years cooped up in a small village in Yorkshire — emerging only occasionally in full purdah to buy groceries from the eunuch in the local post office — before marrying someone shorter, uglier and poorer than me (and with a tiny penis). The fact that Rick is ginger only mitigates the pain slightly.

I know it's stupid and irrational, but the concept of Lucy and my best mate going out together seems to make a mockery of our own three-year relationship. Did she only go out with me to get to him? Was I merely a useful intersection on the way to the ginger with the todger that shatters condoms? Jack Lancaster — the Clapham Junction of relationships.

On the other hand, Rick and Lucy being together might work out very well. It gets me out of the awkward baby situation. If they're together, it presumably means that he's told her about the condom. It might even mean that he's accepted the baby as his and she doesn't have to go through with an awkward abortion. I could be off the hook.

(2) Leila

Screwed up a bit there, didn't I? Not the smoothest way of declaring my affection for her: drunk, with an expletive, in front of her ex-boyfriend and thirty of her colleagues. She still hasn't rung.

(3) Money

Thanks to last year's Christmas bonus (bumper year) and a generous payoff to keep me quiet about a number of Rupert's (bald) fraudulent indiscretions to which I was an accidental witness, I am currently in the black. I am also fortunate to be one of the few city bankers without an expensive cocaine habit. This puts me in the enviable position of not only having bucketfuls of dosh, but also masses of time in which to enjoy it. I don't need to head to the Job Centre just yet.

However, I've decided that I will not squander it on selfish and indolent pleasures, but will use my economic liberation to help me seek my purpose in life.

(4) My purpose in life

Have absolutely no idea whatsoever.

Friday 3rd June

I've been thinking a little more about my purpose in life and have come to the following conclusions.

While everyone wants to be happy, there are many different ways of going about this. Some go for pure hedonism — drugs, sex and rock 'n' roll (girly equivalent — shopping, chocolate and skinny *lattes*). Others get their kicks out of helping others. Others like collecting stamps. It's rather like trying to make a journey from London to Edinburgh: you could drive; you could go by train; you could fly; you could cycle; you could walk on your hands; you could canoe down the Thames Estuary and back up the Firth of Forth. The point is, we're all trying to get to the same place.

So what specifically makes me, Jack Lancaster, happy?

Booze.

Which is why — after much persuasion on my part — Flatmate Fred and I are doing the Circle Line pub crawl today.

'I'm writing a screenplay, Jack. I can't just take time off willy-nilly.'

'That's exactly what you can do when you're writing a screenplay, you willy. You're your own boss. "Hello boss, can I have the day off?" "Yes, course you can, employee of the month. I'll make sure your PA picks up any important messages."'

'But Jack, I've got to a really key bit in the plot.'

'Fred, you promised. Purleeeeeeeease. We have to celebrate my freedom.'

He gave in. We're just off now to exercise our democratic right to purchase and consume twenty-seven pints in a clockwise manner while the rest of the adult world queues for the office water cooler.

Saturday 4th June

I am never drinking again. Never, ever, ever. This is not my purpose in life. This is crap.

Sunday 5th June

I mean it. Never, ever, again. My hangover still hasn't passed. I have Unidentified Beer Injuries all over me. I must have forgotten to 'mind the gap' on the Underground. The wrath of grapes is great.

I'm not even tempted by a little hair of the dog.

Monday 6th June

Why do I drink so much when I am categorically so bad at it? Awful at Physics — give it up for GCSE. Crap at hockey — stop playing. Clinically incapable of heavy drinking — do it on a regular basis. Dr Singh was flattering my stamina when he put me down as a 'moderate' alcohol abuser.

Alcohol is illogical, expensive and harmful. The cream of Britain's youth go off to university to pickle their fine minds in cheap ethanol — a mere dress rehearsal for the rest of our destructive lives. Are we all completely socially inept? Can we not be happy until we've drunk enough mind-numbing poison to loosen ourselves up a bit? Are we all so clever that we need release from our tortured genius?

I put these questions to Flatmate Fred, but he's too busy working to reply. Perhaps he really is a tortured genius.

'Fred, are you a tortured genius?'

'Shut up, I'm working.'

He is a tortured genius. I shut up and watch *Neighbours*.

Tuesday 7th June

Perhaps I was a little bit harsh on alcohol. A spot of internet research brought up this gem from Omar Khayyam, a Persian poet who died in AD 1131.

> Ah, my Beloved, fill the Cup that clears
> Today of past Regrets and future Fears.
> To-morrow? Why, To-morrow I may be
> Myself with Yesterday's Sev'n Thousand Years.

I rather like that.

'Fred, my beloved, fill my cup.'

'Shut up.'

Have resolved to follow Churchill's dictum and take more out of alcohol than it takes out of me.

Thursday 9th June

An email popped into my inbox today from Leila Sidebottom. *Aha*, I thought perceptively, *it's from Leila for me.*

It was from Leila. But it wasn't for me alone. It was a forwarded joke email to ten people. Not a very funny forward — one of those ones comparing a perfect day for a man and a woman — but at least I'd made her top ten. She had been sitting at her desk at work, read a vaguely amusing email and thought, *I know, Jack Lancaster might enjoy this, I'll send it to him as well as nine other people.*

I scanned down the list. I recognised nearly all the names — mainly other people in the bank, or girlfriends I'd heard her referring to. There was no sign of Buddy. Result. If he's not on her joke forwarded email list, then there's no way she's still shagging him.

But hang on, who is this Olli Wynne character at the end of the list? I'd heard her refer to Bens and Toms and Sams, but never an Olli. Is he a new boyfriend? Oh god, has she met someone else already? Have I missed my (very small) window of opportunity?

I email her back to clear this up. 'Hi Leila, how are you doing? Hilarious email! Life on the outside is great. Let's have a catch-up drink soon. Btw, who's Olli? Friend of yours? Jack x'

A cool, calm, electronic communication.

Olli wasted no time in replying.

To: Jack Lancaster [*unemployed@hotmail.com*]
From: Oliver Wynne [*oliver.wynne@kpmg.co.uk*]
Subject: Leila
Thursday 9th June 11.35

Hi Jack, did you press 'reply all' by mistake?! Oops. I'm just a friend of Leila's.
   Met her in a club last weekend. Great girl. Hope we'll meet up sometime.

Cheers, Olli

Cheers Olli — you can sod right off. And 'Wynne' — what kind of surname is 'Wynne'? Wynne the Wynner. Works at KPMG. Accountant. Wynne the Loser.

Saturday 11th June

Rick phones in the morning and I decide to answer it.
   'Hello, Rick.'
   'Easy now, dude. How's it going, izzit?'

'If you're asking how I am, I am very well indeed.'

'Right, shut up you arse, innit. I've been trying to call you for ages. Why do you keep putting me on to answer machine?'

'I don't put you on to answer machine. I've got a clever button on my mobile that silences you instead. Saves me having to smother you under a cushion until the ringing tone dies out.'

'*Très drôle*, mate. *Très drôle.*'

He pronounces the 's' at the end of *très* so it sounds like 'trezz'. I feel like I'm in *Only Fools and Horses.*

'But seriously, Jack, I've got something I really need to talk to you about. That's why I've been ringing nonstop for the last two weeks, izzit.'

'Is it, Rick? I don't know.'

'Oh please, shut up. Can I come round, dude?'

'I don't know. Can you?'

'Oh sod off. I'll see you in half an hour.'

I'm going to enjoy this...

Rick turns up looking really nervous. Flatmate Fred is out food shopping (for once).

'Horrible weather, innit.'

'It is, isn't it?'

'Much nicer during the week, izzit.'

'It was, wasn't it?'

He meanders aimlessly through the sitting room in our flat, picking up bits of newspaper and replacing them, fingering CDs and reordering them.

'Keane, *Hopes and Fears.* Overproduced and overrated if you ask me, innit.'

'I quite like it actually.'

Long pause.

'Jack?'

No answer.

'Jack? Dude?'

'Yes, Rick.'

'Jack, the thing is...'

'What's the thing, Rick?'

'The thing is...' He reverts to radio advert voice here.

'ThethingisthatIreallylikeLucyandImseeingher.'

I try to look crestfallen and seething with quiet anger, but I'm a crap actor. I have to turn away so that he can't see me sniggering under my hand. But the snigger sounds like a sob.

Rick rushes forward, 'Oh, Jack. Dude. Dudos. I'm so sorry.'

'Dude, I'm only playing.' I turn round and clap him laughingly on the back. 'That's bloody fantastic news. I'm so happy for you.'

Understandably he looks more confused than normal. Rick is a fine friend, but his IQ rarely rises above room temperature.

'So you knew already, innit?'

'I certainly did. Remember that evening the two of you were eating oysters together in St James's two weeks ago? I was in the same restaurant with my dad.'

'Yeah, those oysters were a little aphrodisiac for later. Not that we needed them, innit.'

'Rick.'

'Sorry, dude.'

And then we sit and talk for ages and I'm left in no doubt that Rick really does feel for Lucy. She wants to keep the baby and he's told her that there's a strong likelihood that it's his. He seems so enchantingly besotted by the luscious little frollop that I don't have the heart to tell him that the entire baby charade was an elaborate ruse by said frollop to lure me back. We're having a better conversation than we've had for months and I don't want to spoil the moment.

'This has been a little bit strange, innit,' says Rick as he stands up to leave after several hours.

'Yep. It has. Strange, but nice. Bizarre, but therapeutic. I'm very happy for you both. Send my love to Lucy.'

'Oh, I will. I'm sure she'd love to see you some time, now that things are settling down a bit.'

Rick's just walking down the stairs when he turns on his heel.

'Just one more thing.'

'Yes, Rick.'

'She does give the most fantastic head, izzit.'

I know this should enrage my alpha-male jealousy, but I really don't care any more. He's also hit upon an irrefutable fact: Lucy gives the best head known to man or beast.

'Yes, mate, she certainly does. She certainly does.'

And with a wink and a 'toodle-pip', he trots off for his next one.

Monday 13th June

I'm really not superstitious, but there's definitely something portentous about the date thirteen in my life. In March it was me telling Lucy's dad to fuck off on the phone. In April it was my first major dressing-down from Mr Cox. In May it was my conversation with Rick about my/his/our baby.

And in June? Why, Leila again, of course.

After my little 'reply all' fiasco last Thursday she eventually emailed me today to suggest a drink in the evening. Was I free? No, I wasn't, but I'd make sure I was free for her. Claire (doctors 'n' nurses) would just have to postpone. Sorry.

She comes bounding into the bar, all laughter and smiles and looking, well, looking downright shaggable.

'Jack, how are you? Sorry I haven't been in touch for ages. It's been hell at work. Absolutely run off my feet.'

'I'm sorry to hear that,' I say, barely able to hide my smirk.

'No, you're not,' she laughs, 'you lazy good-for-nothing. How is life on the outside, as you put it? One of my friends in your "reply all" email thought you'd just been released from jail.'

'Ha ha. No, life away from the office is good. I've been working out my purpose in life. Mainly I've been reading and walking and shopping and writing and drinking and visiting museums and doing all those little things you don't have time for normally.'

This is almost true. Mainly I've been drinking.

'So, what is your purpose in life?'

'Oh, I don't know. Have one point eight children, drive a Volvo, get a mortgage, be a godfather to someone... That kind of thing.'

We laugh, and then she looks serious for a moment.

'Jack, I want to ask you something.'

Oh god, this seems to be the week for people asking and telling me things.

'Yes, Leila. Anything.'

'When you came into the office drunk last month and said that you, erm, fucking loved me, you didn't mean it, did you?'

Hearing her say the word 'fucking' is so beautifully dirty.

'Oh no, of course not,' I laugh nervously. 'Don't be silly. Of course, I think you're brilliant and stuff, but no, I was just really wasted.'

'That's such a relief. I was so worried. I didn't want to spoil our friendship with awkwardness.'

'Don't be silly, Leila. You and I would never be awkward together. We're just great friends.'

What the bloody bollocks am I thinking of? I am managing to say the exact opposite of what I feel.

We chat on through this hiatus. Olli keeps on coming up. She's got a definite case of mention-itis.

'So, who exactly is this Olli?' I ask eventually. 'I've never heard you mention him before.'

'That's because I've only just met him. We're kind of dating, I guess.'

'Kind of dating? How does that work?'

'It's what grown-ups do in London, Jack. They go out to drinks and dinner and theatre shows.'

I don't want to be a grown-up in London. It sounds rubbish.

'That sounds fun. Perhaps we should go on a date sometime.'

'But we're having drinks now, aren't we? In a non-date-date type of way.'

'True, good point. Anyway, I thought you were meant to be celibate. How can you date celibately?'

I've had a little bit too much to drink.

'That's beside the point. It's not all about sex, you know, Jack. You men are only after one thing.'

'That's absolutely not true. That's a nasty little stereotype propagated by girly magazines. We men also want someone to hold, to cuddle, to snuggle, to wake up with on Sunday mornings and read the papers with on Sunday afternoons. We're just too embarrassed to admit it openly.'

Leila looks at me a little strangely.

'Listen, Jack,' she continues. 'You're my friend. A very good friend. One of my best, in fact. And, as one of your best friends, I urge you to get out on the dating scene as soon as possible. It's a lot of fun. Perhaps you'll find your purpose there.'

I really, *really*, want to shag her.

Wednesday 15th June

'What's your purpose in life, Fred?' I ask.

For once, he's not too busy writing to talk to me.

'I don't know, Jack. I just don't know. I used to think it was to write this screenplay, but I'm beginning to wonder whether it's really worth it. I mean, what's the point? No one publishes it, and I look like a moron. Someone publishes it, so no one goes to watch it. It's a rip-roaring success — I have to come up with another idea, and I think I've only got one in me.'

'Oh, come on Fred. It's an awesome idea. *Romeo and Juliet* updated into a modern university setting. Everyone's going to love it. What else is bothering you?'

He looks down at his feet.

'I haven't been laid for ten months.'

'Ten months? That is a long time.'

'Yep, two more and I'm a technical virgin again. It's also been seventy-five days and seventeen hours since my last non-solo orgasm.'

'But that's ridiculous. You know that everyone fancies you.'

'Do they? Well, I don't fancy everyone. Perhaps that's my problem.'

Perhaps it's everyone's problem, I mused. This always strikes me as bizarre in the UK. The media prattles on about how much sexual action we twentysomethings are getting. But in my experience we're all mouth and no trousers. All fart; no poo. Close; no cigar.

While people in relationships have a great deal of sex, male singletons just spend their entire time thinking about it.

Shall I buy a new pair of jeans? Yes, it will give me more chance of pulling at the weekend. Shall I get a haircut? Yes, ditto. What should I do as a career?

Barrister is a sexier profession than an accountant, but less secure. Journalists get paid less than bankers but they're more interesting. Firemen get laid the entire time, but what would I tell my parents? Shall I make my bed and dim the lights in my room before I go out tonight? Yes, it will impress any girl I bring back. If I buy this aftershave/mobile phone/digital camera/DVD player/designer coffee cup, am I going to get more sex? No, but I'll try it anyway. If I spend half my weekend jogging around Hyde Park with my iPod and a look of absolute agony on my face, am I going to impress the ladies? No, never. If I join the gym and do fifty sit-ups three times a week, are girls going to notice my six-pack through my shirt and fling themselves uncontrollably at me in clubs? Well, it would be nice...

Our hormones run us, and our hormones ruin us. While our every subconscious move is designed to get us one step closer to the bedroom, we rarely put our best-laid preparations into best-laid action. We spend too much time setting the scene and too little treading the boards.

Sometimes one longs for a far-off day in the 2040s when we can think logically with our real brains. I am rather looking forward to hanging up my slippers by the fireside, my seed sown, my genes appeased, my hormones sated and basking in the importance of being impotent.

Or, as Flatmate Fred puts it, 'Octogenarians should count themselves lucky. It's only when you've got no ink left in your pen that you can start working out what really matters in life.'

Friday 17th June

Decided that Leila could shove her dating advice. I'm a man and I want to do manly things like boys' nights out in cheap, cheesy clubs. This is my purpose in life.

It was the old crowd again — Flatmate Fred, Jasper, Rick and me. No Buddy — he has been relegated to the rank of former friend. Lucy Poett had gone home to the country to visit Mr and Mrs Poett.

We were lazing around, quaffing £7 bottled beers in a corner of Mad Barry's and watching lithe beauties walking about. It actually hurt how attractive they were. The prospect of never getting near to any of them hurt even more.

But then one in particular caught my eye. I had to go up to her. I simply had to. She was even fitter than Miss P. M. Gilmour. I would regret it for the rest of my life if I didn't.

'Sorry, er, I wouldn't normally do this, but you are literally the most beautiful creature I've ever seen in my life. I just wanted to tell you.'

'Thank you,' she says. 'That's sweet of you.'

'You're welcome,' I say and sit back down again with the others.

Five minutes later and she walks past again, beckoning me over with her finger.

'Come up and see me and make me smile,' I can see her miming in time to the music.

I go over and see her, and do my best to make her smile. It appears to be working. Twenty minutes later, we're twirling around the dance floor. Twenty-five minutes later, I'm kissing her. Forty minutes later, we're sitting down in the corner and still kissing. I can see Jasper and Flatmate Fred dancing either side of a girl to 'Karma Chameleon' out of the corner of my eye. I hope Jasper backs off and lets Flatmate Fred get laid before his celibate year is up.

Fifty-five minutes later, and Iona (*Must remember her name this time, must remember her name... Iona, Iona, Iona*) asks me to walk her home.

'Cadogan Gardens — just round the corner.'

Wahey, wahey, wahey.

'That's a pretty cool place to live.'

'Yeah, it's my mum's, but don't worry — she's away.'

Her voice goes up at the end of every sentence. She looks and sounds very different outside the club.

'You don't mind living with your mum still?'

'No, it's just until I finish school.'

'Sorry, *finish* school? Like art school?'

'No, durr-brain, just normal old boring school. Doing my AS levels next year. I'm predicted ten A stars for my GCSEs when results come out in August. And then, after my A levels, I'm going to study Law at Oxford, and then I'm going to be a barrister, and then I'm going to be a judge.'

There's no doubt that she's very clever. There's also no doubt that she's very young... and very annoying.

'Congratulations, that's brilliant. Well done you.'

'And how about you, Jack? You didn't tell me which school you're at?'

Can I? Should I? I shouldn't. But God, she's fit.

Fortunately, I was saved any more moral dilemmas at this point, as I tripped over her pashmina and rolled into the gutter. A definite low point of my life — in the gutter while a sixteen-year-old fittie looked down pitifully on me. I couldn't even pretend to be Oscar Wilde — this was London, and there were no stars to look at.

Fortunately Iona took this as a cue that I was absolutely poleaxed and helped me back to hers, where I gratefully went to bed alone in her mum's room.

Saturday 18th June

Iona, Iona, Iona were my first three thoughts upon waking up in a strange room.

My fourth thought was, *That's Norah Jones playing 'Don't Know Why I Didn't Come'.*

My fifth thought was, *I know exactly why I didn't come last night. I walked a barely legal girl home, got moral pangs about her age and then fell into a gutter.*

My sixth thought was, *Who is this (very attractive) woman in her early forties looking at me as if I'm something the cat dragged in?*

It was Iona's mum. Iona appeared behind her, wearing pyjamas with Winnie the Poohs on them.

'Mumsies, this is Jack. He very kindly walked me home last night because I was a little bit tipsy-wipsy.'

Thank god I didn't sleep with her.

'It's a pleasure to meet you Mrs Iona,' I say, stretching out my right hand and trying to keep myself decent with my left.

'Oh, the pleasure's all ours,' purrs Mrs Iona, apparently won over to the tale of the knight in shining armour. 'How can I thank you enough for looking after Iona? You must give her your number so that we can stay in touch.'

Aaaaaagh!

Someone who had got lucky was Flatmate Fred. When I got back from my Stride of Pride I found him and Jasper having breakfast with a mystery girl.

'Good jail bait?' asked Jasper.

'Indeed, no,' I replied. 'I did the honourable thing and passed out alone.'

'You fool,' said Flatmate Fred. 'Surely you know that they're old enough when they leave school.'

'And when do they leave school?'

'At half-past three.'

I gave him a confused smile and crashed into bed.

Sunday 19th June

'Ten months of celibacy and I've just broken my fast with a threesome — every guy's lifelong dream.'

'Fred?'

'Yes, Jack.'

'Isn't the dream threesome meant to be with two girls and not with one random girl and a failing actor called Jasper?'

'Well, yes, ideally. But Jasper had nowhere to stay. It was a rutter or gutter evening. A score or floor soirée.'

'Fred, you're a horrible person.'

'So, we decided to give the dog a bone.'

'Rank.'

'Even though she was almost clinically ugly.'

'Disgusting.'

'And two's always better than one, in any case.'

'Foul. Even if one of those two is a guy?'

'Yeah, of course.'

'Fred, are you gay?'

'Shut up.'

'Did you touch Jasper at all? Apart from high-fives, obviously.'

'No, really — I mean it. Shut up.'

Rang my dad later to wish him happy Father's Day.

'Oh you soppy sausage, Jack. I hope you're not doing anything embarrassing like buying me a huge present and taking me out for a nice meal. Horrendous commercialism, the lot of it.'

'No, but I have got us tickets for Wimbledon tomorrow.'

Monday 20th June

The perfect day at Wimbledon. The sun shone and Daddy paid for the strawberries. Watched a bevy of gorgeous Russian teenagers up close on the outer courts before taking our centre court seats to watch a Brit lose the first two sets to a wild-card entry from Slovenia and then overcome him 12—10 in the fifth. My retired dad with his unemployed son. We can spend all the time we like together now.

'I meant to ask you,' said Daddy on the way home. 'How's your search for a purpose going?'

'Pretty badly really. Tried pure hedonism. It doesn't work. As soon as I get drunk, all I want is a girl to share the moment with.'

'And how are the girls?'

'Equally bad. I'm fine at expressing my emotions with people I don't care about. But rubbish when it comes to someone I actually like.'

'What about that Leila girl you mentioned?'

'Messed up completely.'

'And other girls? Are you dating?'

'Don't you start, too.'

'And career plans?'

'Hmmm, nonexistent.'

'And Rick and Lucy?'

'Together.'

We look at each other.

'Poor bloke,' we say simultaneously. We collapse into laughter.

'Yes, don't tell your mother, but I was never a great fan.'

'Fortunately, Rick's got the patience of a saint, innit.'

We laugh again and sit in happy silence for a while.

'Daddy, you know how you once said I could ask you anything?'

'Yes, although I don't like the sound of this.'

'Er, do you still have, er, ink in your pen? Does the twitch subside as you get older? Are you still shackled to a mad beast? Does it become clear who's right for you and who isn't?'

'Chin up, Jack. Give it time. You'll be fine.'

'You haven't answered my question.'

'I'm aware of that, Jack,' he says, with a twinkle in his eye.

Friday 24th June

Midsummer's Day and I've resolved to start playing the dating game. Rick has Lucy, Leila might or might not have an accountant, Flatmate Fred's got a Jasper sandwich and all I've had or almost had recently is a sixteen-year-old whose mum fancied me.

This is a crap situation and it's got to change. But how the hell do you go about dating in London?

There was a time when finding a girl was easy. In your youth you played doctors and nurses. In your teens you turned up to a sleepover with a large enough sleeping bag and waited for the alcopops to transform you into a charming Casanova. By university you had your own room, and the size of student beds made intercourse inevitable, if not always accomplished. And, just as you'd blown your chances with one year group, a brand new team of replacements would arrive in September. You may get older every year, but eighteen-year-old freshers are always the same age.

And then suddenly you're in your mid-twenties, and you enter the Wasteland. When I left university I had Lucy. When I left Lucy, Leila preoccupied my thoughts. And now I have no one.

I really need a date. Perhaps one of them will turn into a girlfriend and we can work out our purpose in life together.

'Fred, have you got any attractive friends?'

'Shut up.'

I'm going to ring Claire (doctors 'n' nurses).

Saturday 25th June

Claire's house party. Got three numbers. Result.

I hate asking for people's numbers. To the first one (Lizzy) I offered a lame excuse about wanting to help her get a job in banking. The second (Sarah) I stole off Claire's mobile because I was too scared to ask myself. And with the third (Jean) I embarked on such a pathetic Hugh Grant detour — 'Er, Jean, yes, I just wanted to say, really, that, er, I mean, that, well, I enjoyed meeting you and...' — that she interrupted and grabbed my phone off me.

'Look, do you want my bloody number or not? You've already got two others, so you might as well have mine, too.'

Direct. I like it.

There was also someone there called Miranda who refused my request point blank.

'There's no point, is there? You'll just wait three days and then send me a witty little text. I'll wait another day before I reply. Then we'll meet up, spend £30 on crap food and I'll fancy you no more then than I do now, which is not at all. So let's just leave it, shall we?'

Very direct. I preferred Jean's answer.

Rick's twin Katie was there too, but I'm still in her bad books for not getting back to her. First Kiss and First Shag were also hovering, but I'm in their bad books as well for not seeing them for ages. Why are women so bloody political? They've made no effort to see me for ages, either.

Never mind. Three lost, three gained. It's a score draw.

Monday 27th June

I'm beginning to tire of my listlessly lethargic Lothario lifestyle. When you're in a proper job you cram a huge amount into your spare time. When you're lazing around at home you can make a trip to the supermarket take up the entire day. Your free time isn't free time any more. It just becomes a new routine. I actually miss the structure.

It's almost the end of the month and I appear to have done next to nothing with my time.

In fact, it's been a month of almosts. I almost died of testicular cancer, but didn't. I almost completed the Circle Line, but couldn't. Almost gave up alcohol, but didn't. Almost told Leila how I felt, but backed out. Almost started dating. Almost pulled a schoolgirl. And got absolutely nowhere close whatsoever to working out what my purpose in life is.

Perhaps I should get a useful job — join the big debates over society's future. Perhaps I should start reading the newspapers properly and see what's going on in the big wide world beyond my piss-boring, selfish little existence.

Perhaps.

Tuesday 28th June

Right, I'm going to text Lizzy, Sarah and Jean. It's been two and a half days. Perfect timing, even if I say so myself. After one day they're just beginning to regret giving their number out. If you text then, they'll think you're a desperate loser. After two days the fear is just setting in that you might never get in touch. The trick is for your text to arrive just as they're beginning to analyse what they did wrong to put you off. You have to lift their mood just as it's starting to sag. Wait any longer and you've lost them.

This was my text: 'Hey [*insert Christian name here*], really good to meet you at Claire's. Wld be fun to have a drink some time if you're not too busy. I hear Sunday night is the new black... Jack x'.

For simplicity's sake I sent the same text to all three of them and tried to ignore my phone for the rest of the day. I had to restrain myself from texting again five minutes later, saying, 'Look, are you coming or not? Put me out of my agony.'

I hate the in-between bit. It's like finishing an exam and waiting two months for the result.

Wednesday 29th June

Still no reply from any of them. I detest modern technology. It makes you compulsively check everything — email, voicemail, text messages. When someone contacts you, you're disproportionately delighted. And when no one does, you're a picture of abject misery. It must have been so much easier when your messages had to trot across country-wide staging posts and not zing through satellites.

Thursday 30th June

Beep, beep.

Aha, this will be one of the cheeky little maidens now. I wonder which one.

It was Rick. 'M8, nt sure how to say this, but me and Lucy r getting mrrd, innit. We'd luv u to b bst mn. Rick.'

JULY

Friday 1st July

I've just noticed that the last three months of my life have all ended in emotional cliff-hangers. At the end of April, Lucy announced that she was pregnant. At the end of May, I discovered that Rick and Lucy were an item. And now, at the end of June, I discover that Rick and Lucy are so much of an item that they're planning to get married.

I have to hand it to the two of them: they've got a unique sense of dramatic timing.

Although the content of Rick's text yesterday was understandably surprising, the tone was familiar enough. If Rick wanted to tell his best mate that he was planning on marrying his ex-girlfriend, it would strike him as only natural to use an illiterate text full of 'innits' and smiley faces. In fact, 'innit' was just about the only thing he'd spelled out in full. I mean, what kind of word does he think 'M8' is? And 'luv'? Where's the love in that? With predictive text messaging there's really no excuse for these horrors. 'Cu', 'wld' and 'cld' are just about OK. Anything else is right out.

But I digress. I wanted to shoot the messenger, not the message. So I rang up to ask for an explanation.

'Ah, Jack. Glad you called. Was worried when you didn't get back to me yesterday. Are you happy to be best man?'

'Delighted, Rick. Ecstatic, overjoyed, elated, jubilant and euphoric. I am over the moon and strumming a harp on cloud nine.'

'Wow, I wasn't expecting you to be that happy about it.'

'I'm not. I'm markedly unhappy about it. Isn't it just a little bit hasty, a wee bit precipitous, a fraction rushed? What else have you done since I last saw you apart from get engaged? Gone to Mars, sold a multi-million-pound start-up, found a cure for AIDS?'

Silence.

'OK, perhaps you wouldn't mind explaining how it happened?'

'Well, it was Lucy's dad's idea, really.'

'Ah, Mr Poett. How romantic. Why don't you marry him instead?'

'Would you shut up a moment. While you were out fiddling with jail bait a couple of Fridays ago, Lucy went home and told her dad that she was four months pregnant. He hit the roof. Assumed it was you. Wanted to sort you out good and proper.'

'Rick, Mr Poett's a stockbroker, not the godfather.'

'Anyway, the point is that Mr Poett was livid.'

'And what — when Lucy told him that the father of his grandchild was you and not me, he calmed down and said, "I have not lost a daughter, I will gain a son"?'

'Er, pretty much, yeah. You know what these stuffy upper-middle-class parents are like.'

'Rick, your dad's a QC.'

'Yeah, well anyway. Her dad says that Lucy has his blessing, on condition that she marries me immediately.'

Blimey, not so much a shotgun wedding as a scattergun wedding.

'And you want to marry her?'

'Yep.'

'Do you love her?'

'Yep.'

'You love her so much that you've stopped saying "izzit" and "innit" every second sentence?'

'Yep, it drove her crazy, innit.'

'Well, that is true love, then.'

'It's a small sacrifice to make. So, come on, are you going to be my best man?'

'Dunno. I need time to think, OK?'

Saturday 2nd July

On reflection, Mr Poett's attitude makes me very angry indeed. I've got half a mind to get hideously drunk and tell him to fuck off again over the phone.

I mean, who does he think he is? Some kind of latter-day Mrs Bennett ordering his errant daughter down the aisle? He is a relic of the dark ages, a snob of the worst kind who can't face the realities of the modern era. Single mothers are everywhere. What does it matter whether Lucy Poett becomes Lucy Fielding and starts wearing a wedding ring? There's no more chance of her and Rick staying together just because she changes her surname and has a couple of extra wedding-gift fish knives from distant relatives.

It's no longer social death to be born out of wedlock. Bastards are people like Mr Cox, who treat their employees like dirt. Bastards are people like Buddy Wilton-Steer, who badmouth their ex-girlfriends. Bastards are fathers like Mr Poett, who try to pressurise their daughters into socially acceptable arrangements that won't get the neighbours talking. Bastards are hypocritical fools like Rick, who go along with it. Bastards are not children who are brought into this world by two parents who were too wise to make a spur-of-the-moment lifelong commitment.

Their child isn't going to thank them for a marriage of convenience a couple of months before it's born. It's the fact they're having the baby that is important. Not the marriage. Why can't they just concentrate on that? Babies can't be unborn.

It's none of my business, but I really need to talk to Lucy about this.

Sunday 3rd July

'It's none of your business, Jack.'

'Look, please, Lucy. I'm not trying to get in the way; I'm just trying to help. For old times' sake. Please can we talk about all this?'

'OK, let's meet up next weekend.'

'Not sooner?'

'No, next weekend.'

Bint. She always did get her own way.

I'd just put my mobile down when it beeped and two texts arrived. One from Lizzy, another from Sarah. *Result*, I thought.

Actual context of texts was less of a result. They were identical. They read like this:

'Thanks for texting us both. Sunday is indeed the new black, the new rock 'n' roll… Which is why I have no intention of spending it with you. It's not me; it's you.'

Oh dear, I really am a tit. Perhaps I should have realised that sending identical texts to two friends was a stupid error.

Anyway, you lose some, you lose some humiliatingly. To be honest, they were both last-window girls. There's still Jean.

Monday 4th July

'Fred, you know how when girls live together in close proximity, their periods start synchronising?'

'Yes, I'm aware of that.'

'What do you reckon the male equivalent is? Do you and I get elated and depressed at similar times? Do we get sudden urges to go on CD shopping sprees and gorge on curry and beer? Do we go on and off sex at the same time?'

'Jack, get a sodding job.'

'Is Freddie-weddie missing Jasper-wasper?'

Silence.

'Seriously, Fred. I really don't mind if you're gay. You can tell me, you know. If you're a milky way, ginger beer, Inspector Taggart, it really is fine by me.'

'Seriously, Jack, you're really beginning to piss me off. I can't do anything with you moping around the house like this.'

Wednesday 6th July

Decided that I was going to try and get a letter published in as many different national newspapers as possible.

Started with *The Sun*.

Well done my *Sun* for your brilliant piece on the European Union. How

dare those fat cats in Brussels force me to drive on the right side of the road! Paws off our democracy!
Jack Lancaster, London

Moved on to the *Guardian:*

Congratulations to the Foreign Secretary for his lucid and erudite description of what any future European Constitution really means for Britain in Europe. The sooner the electorate has the chance to shatter the ridiculous myths perpetrated by the Murdoch press and endorse the Constitution in a free and fair referendum, the better.
Jack Lancaster, London

And then the *Independent*:

Sir,
On reading your balanced appraisal of the merits of the draft European Constitution this morning, I was again reminded of the free-minded excellence of a newspaper whose hands are not tied by the whimsical views of its proprietors. I do, however, feel duty bound to point out that it is articles I-40.3 and III-212 which provide for the creation of a European Armaments, Research and Military Capabilities Agency, and not I-40.2 and III-213 as your report stated. In addition, the escalator clause — which would ascribe further competences to the EU without recourse to national governments — is more usually referred to as the *'passerelle'* (Article I-22.4).

Jack Lancaster, London SW3

And finally the *Daily Telegraph*:

From Mr Jack B. H. N. Lancaster

Sir,
Few political events arouse as much ire in the hearts of right-thinking

Englishmen as the mendacious attempts by this discredited Government to sign away a thousand years of history through the back door. Did my relatives die in vain at the battles of Crécy, Trafalgar, Passchendaele and Britain?

Yours faithfully,
Jack Lancaster
23 Onslow Mews, London SW3

Thursday 7th July

Unbelievable. The whole ruddy lot got published. Am deliriously happy. Even Flatmate Fred acknowledged that this was a triumph. *The Sun*'s giving me £25 for writing its Letter of the Day. Perhaps this is to atone for the fact that their letters page — 'The page where you tell Britain what you think' — is squeezed on to page 36 between an advert for the page 3 calendar and the quick crossword. I get the impression that Britain doesn't give much of a toss about what you think.

Equally unbelievable was the phone call I received in the afternoon. I normally hate being called from a withheld number. For a start, you don't know how to answer it. 'Hello' sounds a bit informal. 'Hello, Jack Lancaster' makes it sound like you're in a call centre. And, despite the initial excitement that it might be someone interesting, it normally turns out to be one of your bored mates abusing the office phone at work.

This time, however, it was someone interesting.

'Jack, hi, this is Frankie. We used to play rugby together at school.'

'Frankie, hang on… Yes, Frankie Boal. How are you doing? Have you learned to catch the ball yet?'

'Ha, very good. Have you learned to pass it properly yet? Listen, mate, you know I'm working for the Leader of the Opposition at the moment? Well, someone told me that you were out of a job, so, well, anyway, here he is — he wants to talk to you…'

Shit. I'm about to talk to Alex de Montfort, the bumbling, bumptiously plummy MP for somewhere in Oxfordshire and the new leader of the Conservative Party.

'Cripes. Which way up do I hold this thing? Ah, there we go. Right, Franco, am I connected?'

'Hello? Mr de Montfort?'

'Ah, here we go. Jack, Jack Lancaster? Listen, one of my useless staff has passed me a copy of this morning's press cuttings. Your name seems to appear in almost every comment section. Are all those letters yours?'

'Yes, sir.'

Why am I calling him 'sir'? I'm twenty-five.

'Well, I think it's bloody marvellous, Jack, I really do. You're just the kind of swivel-eyed, deviously crafty, Machiavellian schemer which the Tory Party requires in these dark years of opposition. I'd like you to come and work for me. Can you start on Monday?'

'Of course, sir. I'd be honoured. But don't you want any references?'

'Not worth the ruddy paper they're written on. Franco tells me that you can spin-pass a rugby ball off both hands, and four national newspapers tell me that you're a tub-thumping genius. On condition that you stop calling me "sir", I think we'll get on very well.'

'Thank you, sir.'

Saturday 9th July

'It's none of your business, Jack.'

'You've said that before, Lucy. It was wrong then and it was wrong now. You're not going to make it any less wrong by repeating it over and over again.'

I was at my planned rendezvous with Lucy to talk about the Rick/baby/marriage situation, and it wasn't going very well.

'Look, Lucy, when you tried to lure me back with your elaborate pregnancy ruse, you told me that I was the one for you. Doesn't that at least give me the right to voice my opinion on your current situation? I'm only trying to help.'

'Trying to help me or trying to help yourself? Aren't you just jealous of two people who are sorting their lives out? From what I hear, yours is going down the toilet.'

'You said toilet, you said toilet.'

'It was an expression, Jack. Please grow up.'

'OK, fine. I am mildly jealous. But that's not my motive. I'm happy that you and Rick want to be together. He's convinced me that he loves you. And ultimately I just want both of you to be happy. I think it's great that you're keeping the baby and I think it's great that he's prepared to be a good father. But I also think that getting married on a whim simply because your dad wants you to is a huge error.'

'Oh, that's what you think, is it?'

'Er, yes, that's why I said it.'

'Well, fine, yes, my Dad *did* hit the roof and it *was* his suggestion that we got married, but it's also what Ricky and I want.'

She's calling him Ricky. Ugh, that makes me feel sick. No one makes up nicknames for my best mate.

She continued: 'Marriage isn't about wild romantic sparks, Jack. It's about cellulite and school fees. I've realised that now. You and I had wild romantic sparks but I don't think we could have lasted as a married couple. Ricky and I can. I love him in a solid, constant way that isn't going to change. I can imagine waking up next to him when I'm old and ugly and still loving him as much as I do now. We're going to have a very happy family together. This baby has just fast-tracked us into realising something that has always been there.'

There was a knock on the door of my flat.

'Oh look,' I said. 'It's Ricky. Come on in.'

He looked at me weirdly.

'Easy, mate. How's things, izzit?'

Lucy coughed behind me.

'I mean, hello, old bean. How are you? And hello, my little honeybee. I was wondering if you were still here. How are you and honeybee junior?'

He walked over to Lucy and rubbed her tummy gently. She settled into the crook of his arm and looked up adoringly at him.

'So, mate, have you decided whether you're going to be my best man or not?'

I looked at the two of them and smiled. Rick and Lucy — the happy Fieldings.

'Rick, it would be an honour.'

'Good man. You better start organising my stag party, then. We haven't got long.'

Sunday 10th July

After more than six weeks of blissful unemployment, it would seem that I'm going back to work tomorrow.

To be honest, I'm less than ecstatic at the prospect. I know I should be grateful for the exciting opportunity. I know that I might have hit upon a new purpose in life. It's just possible that this will be my springboard towards becoming the Rt Hon Jack Lancaster MP, Prime Minister, First Lord of the Treasury and Minister for the Civil Service.

But then I'm not sure I can be bothered to get up early in the morning, put on a blue tie and an ironed shirt and spend the entire day with a bunch of hacking politicos.

I mean, what do I know about politics? The student politicians I met at university were a bunch of talentless arseholes. They were prematurely balding, prematurely middle-aged and perennially fat. Then, at least, I had very little in common with any of them.

Monday 11th July

Felt jet-lagged when I woke up this morning. Realised that for the last six weeks I've been operating on Islamabad time — getting up at midday and going to bed at 4am.

When I eventually emerged bleary-eyed from Westminster tube station, I found myself in the middle of a full-blown war between the Countryside Alliance and a bunch of animal rights' protesters. Will they ever give up?

'You only married your wife because she reminds you of your horse,' went up the shout from the soap-dodgers on one side of Parliament Square.

'Hunting foxes is a right, is a right, is a right, hunting foxes is a right, not a privilege,' came the chanted retort from a very privileged group of green wellies and Barbours on the other side. The black Labradors whinnied in time.

Why can't you all just get a job? I thought as I strode purposefully into Portcullis House in my pinstripes and dark blue tie.

Felt less purposeful when I had to undergo a full body search ('Sorry, guv, we can't be too careful after what happened last time'), and then wait two hours for de Montfort's private secretary, Kim, to let me into the complex.

Kim, though, was lovely and gave me a whistlestop tour of both houses before showing me to de Montfort's plush private office.

'You sit here, Jack, in Frankie's seat, as he's away on holiday, next to Dominic, who's Alex's diary secretary. Penelope here manages the press office, Nicola coordinates the international policy unit, Marianne liaises with CCO, and Arabella and Isabella help with correspondence.'

I feel like I'm being introduced to the board of the local pony club gymkhana.

'Hello, everyone.'

They're all in their forties, but they're all very attractive (apart from Dominic, who looks like the product of a few hundred years of inbreeding).

'And Kim... What exactly do I do?'

'Ah, glad you asked that. When this phone rings, you answer it. Ninety per cent of the time it will be a complete weirdo. Try to get rid of them firmly but politely. Occasionally, it will be someone important, although you won't always be able to tell the difference. Put them on hold by pressing this button and then dial the necessary extension. Otherwise, I'm afraid your job consists of photocopying, filing and envelope-stuffing.'

'And how much do I get paid?'

'Paid? Jack, this is politics. We're all believers. But we'll give you a bit of money for lunch every now and again.'

Never mind. Wasn't John Major a bus conductor at one point?

Tuesday 12th July

Yesterday they protected me from having to answer the phone. Today I had no such luck. The first call came through at 9.01am.

'Hello, Citi— I mean, hello, Alex de Montfort's office.'

The office is deadly quiet. I can feel everyone listening to me.

'Hello, can I speak to Mr de Montfort, please?'

'I'm afraid he's in a meeting. Perhaps I can help?'

I have absolutely no idea where de Montfort is. I haven't even met him yet.

'Oh, perhaps you can. I've found Mr Blair's weapons of mass destruction. They're under my kitchen sink.'

'Right.'

'You don't believe me. No one believes me. But I'm telling you it's true. They're emitting deadly radiation into my wok. They're poisoning my stir-fry.'

'Sorry, I don't have time for this.'

I hung up.

Arabella: 'That was a bit abrupt, Jack.'

'You mean I have to sit there and listen to a mad old woman tell me about the WMD in her kitchen?'

'If they're a voter, yes.'

'Even mad voters?'

'A mad vote's still a vote.'

Perhaps she's got a point. It would be foolish for the Tories to alienate their natural constituency.

Spent the rest of the day talking patiently to dozens of eccentrics. A minor triumph at 5pm when an old man rang up and started singing, 'Who Do you Think You're Kidding, Mr Hitler'. I put him on speakerphone so that the rest of the pony club could hear him.

Titters all round. Perhaps I can do this job.

Wednesday 13th July

Look at today's date. Utter embarrassment.

11am, and I had already endured two hours of mind-numbing lunacy when Kim asked me to throw out four half-empty bottles of corked red wine.

'Sure,' I say. 'Not a problem.'

I have a degree in Classics; I'm sure I'm up to throwing out a few bottles of wine.

I'm just walking towards the corridor when Dominic (who is a tosspot, I've now concluded) suggests that I have a swig.

'Go on, Jackie. Have a swig. Don't waste the wine. It's almost midday.'

And so, comic genius that I am, I insert all four corked bottles into my mouth and stumble comically into the corridor... straight into a circle which comprises de Montfort, de Montfort's speech-writer and four of his closest advisers preparing for Prime Minister's Questions.

I recover quickly.

'Lancaster, Jack Lancaster. Just started here. We spoke on the phone.'

De Montfort takes my outstretched hand.

'Pleasure to have you on board. Cripes, Jack — job's driven you to drink already, has it?'

I look down at the four bottles in my left hand. One of them is leaking into the cream carpet.

'No, sir. Ha ha, sir. Sorry, sir.'

I went and hid in the kitchen for an hour and dreamed about having a proper, well-paid job in a large corporate bank.

Friday 15th July

My skill basket has been widened to include correspondence. Not sure if this signifies a promotion from tea-making, wine-recycling and phone-answering, but it adds a bit of variety to the tedium.

De Montfort gets a postbag of well over a hundred letters per day. Some of these are from concerned, well-meaning pillars of society who just want to make a point:

'Dear Mr de Montfort, I'm sorry to bother you as I'm aware that you're a very busy man. I wouldn't normally write to a public figure, but I've been driven to my wits' end and I don't know where else to turn... '

However, the vast majority are from absolute nutcases:

'Dear Mr Monty, Not many people are aware of this but Mr Blair is in fact an alien clone run by Martian puppeteers. I was wondering what the Conservative Party policy is on this distressing phenomenon... '

'Dear Mr de Montgomery, What are you going to do about the vast amount of dog faeces on the streets of Milton Keynes?'

These are often in green ink and can run to many pages. But the most distressing thing is that every letter merits a full and detailed reply. It's the same principle as being pleasant to all callers, however barmy. And we're not even allowed the pleasure of writing entertaining replies. We have to use a template for every conceivable scenario which leaves little scope for individual flair.

Dear [*name*],

Thank you for your letter of [*date*]. Mr de Montfort has asked me to reply on his behalf.

I was interested to read your views on speed cameras/Europe/ asylum seekers/dog faeces/Martian puppeteers.

As Conservatives, we [*insert policy template*]
[*insert personal message, if appropriate*]

I hope we can count on your support at the next election.

Yours sincerely,
Kimberly Dimsdale
Private Secretary to Rt Hon Alexander de Montfort MP

This is then photocopied for the file (by me) and posted using taxpayers' money (by me). And they wonder why they don't have enough money to pay me.

Sunday 17th July

Jean phoned but I was too scared to answer. She left a voicemail.

'Hi Jack, it's Jean. Remember me from Claire's party? Sorry I've taken ages to get back to you. I've been away on holiday. Anyway, I'd love to have a drink sometime. Sunday is definitely the new black, but guess it's a bit last minute now. How about this Wednesday?'

Wahey, she sounds like a nice girl. Was too scared to ring her back, so texted instead. We're going for a drink on Wednesday.

Tuesday 19th July

Had a truly huge number of weirdos phone me up in the morning at work.

One batty old lady: 'Hello. Is that Mr de Montfort?'

'No, but you're through to his office. Perhaps I can help?'

'Oh, Mr de Montfort, what an honour to speak to you personally.'

'Sorry, this isn't Mr de Montfort. I'm one of his researchers (*sounds better than "unpaid tea-maker"*). What can I do for you?'

'Oh, Mr de Montfort, how are you? I saw you on telly last night. You were magnificent.'

'Listen, I'm not him, OK?'

'Oh, Mr de Montfort, you do sound sexy when you raise your voice.'

I heard a titter at the end of phone. The batty old lady was Flatmate Fred. The bastard.

'Fred, fuck off.'

'It was my flatmate,' I explained, as Arabella looked over quizzically in my direction. 'Bit of a japester.'

Five seconds later and the phone rang again.

'Look, Fred, please just fuck off, I've got work to do... Oh, Sir Geoffrey... I *am* sorry, we've had a host of prank callers... Yes, I'll make sure that gets passed on to Mr de Montfort... and I am sorry again for telling you to fuck off... All's forgiven? Thank you very much, sir.'

Arabella shook her head in matronly disbelief as if I'd just pulled a thirteen-year-old at the gymkhana.

Wednesday 20th July

Dating day. I am entering the adult world of London singletons.

I've put on my lucky boxers, dabbed on some of the aftershave that Lucy gave me for Christmas, checked my free university condoms haven't passed their expiry date and I'm standing at a neutral, halfway tube station trying to look sophisticated and hoping I'll recognise Jean again when she walks past me.

But how do you look sophisticated when you're frantically scanning every face for signs of recognition? Do you lean against a pillar with your legs debonairly crossed, or does that make it look as if you're dying for the loo? Do you stand outside the station or in the harsh glare by the ticket barriers? Do you bring something to read while you're waiting for your date (she's bound to be late — it's her prerogative)? And, if so, what? A newspaper — nails your political colours to the mast. A magazine — too metrosexual. A book — what kind of idiot takes a book on a date?

I do.

Oh God. Isn't that her over there?

'Jean?' I ask, waving my copy of *Paradise Lost* for no particular reason.

'Er, no.'

Damn. The girl who wasn't Jean was very attractive. I start chatting to the other guys who are also loitering in their lucky boxer shorts — the hordes of the desperate and the great unwashed, scrubbed up for the evening.

But when the girl who is Jean finally turns up, I'm so deeply embroiled in composing a text to Flatmate Fred about the fit girl who wasn't Jean that I miss the girl who is Jean altogether. And, just as I'm leaning in to kiss her on the cheek, the fart that I've been trying to suppress for twenty minutes escapes noisily.

It's an inauspicious start to the second stab at creating a good first impression.

But things pick up from here. The conversation begins to flow   not that it really seems to matter on a first date. It's just background white noise while you try to work out if you fancy each other or not.

But it's not really going anywhere. Perhaps some more booze? I bought some food in the pub and the first round, but she makes no move to return the favour. Can I offer another round or does that appear desperate? *I am desperate.* Will she think I'm trying to get her drunk? *I am* trying to get her drunk. But no, she holds out resolutely to the end, nursing her double G&T for three hours like it's a newborn child.

And so it comes to the awkward little walk back to the tube station, the pause, the 'I-had-a-lovely-time moment', the launch for one cheek, and then the other, and then the split second when I wonder about throwing the face in and going for the lip jackpot.

141

I don't. It's a shoddy show. Now I'll have to wait a tactical two days and text her again.

Dating is crap. I want to invoice Jean for the £27.85 I spent on the two of us. And I still really want to shag Leila.

Saturday 23rd July

Claire (doctors 'n' nurses) rings.

'Soooooo, how was your date with Jean?'

'It was fun, yeah.'

'Come on, you can do better than that. I want to know all the details.'

'Come on, Claire. You're her girly best mate. She must have told you all the details already.'

'We-e-ell, yes. So, do you like her, then? Isn't she absolutely stunning?'

What is it with girls and their friends? They always describe them as stunning even if they're the fattest, ugliest moose-bag ever to have set foot on the planet. Sure, Jean's not a moose-bag, but she's not 'stunning' either.

'Yeah, she's all right.'

Not a ringing endorsement, I know. Just not convinced that I'm cut out for this dating malarkey.

On a brighter note, it's Rick's stag party tomorrow. Given the short notice of the whole jamboree, I've limited the numbers to Rick, Jasper, Flatmate Fred and me. I've also eschewed traditional entertainments of eyebrow-shaving, French-maid strip-o-grams, Dublin piss-ups, paintballing, etc. in favour of a more genteel day out.

Sunday 24th July

'Sorry, where the bleeding bollocks are you taking me?' said Rick, somewhat ungraciously, when we arrived at his flat in the morning.

'Cartier International Polo day in Windsor. I thought it would be a nice surprise.'

'Well, it's a surprise all right. That's not even in Zone 6, is it?'

'Come on, Rick,' chipped in Flatmate Fred. 'It will be a laugh. Just imagine how many chinless tosspots we can laugh at. Jack's arranged a driver and a shedload of booze.'

'And picture how proud Lucy will be when she finds out that you spent the day with royalty,' added Jasper.

Spot on, Jasper. Rick was converted and we were soon heading west on the M4, swigging cheap champagne out of the bottle.

'This is fantashtic,' said Rick, as the car swung into Windsor Great Park. 'You are the most fanstashtic fwends in the entire world. Have I ever told you that?'

We walked through the rows of parked Ferraris and sports cars. Fuel injection penis substitutes on all sides.

'So how does polo work?' asked Jasper.

Flatmate Fred: 'Well, essentially what happens is that you get really drunk and then chat to fit girls by the side of the pitch. When the teams change ends, all the spectators get to walk on the pitch and replace the divots. This is called "treading in". It's basically a way of mingling with more fit girls before heading back to the bar for the second half.'

'Awe-bloody-some,' said Rick, 'I like polo already.'

It was awe-bloody-some. We were in totty wonderland. Promotional girls in tight T-shirts and short skirts strutted their stuff. I have no idea what they were selling — probably more Ferraris — but they could have sold ice to Eskimos. It was paradise.

But by mid-afternoon Rick was getting restless.

'Come on guys, I want to do something really crazy. This might be the last time we're all together like this. This is one of my last tastes of freedom, innit.'

Flatmate Fred: 'Izzit. Rick, you're getting married, not joining a monastery, innit.'

'It's my stag party and I'll say "innit" if I want to.'

'OK, Rick, OK,' I simper. 'Why don't we all get naked and run across the pitch?'

What am I thinking of? I am a responsible member of the private office of Her Majesty's Official Opposition. For God's sake, the Queen herself is here watching.

'Jack, you're a bloody genius.'

'Yes, marvellous idea, simply marvellous,' says a pink-shirted toff next to us.

'Shut up, you toffee-nosed wanker. No one asked your inbred opinion.'

'Isn't it rather cold for you boys?' giggles one of the promotional girls.

It was at least thirty degrees.

'Right, that does it,' says Rick.

And the next thing I know the four of us are naked and ducking under the pitch's perimeter fence. There's not a thread on us and we're streaming towards the middle of the action. Rick is leading the way like a bucking young stag. I am the responsible best man bringing up the rear. And Jasper is just in front of Flatmate Fred, who appears to be struggling with a half-mast erection. There is a huge cheer from the crowd. Win the crowd and we will win our freedom. We are gladiators. We are the four naked musketeers. We're young, we're free and we're very, very drunk.

One of the horses looks so intimidated by Rick's approaching manhood that it whinnies and bucks its rider. Rick leaps on to its back and starts to trot towards one of the goals, his bits hanging down the saddle towards the crowd. Jasper and Flatmate Fred collapse in a heap of laughter and are dragged off the pitch by security guards. I manage to sidestep two other guards — the crowd roars again — before I am brought to the ground by a bone-crunching tackle. The crowd groans.

I'm a slain gladiator. I'm just being led off the pitch by the centurions when I hear a familiar voice in the front row of the corporate stands.

'*Salve,* Jack Lancaster. What a delightful surprise. It was only the other day, if not the day before the other day, that I was thinking to myself, open brackets, the managing director of a successful investment bank, close brackets, I wonder what young Lancaster is doing to advance his *curriculum vitae* these days. *Et voilà*, it would appear that we have an answer. *Ecce*, behold, bear witness: a trouserless Lancaster on the playing fields of Windsor.'

'Mr Cox, you crapulent piece of manure. I was hoping I might see you again one day.'

'Indeed. We must stop meeting like this — you with security guards restraining you, me with better things to do with my time. You have entertained the crowds. Leila Sid-day-bot-tome and I are entertaining clients. This, I'm afraid, is *vale*, if not *au revoir.*'

And, rod a dog, there was Leila, waving and grinning from a pitch-side table while one of the bank's corporate clients stared at her cleavage. I looked down at my muddy and reticent Mr Happy and he winked back at me. Nothing for it — I was busted in more ways than one. I waved back to Leila and was led off to the police station for a reunion with the others and an official caution.

On balance, an excellent day.

Monday 25th July

'How was your weekend?' asked Arabella, as I stumbled rather inelegantly into the office this morning.

'Oh, you know, the usual,' I mumbled.

'So you usually go to polo events, strip in the Queen's back garden and end up with your naked picture plastered over the internet, do you?'

Oh buggeroonies. I went over to Arabella's computer to see her looking at an unmistakable picture of me being led off the field by two scowling security guards. 'Hung like a horse' was the blog's caption. Fortunately, they'd pixelled out my sensitive parts so you couldn't see that a combination of alcohol and fear meant that I was actually hung like a very cold hamster.

Arabella, however, thought it was marvellous.

'It's simply marvellous,' she gushed.

'Yah, what an absolute hoot,' trilled Isabella.

'Yah,' hooted Arabella. 'This is just the kind of fun, in-touch person we need in the New Conservatives.'

They're absolutely right. Jack Lancaster — the fun, in-touch person who spends his weekend getting naked at polo matches. I am the saviour of the Tory Party. I am the proud inheritor of the legacy of Disraeli, Churchill and Thatcher. I am an absolute wanker.

Tuesday 26th July

Only two days left until Parliament adjourns for the summer. There is a festival mood in the place — probably because the MPs are about to gallivant off to Tuscany for a couple of months and we don't have to look at their puggy little faces any more.

I had a very long, boozy and subsidised lunch — thanks, taxpayer — and then returned to my correspondence pile.

The first 'letter' was written on loo paper and addressed to 'Mr de Mountain'. Right, I thought, I'm going to enjoy this. I mean, anyone who writes on loo paper deserves everything they get. No ruddy Conservative templates for me this time. On official headed notepaper I typed:

Dear Mrs Fothergill,

Thank you for your communication of 22nd July addressed to Mr de Mountain. I assume this was intended for the Rt Hon Alexander de Montfort MP, Leader of the Conservative Party and of Her Majesty's Opposition.

Mr de Montfort is a very busy man and has better things to do than respond personally to your menopausal whingeing. I hope you don't mind me replying on his behalf.

It is a shame that you are having trouble with your pension, but I don't know what you expect Mr de Montfort to do about it. You have the misfortune to live in the north of England; Mr de Montfort has the honour to represent a southern constituency. Even if he were interested in the minutiae of your tedious life, parliamentary protocol decrees that MPs should not interfere in their colleagues' bailiwicks (you'll find 'bailiwick' under 'b' in a dictionary).

As you are no doubt unaware, Mr de Montfort has no real power, in any case. His role is to make weak jokes in Prime Minister's Questions, and then wait until the Government does something stupid. Real power in this country resides with the media and the Civil Service. I'm afraid that the little people like you don't really get a look in.

So I thank you for taking the trouble to write to us, and I thank you not to trouble us again. In the future, perhaps it would be financially wiser to save the postage and invest in some better-quality loo paper instead. It would be a pity to waste any more rainforests with your literary faeces.

Yours sincerely,
Rt. Hon Alexander de Montfort
p.p. Jack Lancaster
PS I'm sorry to hear about your cat.

Thursday 28th July

Feel rather bad about that letter now. I don't think I should have sent it.

I am, however, still a huge hit with Arabella, etc. over my polo exploits. They have asked if I'd like to stay on over the summer. There's even talk of them giving me a proper position and a respectable salary. Will have to think about it.

Saturday 30th July

Just had a call from the political editor of the *Sunday Times*. Mrs Fothergill rang them up. I'm going to be on the front page tomorrow.

I am for the high jump.

AUGUST

Monday 1st August

John Humphrys: 'And now, we've got Jack Lancaster in the studio. In case you've been on Mars for the last two days, Mr Lancaster is the man responsible for a twenty per cent slide in the approval ratings of his boss — perhaps I should say former boss — the Conservative leader, Alexander de Montfort MP. His extraordinarily insulting letter, written on headed notepaper from the Leader of the Opposition, was given by its recipient, an elderly lady called Mrs Fothergill, to a Sunday newspaper, which published it in full.'

I'm sweating like a paedophile in a playground. Six million people are listening to this. The only thought going through my head is *Six million people are listening to this. Don't swear, Jack — don't bloody, pissing swear.*

He continues: 'Mr Lancaster, your letter describes Mrs Fothergill as 'whingeingly menopausal'. What on earth did she do to justify that kind of abuse?'

'Nothing, John, nothing at all. I would like to make excuses — I was tired, I'd had too much to drink at lunchtime, etc., etc. — but the truth is that what I wrote was inexcusable. I cannot apologise enough for the hurt that I've caused Mrs Fothergill and the Conservative Party.'

This is going OK, isn't it? I am trying to imagine Humphrys taking a dump, which is making me less nervous.

'Inexcusable? It certainly is. Mrs Fothergill is the widow of a decorated war hero and you call her contribution to the democratic process 'literary faeces'. I put it to you that your letter is patronising, smug, haughty and intolerably rude. Doesn't it embody everything which has made the Conservative Party so unelectable for the last decade?'

'I think it probably does. That's why I voted Rock & Roll Loony at the last election.'

'You're not even a Conservative?'

'No.'

'So why did Mr de Montfort give you a job?'

'I'm not sure. Although I imagine he's probably asking himself the same question right now.'

'I don't doubt it. Right, the time now is 8.27. I think we've got Mrs Fothergill on the line. Mrs Fothergill, what would you like to say to Jack Lancaster?'

'Mr Lancaster, you're a horrible piece of work. It's people like you who have brought this great country to its knees.'

'And what do you say to that, Mr Lancaster?'

'I think I agree entirely, John.'

Tuesday 2nd August

It's been something of a nightmare, to tell the truth. I didn't sleep for sixty hours. The flat was besieged by reporters and photographers. I've appeared on the front page of almost every newspaper (except *The Sun*, which splashed with a soap star's breast enlargement — perhaps they're being loyal to their former Letter of the Day writer).

At lunchtime de Montfort rang personally to vent his anger, just as Flatmate Fred was pouring dirty dishwater on the reporters outside.

'Lancaster, you were good on *Today*, but you're a first-class fool. Do yourself a favour and piss off out of all of our lives.'

'Thank you, sir. Yes, sir. Sorry, sir.'

I don't think I'm ever going to be Conservative Prime Minister. And, worst of all, I've got no one to blame except myself.

Wednesday 3rd August

'You've got no one to blame except yourself.'

'I know, Daddy, I know. I am a complete fool.'

'Jack, for the first time in my life, I'm utterly ashamed of you. I don't mourn the damage you've done to the Conservative Party, but I can't believe you've sabotaged your reputation in this way. You've made your mother and me look extremely foolish. We're both utterly ashamed of you.'

Ouch, that really hurt. There is something in the raw, moral goodness of the man that prevents him from being unduly unpleasant to anyone.

But, bizarrely, my dad's reaction has been relatively atypical. Maybe it's a generational thing. Most of my friends now think I'm a hero. People I haven't seen for years have tracked me down. Jean has been texting furiously trying to arrange a second date with the celebrity of the hour.

Leila sent me an email: 'Now I can understand why you left the bank, you irresponsible reprobate! Yesterday polo, today the Conservative Party, tomorrow the world. Let's meet up soon. Keep on entertaining me in the meantime!'

One newspaper even ran a leader praising my 'refreshing honesty in the hypocritical world of politics… It was the letter which we have all wanted to write — perhaps all should have written — but have never had the courage to put our fingers to keyboard.'

They're wrong, of course, and the rest of the press tore me to shreds. It was a bloody stupid letter to write. Mrs Fothergill was an innocent, defenceless victim. But my forced display of public self-flagellation was equally unedifying.

Now that I've emerged from the other side of the whirlwind, I can see the episode for what it really was: a pointless and self-serving merry-go-round for a media and political circus which picked me up and spat me out with the rest of their five-minute wonders.

Thursday 4th August

Thank god, I've disappeared from the papers altogether. The Prime Minister has been implicated in some scandal or other and de Montfort's approval ratings have soared back up. The millions of breakfast-table voyeurs now have someone else to disparage over the marmalade. The unknown twenty-five-year-old has been replaced and there are only 11,579 Google hits for 'Jack Lancaster letter' to remind me of the sordid episode for ever.

Friday 5th August

Two phone calls. First, Arabella from de Montfort's office:

'Oh Jack, you silly billy. You were fabulous on the *Today* programme. Of course, it was jolly rotten of you to write that kind of tosh in the first place, but I just thought you should know that there are no hard feelings.'

I think the dreadful old bag fancies me.

Second, Rick:

'Mate, have you written your speech for tomorrow yet?'

'Tomorrow? What's happening tomorrow?'

'Ha ha, very funny. I'm getting married, innit.'

Oh shit.

'Yeah, of course, mate. Wrote it ages ago.'

'Good, nothing too embarrassing in it, I hope. You're not going to bring up the sheep story again, are you?'

Hmmm, I will now.

Saturday 6th August

'And look, it's the celebrity best man, saviour of the Conservative Party.'

'Hello, Mr Poett. How are you?'

'Very well, Jack, thank you. And thank you for your delightful apology note after our late-night conversation back in March. Such a shame that you didn't extend your rigorously polite epistolary style to your professional life.'

'Hmm, point taken, Mr Poett.'

'And Jack?'

'Yes, Mr Poett.'

'You dated my daughter for three years. Today you're the best man at her wedding. Perhaps you could stop calling me Mr Poett like a guilty schoolboy.'

'Yes, er, Archibald. Certainly.'

'Archie, Jack, Archie. Come along. Let's get to the church. It's a beautiful day for a father to be giving away his daughter.'

It was indeed a beautiful day. The sun shone as friends and families streamed into the picturesque Wiltshire church.

'Bride or groom?' asked an usher whom I'd never met at the church entrance.

'Well, I used to shag the pregnant bride, but I've known the groom since we used to soil our nappies together, so, on reflection, I'll probably go and sit at the front in the best man's seat.'

A bit harsh, but I was fractious and nervous.

But from then on the service was perfect. Lucy looked more beautiful than ever in a dress that did its best to disguise her bump. Jasper played the organ. Rick's twin sister Katie was one of the bridesmaids, I didn't lose the rings and Rick managed to say 'I do' and not 'izzit'.

Later we trooped back to a marquee in the field adjacent to the Poetts' house. And, after I'd judged that the guests had drunk sufficient quantities of expensive poison, I rose to my feet:

Ladies and gentlemen, as some of you might be aware, I have recently acquired something of a reputation as a letter writer. I hope you will forgive me if I give this speech in a medium in which I feel at home:

Wiltshire
6th August 2005

Dear Rick,

Our friendship has always been a competitive one. When you were two years old you deliberately peed on my trousers at nursery school. I hit you and forgave you. When you were eight, I spotted you cheating off me during a French test, so I wrote out the wrong answers on purpose before changing them at the last minute. You hit me and forgave me. When you took my place in the under-13 rugby team, I threw your gum shield into the urinals. I haven't told you about this until now, but I hope you can forgive me without hitting me [*pause for polite laughter*].

This rivalry has never really died down. Recently you pointed out that I was beginning to lose my hair. Well, if I was as ginger as you, I'd want to lose mine, too [*pause for sustained laughter*].

But now that you are marrying my first real girlfriend, I graciously concede defeat [*pause for uproarious laughter*]. Lucy is very lovely and very beautiful... and a million miles out of your league. Treasure her well or half of Britain will be tapping you on the shoulder to ask to swap places.

You are more than a best friend to me, Rick [*pause to achieve desired catch in voice*]. You are my brother. I wish you and the lovely Mrs Fielding all the happiness in the world.

Jack

PS [*Pause, grin and wink*] I know I just said that you were a brother to me, but your sister Katie does look absolutely ravishable as a bridesmaid.

I sat down to thunderous applause as Katie's face turned the same colour as her hair.

Three more speeches, two bottles of champagne, six regrettable karaoke performances, one honeymoon departure and eight hours of dancing later, I was lying post-ravish beside the ravishable bridesmaid Katie in Lucy's childhood bed, sobbing quietly into a pillow and clutching the teddy bear I'd given Lucy for our first anniversary to my heaving chest.

A very strange day.

Monday 8th August

So why exactly was I crying post-ravish on Saturday? Well, the most prosaic reason was that Katie was agonisingly rough with her handiwork. I don't mean to be crude here, but a penis is not a gearstick. It only really likes to move in two directions. And you certainly don't find reverse by pushing it down violently and shoving it into the top left corner of its axis.

I suppose it's the age-old conundrum for a man. Do you let a woman continue to chafe you raw in the hope that the orgasm might validate the purgatory? Does the end justify the means? Or do you quietly and sensitively show her how to do it gently? Women are always taking the mickey out of us for requiring a map to find their clitoris. (Men are fine with maps, we just don't like to ask directions.) I think it's time that we struck back.

But of course, I was also crying because I'd realised that I'd lost Lucy for good. I didn't really want to sleep with Katie. She was just Rick with longer hair, fit from afar, far from fit, a substitute for all that I'd been through with Lucy. I wouldn't want Lucy back in a million years, but I've got to the stage now when I can remember the reasons why I liked her in the first place. I suppose this is the final stage in getting over someone.

All of which are very generous thoughts, but I can't help wondering whether I really meant all those nice things I said about Rick and Lucy at the wedding. A large part of me wanted to stand up and give vent to the vilest, most cynical speech ever witnessed at a festival:

'Ladies and gentlemen, we are gathered here today because the bride slept with the groom as a way of making the best man jealous. We are here to celebrate the happy fact that the bride is pregnant and the father of the bride is so bottom-clenchingly middle class that he forced her to marry her one-night stand. Ladies and Gentlemen, I give you the happy couple (and I give them half a year).'

But that would have caused quite a scene in rural Wiltshire, and Archie Poett and I would no longer be on first-name terms.

Friday 12th August

Now that my life is back on a boringly neutral plateau again — no annoying boss, no pestering ex-girlfriend, no immediate love interest, no testicular cancer, no fights with friends, no political ambitions, no real purpose — I suppose I should set about working out what to do with myself for the next forty-five years until retirement. This is the strange thing about life after university. It's feels like you've just fallen off a conveyor belt of nonstop academic landmarks, and are launched in one fell swoop into the rest of your life. It's suddenly up to you, and not your tutors or your parents.

But I've really got no idea at all what to do next. The things I enjoy and do well — socialising, drinking, writing amusing emails — are not really transferable economic skills. I think the sad truth is that to make money you have to work with money. And money per se is indescribably boring. Worse still, it's impossible to know which job will suit you until you try it out. And as soon as you try it out you're stuck with contracts and inexplicable gaps in your CV. It's like jumping straight from a first date into marriage.

What do you do with a BA (Hons) in Latin, anyway? Classical Civilisation is very interesting, but it doesn't really lead you down a career path in the same way as studying Economics, or Law, or Medicine. We have no real skills beyond copying other people's essays. You can do anything or nothing with an arts degree. It opens every door and no door.

I've even thought about going back to university and learning some more useless facts. It was so much simpler there. You could have breakfast in the afternoon and dance midweek to Abba in sweaty student clubs. You could impetuously decide that you had had enough of working at 3pm and leave the library for a game of tennis. One of the hardest decisions you had to face on an average day was whether to have chicken or minestrone Cup-a-Soup.

If I went back and did a Master's I could be a legend again. I would stand out from the rest of the sad grads. I could have my pick of the nubile teenagers. I could wake up every morning feeling a little fresher.

But then I'm far too late for this academic year. And I've got absolutely no idea what to study. And what nubile nineteen-year-old wants to go out with a balding former banker when she could have a hot young stud at the peak of his sexual prime?

Perhaps I need an older woman. Where is Mrs Iona in these times of trial?

Sunday 14th August

I finally arranged to see Jean again in the evening.

I was nervous. I was aware that I was entering dangerous territory with a second date. You can't have a second date with someone and not kiss them at the end. It's against the rules.

But my problem is that I am incredibly bad at kissing someone for the first time. I hate rejection. I hate throwing the face in. I don't like doing something unless there is a statistically high chance of success. There must be something of the banker still in me.

And I think the worst bit is that split second just as you're leaning in. It seems to last a lifetime, and there's that agonising fear that she might turn her head away at the last minute, leaving you hanging like a mutant teenager with your tongue lolling out.

All these thoughts are still running through my head as I'm walking Jean back to the tube at the end of the evening. I look at her sideways. She's attractive. She's a very nice girl. But I can already see the future — we'd go out for three months, become fond of each other and then I'd feel trapped and try to extricate myself without hurting her. She's got lots of good qualities, but none of them are enduring. And what's the point of starting when you can already see an inevitable end?

'Jack, are you listening to me?'

'Sorry, I was miles away. What were you saying, Jean?'

'I was asking whether you wanted to kiss me.'

Direct, as ever. We're standing outside a tube station. There is a *Big Issue* seller next to us. A bunch of teenagers walks past giggling.

'Er, yes, that would be quite nice actually.'

But it's far from nice. I mean, I've had some bad snogs in my time. I remember my first one with Mel aged fourteen. We were both wearing train tracks. We didn't come up for breath for fifty minutes. Every time I opened my eyes, hers were staring into my left eyebrow. I remember seeing Rick and Flatmate Fred jigging around behind her giving me the thumbs-up. It was like we had been waiting all our lives for this moment (I guess we had) and we were going to cling on for dear life. And I think we were both scared that stopping meant having a conversation, and that is the worst thing imaginable for a fourteen-year-old.

But eleven years on, here is Jean pipping Mel to the post. It's the most rancid kiss I've ever had in my life. And there is nothing worse than a bad kiss. I want fireworks; I'm getting a tumble-drier. I'd like some delicate nibbles; she is trying to vacuum out my oesophagus. I'd appreciate some delicate teeth work; she's taking penalty hockey flicks at my tonsils. It's utterly repellent. It's about as sexy as cooking beans on toast.

I close my eyes and try to imagine Leila, but it's still not working. After thirty seconds, I can take no more.

'Jean, this has been lovely.'

'Yes, it has. And you're an amazing kisser. Call me soon, lovely boy.'

With all due modesty, I think I am a rather good kisser. But it takes two to tango, and I plan never to waste my talent on Jean the Dyson again.

Tuesday 16th August

'Fred, why is it that everyone we like at the moment is completely unfanciable and everyone we fancy is completely dislikable. Why do we continue with the torturous amateur dramatics of the dating game? Why do we love our friends and fancy unsuitable strangers? Why do we think like heroes and act like cads?'

He looks up from Act II of his screenplay.

'Jack, you're in love with Leila. She's the one girl who you adore *and* fancy. She seems to bring out the best in you. Why can't you just admit it to yourself and then admit it to her? Then you'll get closure, and then you can move on, and then you can get a bloody job and join the rest of humanity again.'

'What, you think she'll say no?'

'I've got absolutely no idea. But you're never going to find out if you don't ask her.'

Actually, he's right. It's piss-simple, but he's hit the nail on the head. I always skirt cowardly around the issue, hoping somehow that she'll pick up on my feelings through a fog of alcoholic obfuscation and subtle hints. For all our conversations and our friendship and our closeness, I have never wholeheartedly told her how I feel. Instead, I sit here at my laptop, recording my grubby little thoughts in my diary, frustrating my feelings and feeling my frustrations, refusing to set myself up for failure, unwilling to take a leap in the dark, living the cosy fantasy because I'm too scared to try the reality.

I haven't spoken to her properly for ages. We've let the closeness slide. I'll see what she's up to at the weekend.

Saturday 20th August

Leila has offered to cook for me at her house in Shepherd's Bush.

I spend ages getting myself ready to go out. Every hair is in place, every orifice scrubbed, deodorised and perfumed. My lucky boxer shorts are washed, pressed and sparkling.

Eminem is helping to psych me up. I'm jigging around my bedroom using my aftershave as a microphone. The crowds are loving it. I've only got one shot, one opportunity, to seize everything that I ever wanted, one moment. Yo! I've got to capture it, not just let it slip.

'Yo,' says Flatmate Fred, coming into my bedroom and turning the music down a notch. 'You can do anything you set your mind to, man.'

'Thanks, Fred, very profound.'

'Go get her, Tiger. And, Jack — one thing.'

'Yes.'

'If you don't say anything to her, I'm not letting you back into the flat tonight. This nonsense has gone on long enough.'

'Thanks, mate.'

He gives me a hug.

And so I arrive at Leila's house just off Uxbridge Road. I've never been here before. Her two housemates are out.

'Jack, it's so great to see you. I'm just cooking now. We're going to have a duck.'

'A what? Oh, yes, sorry.'

I haven't spoken to her properly for ages — not since our 'No, don't be silly, of course I don't fucking love you' chat. We've got a million things to catch up about. She wanted to hear about the Windsor polo incident and the Mrs Fothergill letter in full. I told her about Rick's wedding. I left out the bit about Katie.

I feel myself open up to her again. We pick up from where we left off. I can talk to her like no one else in the world. She takes away my cynicism and my juvenility and my snideness. I become the idealistic person I'd like to be. And when she talks I listen because I want to, and not because I have to. She is endlessly and wholly and perfectly enchanting.

We're still there at midnight. I have absolutely no idea what we're talking about by now, but I know it's great. It's just that right level of drunkenness where the conversation really hits its stride. We could be talking about shooting stars, eternal love and the fundamental meaningless of it all; we could equally well be discussing the perfect Pot Noodle. It doesn't really matter; we have an inner rhythm of our own. I just want to hear her voice, swim in her eyes and lie, at mortal rest, between her golden breasts for ever.

But my poor blue balls are in exquisite raptures of agony. I've had an erection for three hours and I really need to go to the loo. And that means trying to pee with an agonising stiffy. It's an awful conundrum. Either you spend ten minutes pacing up and down the bathroom thinking about an OAP wiping his bottom or you opt for the long-distance release.

I go for the latter. I want to get back to Leila and tell her how much I like her, that I want to grow old with her, that I would die to protect her.

A long-distance release involves crouching on the floor at a distance of about one to two metres from the loo, according to a rapid calculus formula based on your angle of excitement and the fullness of your bladder. After many years of unrequited conversations about shooting stars and Pot Noodles, I have the technique almost flawless.

But, just as I'm settling, one of Leila's housemates comes home and flings open the bathroom door. In a normal situation this would have been fine. We would have had a laugh about locks and swapped a few sumptuous observations about men and loo seats. But long-distance releases are no normal situations. Crouched as I am almost two metres back from my target, the bathroom door catches me in the small of my back in the full arc of its parabola. I topple forward, *membus virilis* still in shocked hand as the pair collide in a searing chorus of pain on the rim of the pan.

'Sorry, so sorry,' she trills out, closing the bathroom door rapidly behind her.

Not half as sorry as I am. The force of the door also causes my head to fling forwards, hitting the upturned loo seat and bringing it crashing down on my neck. I am left looking like the victim of a medieval torture, my neck on the block, my head down the pan, my damaged cock in my hand, my life going down the toilet.

I struggle to my feet and make my way back to the sitting room to join Leila and her bemused friend.

'Jack, this is Catherine.'

'Hi, Catherine. Hi.'

Catherine looks at me as if I'm some kind of child molester. How much did she see in the bathroom? She wipes her hand on her trousers after shaking mine.

'Leila, I've really got to go.'

She looks disappointed.

'I'm sorry. Think I'm suddenly a bit drunk. I'll see myself out.'

Sunday 21st August

'So her flatmate thought you were polishing your trumpet in the bathroom?'

'Yeah, Fred, probably. Whatever.'

The memory is almost as painful as my nether regions.

'Ha ha, you and your penis injuries. When you weren't back by midnight, I assumed you'd got lucky.'

'It's not bloody funny at all. I've blown it again. One shot and I was chewed up and spat out and booed off stage. Right now, Catherine will be telling Leila what a weirdo I am.'

'Yep, I reckon you've well and truly blown it this time.'

'Cheers, Fred. Look mate, I want to go travelling. The last refuge of the failure. Get away from all this crap and nonsense. My life's going nowhere. I need to clear my head. Do you fancy coming, too?'

'I'd love to, but I'm really too busy. Why don't you go by yourself? You're a mess at the moment. Get a round-the-world ticket. You'll meet people on the way.'

You know, I think I might just do that.

Tuesday 23rd August

Everything is in place. I have an open-ended return ticket to Lima. Jasper is moving into my room until I get back and I have managed to palm off Jean with the hundred per cent truthful excuse that I am going to be out of the country for a lengthy period.

My bags are packed with books, mosquito nets, malaria pills and condoms. I am off to expand my mind and find the inner Jack Lancaster.

SEPTEMBER

Thursday 1st September

From: Jack Lancaster [*unemployed@hotmail.com*]
To: Buddy; Claire; Flatmate Fred; Jasper; Katie; Leila; Lucy; Mel;
Miranda; Mr Cox; Rick; Rupert; Susie
CC:
Subject: South America — my Lonely Planet

Hola amigos (that's Spanish),

Well, I've now been in South America for a week and I'm fluent in
Spanish. It is not a linguistically advanced language, and I also have
working knowledge of several local dialects, as well as a passable
understanding of most indigenous languages of the region. Frankly,
it's embarrassing having to sit here and write to you in English, so do
the decent thing and master it yourselves next time you have a few
spare minutes. *Gracias.*

A week ago (when I knew no more Spanish than the rest of you),
I embarked on my epic, self-searching, life-affirming adventure at
Terminal Three, Heathrow, near Slough, UK. How remote the tawdry
baubles of the corrupt First World seem to me now as I sit in an
internet café in the Andean foothills.

Anyway, the trip got off to a bad start when my hand luggage was
searched by security staff at Heathrow and two hundred condoms fell
out of my washbag.

'Are you planning on having a lot of sex?' asked the unforgivably
ugly security woman.

'No, they're in case I run out of water containers in the Peruvian
rainforest,' I explained, pointing at the appropriate page in my SAS
survival handbook to illustrate my point. 'They can hold two pints of
liquid each.'

Passed the time on the flight reading the Not-So-Lonely Planet
guide about the countries I'm visiting. Paid particular attention to the

'Dangers and annoyances' section to check up on my statistical chances of being kidnapped, raped or robbed (low to medium).

I only spent two days in Lima (the capital of Peru and the armpit of the earth). As soon as you venture onto the streets, nasty little hordes of ankle-biters would swarm around you saying, 'One dollar, mister.'

'Oh yes, my whaggish whimsies,' I would reply in fluent Quechua, 'a dollar is the native currency of the United States of America and approximately equal to 3.31 Peruvian *nuevo sols*. Now go and play in the traffic.'

I avoided these unpleasant menaces by spending most of my time in the hostel — a beautiful colonial building in the city centre — watching a pirated copy of *Braveheart* and talking to gap-year travellers while drinking Pisco Sour (translation: 'sour piss') which tastes like a combination of tequila, cream and vomit. Briefly contemplated going to a nightclub called 'Heaven or Hell, *Tu Decides*', but took an executive decision to go to bed instead.

The next day I caught a bus to Huacachina via Ica (look it up on a map) and watched an intriguing film called *Death Wish VII* en route. Went sandboarding in the desert dunes and swam around a stagnant lake. A couple of days later, I caught a bus to Nazca and flew over the Nazca Lines (much better in the postcards) and then carried on to Arequipa, which is a pretty town with amazing views of the mountains.

I am now in an adorable little village above Arequipa called Chivay, which is at 3600 metres. I spent yesterday getting altitude sickness and admiring the huge condors. Today I was invited to a local wedding and bathed in the hot springs. Just off now to the only open building in the village — an Irish pub.

Hope you're all enjoying autumn in London. Will write soon.

Love Jack
PS Fred, how's the new flatmate?
PPS Mr and Mrs Fielding, are you back from your honeymoon yet?!
PPPS Hi Buddy, long time, no see. Now rod off.
PPPPS Hello Mr Cox, you crapulent piece of crap. Thought you'd like to hear what I'm up to.
PPPPPS That's it. The rest of you don't get personal PS messages.

Saturday 3rd September

From: Jack Lancaster [*unemployed@hotmail.com*]
To: <undisclosed recipients>
CC:
Subject: South America II — electronic errors

Buenas días, filos de putas,

Well, as you can see, I have learned my lesson and decided to blind-carbon-copy you all in future.

Thank you for your 'reply all' email, Flatmate Fred. Now go away and shag Jasper.

Jack
PS Mr Cox, thank you for your request to be 'taken off this goddamn list'. I would love to, but I don't think I have the requisite technical skills. Sorry.

-----Original Message-----
From: Fred Hardy [*fred.hardy@yahoo.co.uk*]
To: Buddy; Claire; Jack; Jasper; Katie; Leila; Lucy; Mel; Miranda; Mr Cox; Rick; Rupert; Susie
CC:
Subject: RE. South America — my Lonely Planet

Hello everyone on Jack's email list (that's English),

Here in London (that's the capital of Great Britain), things are absolutely crazy. Today I got up at around 8.30am. Then I had a shower and ate my breakfast. I had Crunchy Nut Cornflakes with a splash of semi-skimmed milk. Then I made some fair trade coffee — we can all save the world in our own little way. And then I sat at my desk for eight hours and worked.

Later I am going to a bar where you really get to meet the locals. It's really authentic — it's called Walkabout. The indigenous people here are so friendly and so much more real. So are the sunsets. These are just some of the little details which make living in London in your twenties one of the most rewarding and life-enriching things to do.

I am slowly mastering the English language. My name is Fred. Jack refers to me as Flatmate Fred. I have one sister. She is called Beatrice. I have one hamster. My hamster is called Gnasher. I love school. My favourite subjects are Science and Sport. I would like one blackcurrant ice cream and four gallons of unleaded petrol.

I hope you are swimming in as big pools of you/me as I am.

Love from Fred
PS Take me off this list.

Monday 5th September

From: Jack Lancaster [*unemployed@hotmail.com*]
To: <undisclosed recipients>
CC:
Subject: South America III — in the bathroom

Since I wrote to you last I have mainly being shitting for Britain.

I think it was the 'bacon burger' that I had in the 'Irish pub' in Chivay.

'Would you like it heated?' asked the Irish barman (called José).

'No, I would like it cooked,' I replied.

But I think he wafted it over the lukewarm coals just along enough to galvanise every dormant bacteria in Peru.

Extra hamburguesa con tocino y quesa y mierda (that's Spanish again).

Ten minutes later I was running for the loo. It was like shitting an angry dragon. It reminded me of one of my university essays: wobbly introduction, a couple of cogent points in the middle and a loose conclusion. In the last twenty-four hours, I have gone to the loo twenty-eight times. Fifteen of these trips were poos alone. Eight were voms. And five blessed times I didn't know whether to squat or kneel. All in all, my work in the South American bathroom leaves a great deal to be desired. When evacuation is less controlled than desirable, one requires the balance of an eastern European child gymnast to avoid pebbledashing the pants. I have the balance of a fat Englishman on holiday.

Apologies if you're reading this over lunch. We travellers sometimes forget that normal people at home don't talk about their bowel movements incessantly. When/if I come home, it could be something of a reverse culture shock.

Have to go now. The beast is awake again.

Love Jack (half the man he used to be)

PS Rick, delighted that you had 'so much fun shagging on your honeymoon'. I hope Lucy enjoyed Venice too.

Thursday 15th September

From: Jack Lancaster [*unemployed@hotmail.com*]
To: <undisclosed recipients>
CC:
Subject: South America IV — bottom-blockers

Hola hola,

You might be relieved to hear that I have now taken quadruple doses of bottom-blockers and have had no movement for a hundred hours.

Alas, just as one bodily function began to function properly, another went spectacularly wrong. I have been taking Diamox to help me cope with the altitude. As well as giving you extremely unpleasant pins and needles, this makes you pee incessantly. This would have posed little problem had I not taken a loo-less night bus from Arequipa to Puno (on shores of Lake Titicaca).

Despite taking nil by mouth for the entire day in preparation, there was no way I was going to last the distance. By 3am I could take it no longer. Even *Death Wish IX* couldn't distract me from the constant pressure in my bladder. I took myself off to a quiet seat at the back of the bus and tried to relieve myself into an empty bottle of Inca Cola. As some of you know, I have a huge and unwieldy penis. I was doing the best I could on the bumpy roads when I looked up to see the bus conductor looking down on me.

'What do you think you're doing?' I think he said in one of the few indigenous dialects which I haven't yet mastered.

'I am having a piss with my huge and unwieldy penis,' I replied in fluent English.

167

At which point he decided to throw me out at the next stop, and I had to wait by the side of the road for twenty-four hours until the next bus came along. It is these little events that make travelling in a foreign country such a mind-expanding and varied experience compared with the humdrum routine of daily life back home.

Since then, I have been to Puno (small ming-hole), La Paz (big ming-hole and capital of Bolivia), Copacabana (beautiful), Isla del Sol (stunning) and back to Puno (small ming-hole) again. Off to Cusco for the Inca Trail next.

I would tell you more, but you all lead such drab and meaningless lives in your capitalist sweatshops that it would only make you jealous.

Just off to watch the sunset over Lake Titicaca (translation: 'Lake Breasty-poos'). Hope you're all enjoying London and don't get stuck on the tube for more than a couple of hours today.

Love Jack

PS I did an S-shaped poo today. Perfectly formed. Quite extraordinary. Remind me to show you all the photo when I get back. I am thinking of entering the Turner Prize next year: 'My travels across South America', which will consist of a photo collage of my bowel movements. A dead cert at the bookies, I'm sure you'll agree.

PPS Lucy, sorry to hear that Rick thought *gelato con pistachio* was a Renaissance painter.

Saturday 24th September

From: Jack Lancaster [*unemployed@hotmail.com*]
To: <undisclosed recipients>
CC:
Subject: South America V — Wayne 'n' Dwayne

Hola, those of you who haven't blocked my emails,

Some of you have been expressing concern that I might be rather lonely travelling all alone. You needn't worry; I am perfectly capable of keeping myself entertained.

For example, when someone comes up to me and tries to sell me a crappy trinket, I find it hilarious to smile nicely at them and say things like, 'You must be absolutely off your rocker, me old china plate, if you think I want to part with my hard-earned sausage and mash for that crappy piece of overpriced tack.'

'*Si, signor, si signor,* very good.'

Yes, I am rather good, aren't I?

But there are times, I admit, when it's nice to have some company.

For example, when I bought some jam that went by the brand name of 'Fanny', I longed for a chirpy Flatmate Fred by my shoulder. 'Pass me the Fanny when you're finished, Jack.' How we would have chortled.

But I have met my fair share of travellers. There were the Israelis who went for an early-morning naked swim every day in Lake Titicaca and then jogged up the nearest hill before breakfast, arguing loudly the whole way. There have been Australians heading east en route to Earl's Court and Kiwis heading back west in the other direction. There have been a couple of British city workers trying to 'get away from it all' and a fair number of loser hippies who can't face up to real life. I have met French and Dutch travellers who speak better English than Rick, and Americans pretending to be Canadian.

I have collected dozens of email addresses and made hundreds of promises to stay in touch. I intend to keep none of them. I mean, it's all very well when you're wearing grotty clothes and talking about bowel movements in a South American jungle. But meeting up back in London? Please.

But two people who really have stood out are Wayne 'n' Dwayne. Wayne Buchanan-Dunlop and Dwayne Bernard-Carter, to give them their full names. Both from Essex, both with Burberry backpacks, both on their gap year, both about to start at the Polytechnic of the West of England.

Wayne was born Wayne Dunlop. His cousin was born Dwayne Carter (on the same day). When they were seven years old, their grandmother (Tracey Bernard) won £10 million in one of the first National Lottery jackpots. Wayne Dunlop became Wayne Buchanan-Dunlop; Dwayne Carter became Dwayne Bernard-Carter. Both were put down for Eton. Both should have been put down at birth.

I first came across them in the backpacker town of Cusco, debating whether to pay $100 for a repulsive ethnic jacket.

'There's no point bartering for it, Wayne. We've got so much money. Let's just offer the nice little indigenous chap double.'

'That's not the point, Dwayne. It says here in the Lonely Planet, aka the Bible, that they expect you to barter. They're offended otherwise.'

'Listen, Wayne. Papa's house has more bidets than a man can shake a cane at. Let's just pay the dough and go.'

'But it might clash with your Burberry rucksack.'

I stepped in and told them that the jacket was worth $5 at the very most. I also warned them that they would never be seen dead in it back home. From that moment on, I was their firm friend. They looked upon me as some sort of travelling god who knew the price and the value of everything.

So we decided to do the Inca Trail together. Wayne wanted to do the five-star version with little men who run on ahead with indoor loo tents and heated face flannels. Dwayne wanted to carry all his own pots, pans and tent poles himself. I persuaded them to go for a happy medium.

It was brilliant. Well, apart from meeting half the Home Counties on their gap years, getting overtaken by most of the Israeli army and almost dying from altitude sickness, it was brilliant. On the last day we were woken up by our guide at 4am to walk to the 'Sun Gate' where we sang 'Where the fuck is the sun, do, dah, do, dah' by the Beatles as our promised view of Machu Picchu was entirely obscured in the morning mist.

'Two dollar, please,' said our guide.

'What for?'

'For showing you the Sun Gate.'

'What's the Spanish for "sod off"?' said Dwayne.

'*Soddus offus*, with a lisp on the "s".'

Now back in Cusco. Off to get drunk on Pisco Sour in the Irish Bar.

Love Jack

PS Buddy, that wasn't very nice, was it?

PPS Jasper, I bumped into someone who knew you at university. Guy called Crispin MacLean. Absolute wanker. 'Small world, isn't it?' I said to him. 'Not really,' he replied. 'There's probably a higher statistical chance of me bumping into a friend of Jasper's on the Inca Trail than bumping into Jasper in the library at Oxford.' As I said, absolute wanker.

PPPS Yes, Leila, I do keep a diary normally. But no, it's not nearly as fruity as these emails, so don't worry!

PPPPS Sorry for not replying personally to more of you. The internet cafés here are crap beyond belief. The computers are powered by small, unfit hamsters on treadmills. These beastly rodents often delete my emails before I've sent them. Please keep on writing, though.

Tuesday 27th September

From: Jack Lancaster [*unemployed@hotmail.com*]
To: <undisclosed recipients>
CC:
Subject: South America VI — mugged

Hola gilipollas,
     Yesterday I was mugged, beaten up, threatened with a knife, stripped in sub-zero temperatures and relieved of all my current possessions. At least now I can make an honest insurance claim.
     Wayne, Dwayne and I were all at a bar called Uptown in downtown Cusco. Both of them were chucking daddy's credit cards around, tossing their floppy fringes and flirting with everything in sight. They were doing little to draw attention away from themselves.
     In the early hours, someone came up to us.
     'You want shit?' he whispered conspiratorially.
     'Er, no thanks. I've already had the shits.'
     'No, you want good shit? Hashish, cocaine, heroine, coca leaves? Can get women, too. You like? Five dollar sucky-sucky.'
     'What's the charming little chappie saying?' asked Wayne.
     'He's offering us drugs,' I said.
     'Oh super,' said Dwayne. 'That sounds like such a genuinely travellerly experience.'
     The little chappie asked us to follow him round the corner, where a gang of eight huge chappies jumped on top of us and held knives to our throats.
     'What's this, what's this?' said the biggest of the chappies.
     'That, sir, is a knife. Please fuck off.'
     'Dwayne, shut the fucking fuck up. This is serious. Just do what they say.'
     'You can't really find yourself until you've been in a genuinely life-and-death situation,' retorted Wayne.

'Oh yes,' chimed in Dwayne. 'This is such a really genuine experience. Such a real opportunity to meet the locals.'

The locals enjoyed meeting us, too. We were strip-searched at knifepoint and they took our wallets, our money belts and our passports. Then they kept the other two hostage while three of them escorted me back to our hostel to clear out the rest of our stuff. And then they beat us up for good measure.

Fortunately, Wayne had a tri-band satellite phone secured in the hostel safe and rang his dad, who wired through a couple of extra thousand pounds, so I am now clothed again. No passport, though — which is gutting, as I had collected a nice range of exotic stamps — so have to head back to the embassy in Lima.

Hope London is slightly safer and you are all well in your heated offices and insulated apartment blocks.

Love Jack
PS Fred, could you be a legend and ring my parents and tell them I love them and I'm eating properly, etc. My phone card hasn't been working for the past week and I'm not sure that they do email.

Friday 30th September

From: Jack Lancaster [*unemployed@hotmail.com*]
To: Buddy; Claire; Flatmate Fred; Jasper; Katie; Leila; Lucy; Mel; Miranda; Mr Cox; Rick; Rupert; Susie
CC:
Subject: My father

Dear All,

This is to be my last email from South America. It is possible that some of you have already heard the dreadful news. My dad passed away in the early hours of Thursday morning. I found out just now by email from my mum. I am at an absolute loss for words.

I hope to catch a flight home tomorrow.

I have nothing more to say.

I love you all.

Jack

OCTOBER

Saturday 1st October

I've never seen anything like my mother's email. It seems an inappropriate time to be making jokes, but I think she thought she was writing a telegram charged by the word.

'Jack. Stop. Your father died early Thursday. Stop. Am so sorry. Stop. Please come home. Stop. All love. Mummy. Stop.'

And there it was. Stop all the clocks. Stop everything. Stop my world spinning. Full stop.

But now I'm sitting in first class on British Airways on my way home and I've got absolutely no idea what to think. I feel like I can cry no more. But then I can't put a stop to the host of inappropriate thoughts running through my grieving head:

(1) Isn't it nice to be upgraded for compassionate reasons?
(2) Is it wrong to take advantage of the compassionate upgrade and have more than one Kir Royale?
(3) The air hostesses are so much more attractive in first class.

I am in a state of complete and utter limbo. I don't belong to any time zone. I don't believe my mum's email any more. England is thousands of miles away; it seems like a million. There must be some mistake. The last time I saw Daddy he seemed fit and healthy. Was he run over? Was he murdered? There are a million unanswered questions. And they are trite and horrible and nowhere near the real point.

But then some inner reflex kicks in, and suddenly I understand. My father — who means more to me than anything else in the world — died two days ago. I will never see him again. I am flying home to his cold and lifeless body. He will not be there at the airport with a friendly squeeze on the shoulder.

While I was pissing around in South America like a selfish prat, he passed away. While I was composing stupid juvenile emails, he disappeared for ever. I will never ever see him again. And he died ashamed of his eldest son.

Something inside me snaps and I'm crying black floods of hell. I'm pummelling the seat in front of me with my fists, raging against the dying of my light. Everyone is looking at me, but I just don't care any more. When did their fathers die? All is black and dark and alone. An air steward asks if I'm OK. I shout at him. I'm angry with him for being alive. I run to the loo and crumple to the floor, wrapping my arms around the seat, grateful for any contact, human or otherwise.

It has taken me two free champagne cocktails to understand the awful truth. I hate myself. I am an unworthy piece of inconsequential matter. I require alcohol to connect with any shred of human decency. I don't deserve to be called my father's son.

All is cold and black and dark and very, very alone.

I want the plane to crash.

Sunday 2nd October

The plane didn't crash. I walk through customs at Heathrow and there's a small delegation there to meet me: Flatmate Fred, Rick and Lucy, Katie, Jasper, Claire and Leila.

I try to be strong, but this touches me more than anything else in my life. They've travelled down by tube and organised a car to take me back to Berkshire. They've all made a three-hour round-trip to see me for ten minutes so that I don't have to walk the Arrivals gauntlet alone. I break down into their loving arms. These are my friends. This isn't *Love, Actually*. This is real life. Bless them all to heaven and back.

Later I head out west on the M4, alone in the car. I look out of the window. 1500 people die every day in the UK. Some of those lives will have touched thousands. Some will have passed almost unmourned. Some will be remembered for decades; others, for a couple of hours. But this still means that over 10,000 people are grieving every day in this country.

I feel a sudden connection with this communal sense of loss, this great well of tears. I want to reach out and touch them all, dry their eyes and say, 'Yes, I too understand.' It puts my own loss in proportion. We are all just numbers in a ridiculous cycle of expectation and disappointment.

But I don't want proportion. I'm jealous of the sheer scale. 'One death is a tragedy; a million is a statistic.' I don't want my dad to be a statistic. And I feel that his death is more tragic than all the others put together.

But the tragedy doesn't really sink in until the car pulls into the drive at home. I can already sense the absence. My parents have lived here all my life. There is his car which we washed together. There is the wheelbarrow which he would push around the garden. There are the peeling windows which he never got round to painting. There is a confused dog, wondering why no one has taken him for a walk. He is everywhere, but my dad isn't here any more.

Brother Ben comes out and hugs me. We stand there silently on the drive holding each other, shuddering quietly into each other's arms. There are no words. They've lost their meaning.

And then Mummy comes out, her face lighting up to see her two grown boys. We open our circle to include her. The three remaining Lancasters, shaking quietly in the October gloom.

The dog whines and pushes into the middle, and we all fall about his face, hugging him and telling him what a good boy he is.

Sometimes it's easier talking to an animal than discussing a loved one you're never going to see again.

Monday 3rd October

Daddy had been ill for ages. I'm livid that I was never told, but I'm more angry with myself for not realising. There I was completely wrapped up in my own little world of inconsequential testicular lumps and minor career and girlfriend problems while he'd had terminal cancer since February.

But I can't be angry with Mummy for keeping it from me. She's a changed, softer person. I can sense that she's shredded to pieces inside, but some of Daddy's raw goodness seems to have passed on to her now that he is gone. I feel awful for all the horrible things I once wrote about her.

I look at her and see the woman who fell in love with him thirty years ago, the woman who fell for a man not much older than I am now. I would have loved my father even if he had been a bastard for the trite and simple reason that he was my father. But she chose to love him. She dated him. She fell for him. She married him. She bore his children. She knew him as an adult for five years before I'd even learned to say his name. Whatever shattered emotions I am feeling, she must be experiencing a million times over. I will never find another father, but I will hopefully fall in love, find a wife and have my own family. For her, there is nothing now. Just her two sons.

My father is dead. My mother's love is over. Death did them part.

Friday 7th October

Funeral.

We wanted to have a small, family affair, but our mailboxes and telephones have been jammed with people who knew and loved Daddy as we did. The village church is packed to the rafters.

'We brought nothing into this world, and it is certain we shall carry nothing out. The Lord gave, and the Lord hath taken away; blessed be the name of the Lord,' intones the vicar to signal the start of the service.

And I think: *No, wretched be the name of the Lord. This invisible, omnipotent deity who strikes with jealous randomness. Cursed be his wretched fiction.*

I wait in vain to be struck down by a thunderbolt.

The service drifts on. Uncle James — Daddy's brother — reads from Ecclesiastes: 'Then shall the dust return to the earth as it was.'

And I think: *He's not dust. He never was. He never will be. He's my father.*

And then Brother Ben is on his feet reading in clear, confident tones the poem that they chose together:

> Do not stand at my grave and weep,
> I am not there, I do not sleep.
>
> I am a thousand winds that blow.
> I am the diamond glint on snow.

I am the sunlight on ripened grain.
I am the gentle Autumn rain.

When you wake in the morning hush,
I am the swift, uplifting rush
Of quiet birds in circling flight.
I am the soft stars that shine at night.

Do not stand at my grave and weep.
I am not there, I do not sleep.
Do not stand at my grave and cry.
I am not there, I did not die!

But how can you not weep to words as beautiful and brave as those? I know they've become clichés. I realise that they're probably said 1500 times per day in Britain. But they hit me to the very core of my being. They achieve the exact opposite of their message. I am weeping openly and unashamedly.

We sing another hymn — 'Guide Me, Oh Thou Great Redeemer' — which was sung at my parents' wedding. I try to pull myself together, to be strong for the family, to keep up a good show. I look sideways at my mother for inspiration. She is standing stock still and upright, not singing but letting the words wash over her, bathing herself in their nostalgia. She's crying out of one eye and smiling out of the other. I give her hand a little squeeze, and she turns and says, 'I love you.' It's the first time she's said that to me since I reached double figures. No one at all has said it for months. I start to lose it again.

But I have to regain my composure, as it's my turn next. And as I walk up to the pulpit and open my notes I'm suddenly aware of a sea of faces, some familiar, many not — all sympathetic. I suddenly realise how haggard I must look. I wait for the final bars of the organ to die away and then I speak:

'I am weak, but thou art mighty. Hold me with thy powerful hand.'
My father was mighty in every sense of the word. In recent years, my Mother loved to tease him about his expanding girth. 'You'll just have

to grow longer arms so that you can still cuddle me,' was his typically affectionate reply.

But he was also a man of mighty integrity, mighty patience and mighty love. He is not only the best father that I could have had; he is the best father that anyone could have had.

I know that he touched the lives of thousands of pupils and hundreds of teaching staff who looked upon him as a father figure. There will be a memorial service at Morley Park — the school where he taught with so much love for twenty years — towards the end of this month.

But, if you'll forgive me, I want to talk for a short time today about the very personal relationship I enjoyed with him over a quarter of a century.

In comparison to my dad, I have always felt weak. His is a hard act to follow. There is a poignant moment in *The Lion King* when Simba, crossing the veld in the shadow of Mufasa, compares his own tiny pawprints to the vast tracks of his father.

I have approached much of my life with the same trepidation as Simba. But my father has always been there as a loving Mufasa to me — my man-mountain of bonhomie and integrity. From teaching me to ski and play cricket, to putting up with a brief period in my teens when I temporarily became subhuman, to listening to my recent dilemmas, he has always been there to hold me in his powerful hand. I deserved nothing. I owe him everything. I owe him the world.

And I also owe this to him: Daddy, I will do everything I can to live up to you. I will honour your legacy. Your memories are my memories. You were the rock of my life; you will remain so. I will try to be a rock for the rest of the family. I love you. I always will.

For, even after the sun has set over the horizon, its reflected beams continue to light the scene it's left behind.

The reflection of Charles Lancaster's memory will continue to lighten all our lives for a very long time to come.

Amen.

I find my way back to my seat through the tears. We stand for the final hymn and then there's a departing collect from John Donne: 'Bring us, O

Lord God, at our last awakening into the house and gate of heaven, to enter into that gate and dwell in that house, where there shall be no darkness nor dazzling, but one equal light; no noise nor silence, but one equal music; no fears nor hopes, but one equal possession; no ends nor beginnings, but one equal eternity; in the habitations of thy glory and dominion, world without end.'

Ben and I stand at the front of the coffin. Uncle James and Uncle Tom take the back end. And, with slow, mournful steps, the tears flowing freely now, the Bach Fugue in E flat ringing in our ears, we process down the aisle; Ben and I linked by our inside arms, our dead father hoisted on to our shoulders, like a child lifted above the heads of a crowd, bearing him aloft towards a waiting hearse and a freshly dug grave.

It's all over. All over bar the cremation, the small talk, the unanswered letters and the long, lonely, dark nights of tormented rants against God, Man, and the fundamental meaningless of this nonsensical in-joke of a jamboree which we call existence.

It's all over bar the shouting.

Friday 21st October

I am still at home, helping to put Daddy's affairs in order. It's an extraordinarily drawn-out process. It's the little things that you don't think of — whether to give his clothes to charity shops, which photos to keep, etc.

And, as for me, I'm finding it difficult to know what to think any more. I mean, how long are you meant to mourn? Should I feel guilty about enjoying myself again? How long should I stay around to look after my mother? What would he have wanted?

A couple of things have helped to get me back on track.

The first was a beautiful letter from Leila. It ended with a poem called 'Conclusions', which she claimed to have found somewhere (I rather suspect she wrote it herself). It's not Shakespeare, but I quite like it:

There have been tears and rejections, nights awake hitting pillows and days of listless boredom. I have known regrets and their waste, doubts and their selfish loneliness.

Life, sometimes pointless, and when there suddenly is a point, worthless. And the end so ultimate. Death so final. Eternity as terrifying as nothing.

Yet as long as there is laughter and friends to share it with. New mysteries, old places, eternal truths. Whilst music still sings and nature calms. Whilst words inspire, sleep soothes and people delight. As long as lips touch and hands caress, and events spur to action.

Whilst tomorrow's dreams excite as much as yesterday's memories, whilst anything still means everything to me, until I no longer have breath, you will see me love and live and smile.

Lips touch? Hands caress? That would be nice…

The second was a short letter from Daddy himself, which he wrote two days before he died.

My darling Jack,

I am writing this in the expectation that I won't be seeing you again. I have suffered a sudden decline in my illness, and we have no idea how to get hold of you in South America. When I have finished this letter I will pass it on to your mother. I will ask her to keep it until a suitable time has passed after the funeral.

I do not want you to be sad. Life is too short, too precious. I want you to go out and laugh in my name, love in my name, drink in my name.

I do not believe in an afterlife, but I see myself in you and Ben. That is comfort enough for an old man who has enjoyed his life.

Look after the family. I am proud of you.

All my love, Daddy

PS Don't write any more letters for the Conservative Party.

Strangely, we never spoke about death or religion together. For all our closeness, it was the one taboo subject between us. But I always had a suspicion that he didn't believe in a fundamentalist Christian version of the world.

And the more I think about it — and I've been thinking about it a lot recently — the more I embrace his doubts. I would really, really like to believe in the Bible. I would like to be a spiritual person. Perhaps more importantly, I am terrified by death. It has scared me into countless sleepless nights. And the concept of not existing any more frightens me far more than the fire and brimstone warnings of hell. At least you would still be able to feel something.

But for me, the Bible just doesn't measure up. I'm aware that I'm no theologian, but it seems to me that the Old Testament introduces us to a God who chooses certain people at the expense of others, sponsoring the bloodthirsty Israelites in their smiting and pillaging tours of the Middle East. It's an accident of birth whether you're chosen or not. It's the ultimate old boys' network; the final access issue. We are told to take an eye for an eye and a tooth for a tooth. Goats are to be killed and sent out into the wilderness. Gays are condemned. A man with a discharging penis has to sacrifice two pigeons at the entrance of the tent.

And then suddenly Jesus — a character whom I find inspirational in the extreme — turns up in the New Testament and says, 'Actually, Dad made a bit of a mistake back then. He'd like you all now to turn the other cheek and forgive each other. And also, by the way, he's decided to become all-inclusive and PC and welcome Gentiles as well.'

And then we are left alone for two thousand years with a mountain of conflicting evidence. And for good measure someone also chucks in Islam, Judaism, Hinduism, Buddhism, Taoism and a Catholic vs. Protestant divide.

We've gone from the God who talked directly to his people — albeit in burning bushes and columns of fire — to one who leaves us alone to figure it out for ourselves.

I would love to believe. I really would. It would give me the ultimate sense of purpose in my drifting life. But it just doesn't make sense.

And what's the point of heaven anyway? I mean, John Donne's poem is beautiful. One equal music and all that. But imagine how boring that would become. What is anything without fears and hopes, ends and beginnings, light and dark, contrasts and distinctions? This concept of heaven scares me as much as hell.

My problem with Christianity is not its basic message. It is a beautiful story of love and redemption. My gripe is its portrayal of God as a weak, needy figure who requires our worship and begging supplications.

I'm aware that none of us is perfect. I know that we all do a great deal of wrong. But this emphasis on kow-towing in prostrate guilt before an unknown megalith seems very unhealthy to me.

I think what really tipped it was the born-again acquaintance who rang me up today.

'Did your father believe in God?'

'In a vague sort of way, yes.'

'How do you mean?'

'Well, he was a very spiritual man. He was in awe of the natural world. He believed in responsibility to his fellow man. He was a fundamentally good person.'

'But did he believe that Jesus Christ, the only Son of God, a carpenter from Nazareth, came down from heaven two thousand years ago and died for his sins? Did he confess regularly? Did he say he was sorry for all the wrong he's done?'

'No, I don't think he was that naive.'

'Oh dear. I'm very sorry to tell you, Jack. Your father is going to hell.'

And I thought, *Go to hell yourself, you horrible little creep.* I want nothing to do with a religion that selects its eternal holiday-trip winners on the basis of whether they remembered to say sorry just before they died, a religion that prefers a murdering, but apologetic, rapist to a good man whose mind is too complicated to embrace dogma.

If heaven has no place for a man like my father, then I don't want to go there, either.

But then I read back over what I've just written and feel a horrendous sense of guilt that I could have been so blasphemous. And that's why religion works. It's the fear. It's got a morbid monopoly on our one last unknown. It's a safe bet-hedger.

Does God find the time to read private diaries? I'm for the high jump if he does.

Dear God, if you exist, I am very, very sorry.

Saturday 29th October

I was walking the dog this afternoon in the fields near the house, when I was suddenly aware of a huge sense of inner calm. I'm not sure why. I'm twenty-five and living at home in the middle of nowhere with my widowed mother. I have no girlfriend, no job and no prospect of sex within the next millennium.

But then none of it seemed to matter any more. I can't even begin to articulate this, but I wanted to throw off my clothes and run naked through the fields. I called the dog over and hugged him so hard he whined. This was it, this was life, with its shitty troughs and peaks, its inconsequential worries and concerns, its dark despairs and temporary elations. I embraced it all. I didn't even care that I was still hurting. At least I could still feel something.

A sense of overwhelming curiosity came over me. What would happen next — to me, to my friends, my family, the world in general? I wanted to live, to stay alive out of a simple, nosy interest in the course of events. I threw my head back, my arms spread wide, and laughed and thanked God, or god, or whatever other perverse, innate genius gave us the chance to think these thoughts and connect these emotions with other sentient beings.

The death of my dad has turned me into something of a walking cliché. I have realised the fragility and futility of life, its utter irrelevance and its irresistible importance. I have understood the waste of regrets, of words unsaid, of actions undone, of emotions left to run cold and dry.

I sat down under the old oak in the middle of the field. It's been there since the Crimean War. It had seen my great-great-grandfather. It would outlive me. The dog came and shook dirty water from the horse trough over me and put his wet head in my lap.

We're going to be OK.

Sunday 30th October

Daddy's memorial service at Morley Park.

A beautiful day. The end of British Summer Time, but the start of something new. Hundreds of old boys, staff and parents turned up to celebrate his life. It was uplifting, with none of the fake religiosity of the funeral. It was the perfect end to the bleakest month.

After the service Daddy's replacement as headmaster — Stuart Ackland — comes up to chat.

'Hello, Jack. You're looking more like your father every day.'

'What — fat and balding?'

'Ha ha.'

He looks at me a little uncertainly.

'Jack, I know this is a bit off the cuff, but you know how Roddy Lewis had to leave suddenly…'

'The one who was caught with kiddy-fiddling images on his computer?'

Stuart looks at me even more uncertainly.

'Well, those are unsubstantiated rumours, but Roddy has taken a leave of absence to clear his name.'

'I see,' I reply.

'Well, I was wondering whether you might like to step into his shoes after half term, see us through till Christmas. See how it goes?'

'Stuart, I am a failed banker who has been sacked twice in the last six months. I have a mediocre degree in Classics and no teaching qualifications whatsoever.'

'Jack, this is a private preparatory school. You're perfect. You can start on Tuesday.'

NOVEMBER

Tuesday 1st November

'Boys, welcome back to the second half of the Michaelmas term. I have a couple of notices before you go off to first period. The first eleven is playing our main rivals Summer Meadows this afternoon. It's a half-holiday, so I would like as many of you as possible to come and watch. Tomorrow there will be a nits inspection for all boys in West and South houses who don't have chits signed by their mothers or by Matron. North and East, it will be your turn on Thursday, unless you're in the away match at Brock Hill, in which case you should ask your form master what to do.'

'And finally, I'm sorry to announce that Mr Lewis is unwell [*sniggers from the staff*] and won't be returning for the rest of this term. Fortunately, we are very lucky to welcome Mr Lancaster...'

I feel a hundred and fifty pairs of beady little eyes turn round and stare at me. I'm wearing a battered corduroy jacket and chinos. I look like a tosspot. These little ankle-biters terrify me.

'Turn back round, boys. As I was saying, we're delighted to welcome Mr Lancaster, who will be taking over Mr Lewis's responsibilities for Forms IV, V and VI French. He will also be helping out with the sport and music. Mr Lancaster is an old boy of Morley Park and he comes to us via Bristol University and a very successful career as a city banker.'

I manage to catch Stuart Ackland on the way out of morning assembly.

'Stuart, I haven't done French since A level. I thought I was going to be teaching Latin. There's not a chance that I will know how to teach French.'

'Jack, they're only ten years old, for God's sake. How hard can it be? I did Sports Management at university — I'm now the head and teach Geography. Just take them through the textbook. Norris will show you the ropes.'

'Norris?'

'Yes, Norris Beaumont. He used to teach you, didn't he?'

He certainly did. Mr Beaumont had been a teacher at Morley Park for forty years. He was there as a boy himself. He hated leaving for secondary school, did his national service and then came right back to where he belonged. I assumed he'd retired long ago, but there he was storming down the corridor towards me, all tweed and paunch and eyebrows. And to think I used to be terrified of him!

'Ah, Lanky, old boy. *Bonjour.* Or should I call you *Mr* Lanky now? Fancy having you back here. What fun. Right, French — bloody easy language. English has over 800,000 words; French has less than 100,000. I hear you're a classical scholar these days. French is the same language as Latin, really — just a bit more modern. Don't worry about teaching them a French accent. They'll just speak English like everyone else when they go there on skiing holidays and booze cruises.'

'Right-o, Mr Beaumont.'

'And, just call me Norris.'

'Really, sir, I can't. I spent five years of my life peeing in my pants every time I saw you.'

'Norris, Lanky, Norris. And none of this "sir" nonsense, either. Right, what else do you need to know about teaching?'

'Er, how should I plan a lesson?'

'I recommend the five-step plan, Lanky.'

'And how does that work?'

'Five steps before you go into the classroom, work out what you're going to teach them. One step — vocab test? No, too boring. Second step — grammar test? No, takes too long to mark. Third step — show them a video? No, Mr Lowson's got the bloody machine again. Fourth step — reading comprehension? No, none of them can read. Fifth step — wing it. You'll get the picture.'

I think I'm going to enjoy this.

Saturday 5th November

I *am* enjoying this. I'm happier than I've ever been in my life. It's the first job I've done when I haven't watched the clock and longed for the end of the day. I am getting paid to do something I actually enjoy doing.

My colleagues are a happy bunch of eccentrics who love their jobs. Sure, there are the usual inevitable tensions of any group of people. Geoffrey Aitken, the Latin teacher, thinks he should have been made deputy head over Bob Lowson, the Science teacher. Norris Beaumont is an implacable snob and hates the idea that Stuart Ackland — a former PE teacher — should be Headmaster. Rupert Pearce (Maths) is jealous that Simon Reeve (English) gets to coach the first team football and he's stuck with the under-9 D team. And there is an intriguing little love triangle between Alice Price (Matron), Charlie Blackwell (gap year teacher from South Africa) and Amy Barbour (Junior Form Mistress).

But there is none of the horrendous competitiveness of most other jobs. They tease each other in a light-hearted way. There are no Arabellas or Mr Coxes or Buddy. They are here because they love teaching, not because they love money. It's something that they've chosen to do and not something they've drifted into. It's all about the boys.

And what a bunch of little characters the boys are:

'Thsir, thsir, are you sexing Miss Barbour?'

That, my little chestnut, is not a proper transitive verb.

'Thsir, thsir, why does Mr Beaumont call you "Mr Lanky"?'

None of your business, Fereday. It's Mr Lancaster to you.

'Thsir, thsir, is it true that you're a zillionaire with a really fast car?'

Well, Blenkinsop, you can tell Miss Barbour that if you like.

'Thsir, thsir, how long have you been teaching French for?'

Shit, is it really that obvious?

'Thsir, thsir, why don't you have a girlfriend?'

Boys, how long do you have?

They're young and they're inquisitive and they're full of fun. There is respect behind their cheekiness. Their enthusiasm is infectious. The older ones have told me how much they liked my dad.

And I even love the teaching. My only previous experience was on my gap year in a village in Syria with classes of sixty to seventy kids of mixed ability. The headteacher there was a carbon copy of Hitler and almost as ruthless. He claimed that he only hit the pupils because he cared for them, but it was not an uncommon sight to see the playground strewn with those he had laid out unconscious. The kids thought I was weak because I refused to hit them. Their desire for English stretched no further than 'Sleep with me, pretty girl' to my fellow gap volunteer.

Morley Park is something of a holiday camp in comparison.

And that's all I have time for. Mr Lancaster (still haven't got used to that) is off to prepare the games pitches for bonfire night.

Sunday 6th November

Flatmate Fred rang. It's my birthday on Wednesday and he wants me to go back to the old flat in London, where he and Jasper are going to cook for me.

Flatmate Fred 'n' Jasper. They're beginning to sound like a bit of a roadshow. They've made it clear that I can have my old room whenever I want, but I'm really quite happy in the countryside.

Flatmate Fred is still Flatmate Fred, whoever's flatmate he currently is.

Wednesday 9th November

'Surprise!'

It certainly was. I'd let myself into my old flat with my own key and found myself in the dark. Just as I turned the light on, twenty people jumped out from behind the sofa. I'd never had a surprise party before. I'd always wanted one.

Twenty of my best friends in one flat and the first person to collar me was Buddy.

'Jacko — very long time, no meet, as you guys say.'

'Buddy, wow. How are you? This really is a surprise.'

'Yeah, well me and your Flatchum Fred have stayed in touch a little bit. Thought I'd pop down and see how ya doing. I heard you've sorted yourself out a bit. Got a teaching job, eh? Those who can't, and all that.'

'Yeah, and those who can put numbers in Excel boxes?'

I managed to sidestep him and talk to Rick and Mrs Fielding, who didn't look quite as heavily pregnant as I'd expected.

'Drinking on a school night?' said Rick.

'Literally,' I groaned. 'Have to be back in time for morning assembly at 8.30 tomorrow.'

'So how are the provinces?' replied Rick. 'To tire of London is to tire of life? Do you agree with Oscar Coward?'

Marriage had done wonders for his conversation.

'It was Noël Wilde, wasn't it?' replied Lucy.

'My dear Fieldings, it was Samuel Johnson and he was spouting utter bollocks as usual. I'm bored shitless of London and I've never been so energised by life.'

'But you must miss it. All the theatre, and the culture and the opera. And all the best jobs are here. Everyone is in London.'

'Rick, when was the last time you went to the theatre? And actually, for that matter, when was the last time you had one of London's "best jobs"?'

Lucy giggled. Rick looked momentarily hurt and then guffawed, too. We raised our glasses and drained them. Lucy was on orange juice. Rick seemed to be drinking for the two of them.

'You must be due any day now, aren't you?' I asked Lucy, performing some rapid mental arithmetic.

Lucy looked at Rick, who broke into such a fit of unsubtle coughing that she was forced to answer.

'Hmm, yes. Jack, well, the thing is, Rick got me pregnant in March, actually I got my dates slightly confused. I'm due some time next month.'

So there you had it. Valentine's Day – the day of commercialism, despair, desperation, love and inventing stories. I stared at Lucy. She looked back at me evenly and then broke into a small, private smile of apology. I decided to leave it be. We all do stupid things in the name of love. That was all in the past now.

I carried on mingling, but it wasn't until after midnight that I finally managed to talk to Leila. Buddy had been monopolising her all night.

'So, happy birthday, old man.'

'Ah, thanks Leila, but you've just missed it. I've now been twenty-six for fourteen minutes. You'll have to wait till next year.'

'Never mind. Timing never was my strong point.'

I laugh. Slightly bitterly.

'Hmmm, me neither. Actually, speaking of which, there's something I've been meaning to say to you for well, er, for, let's say roughly forty-two weeks and six days and a couple of hours.'

I can remember exactly what I said next, because I'd rehearsed it in my head a million times. I'd muttered its clauses to myself while stomping up the escalators on the Underground. I'd honed its inflections while running round the games pitches with the under-9 C football team. The monologue had become part of me. It had kept me up for hours in bed at night and awoken on the tip of my tongue in the morning. The curtain was lifting on the first dress rehearsal. My seventh seduction attempt and I wasn't going to bottle it this time...

'Leila, to me you are beautiful in every way. You're funny, you're kind, you're sweet and you're stunning. But it's not simply that you're the most amazing girl in the world — which you are — or that I fancy you to bits — which I do — or that you make me unbelievably happy whenever I'm around you — which you do. I think there's something even better there. There's a hidden side of Leila of which I've caught tantalising glimpses. A Leila I'd like to get to know better. A Leila worth fighting for. Nothing in the world would make me happier than to be your boyfriend.'

I pause, waiting to see the effect of my little oration. She's half-crying, half-smiling.

'Oh fuckity fuck it, Jack. You weren't joking about your bad timing. I've been wondering for months whether you were ever going to say anything.'

She hasn't said no. She hasn't said no.

'So you feel the same way? Why didn't you say something yourself?'

'Because I wasn't sure. And I couldn't work out how you felt. I'm the girl. I'm old-fashioned when it comes to this sort of thing. You know how shy I can be. It's your role to hunt us, isn't it?'

Girls have no idea how difficult our self-appointed role is.

'You're so hard to read, Jack. I mean, one moment you're sleeping with your ex-girlfriend again, the next you're having a one-night stand with the bridesmaid at your ex-girlfriend's wedding.'

Who told her that? I never told her about Katie.

She continues. 'You tell me that you "fucking love me" when you're being thrown out of the bank by security guards. The next time we meet up, you deny it completely. A month later you're running naked across a polo pitch. Then, at the end of August, just as I think you're becoming a normal human being, you come round to mine for dinner. I think it's all going well. I'm bursting inside wanting you to kiss me, and then my flatmate Catherine finds you, well, finds you doing something you shouldn't in the loo. Then you disappear travelling without even telling me that you're going. I mean, you've acted extraordinarily. Is there any explanation for all of it?'

There is one explanation: I'm a dickhead. There's another: I love her. But I'm too scared to say it.

'No, Leila, that's just not true. It was a long-distance release... Well, anyway, never mind. I can explain everything. Can't we just put it all behind us? We can still be together.'

'Jack, you're incredibly special to me.'

'What does that mean?'

'It means that you're incredibly special to me, but I can't go out with you.'

'Why not?'

'I'm back with Buddy.'

I'd stuck to my bit of the script. She'd deviated horribly from hers.

Thursday 10th November

'Thsir, thsir, is it true that it was your birthday yesterday and you're now forty-six?'

'Blenkinsop, shut up.'

'Oh is thsir tired today? Is thsir in a bad mood?'

'Right Blenkinsop, detention. Three hours on Saturday.'

There's no point teaching kids if you can't take out your personal problems on them.

Sunday 13th November

Remembrance Sunday.

There's something in the simple beauty of the service that always hits me. The last post, the music, the poetry:

> They shall not grow old,
> As we that are left grow old:
> Age shall not weary them,
> Nor the years condemn,
> At the going down of the sun
> And in the morning
> We will remember them

But when we all stood in the school chapel for the minute's silence, I found it impossible to concentrate on the war dead. It wasn't Blenkinsop with his beeping digital watch a couple of rows in front. It wasn't Anson and his blasted sniffling in the front row. It wasn't even Alice Price giggling next to me because Charlie Blackwell was pinching her arse and saying 'Oooh, Matron' and then blaming it on me.

I found it impossible to concentrate because I was thinking about what an idiot I am when it comes to Leila. I am all blast and bombast and no results. And then I felt like even more of an idiot for thinking about her when I was meant to be thinking about the millions who sacrificed their lives so that I could sit there and think about girls.

That's the problem with our generation. We've got no cause, no belief, nothing worth fighting for. Our grandparents had world wars. Even our parents had the 1960s and Vietnam. What do we have? Fox-hunting and PFI partnerships. It's not much to get worked up about.

We want everything and we are left with nothing.

I was just coming out of my haze as the service ended and we were filing out of chapel.

'So, Lanky, what are we doing with the boarders this afternoon?'

'The boarders, Norris?'

Yes, Mr Lanky, this is a Sunday in a boarding school and the boys need to be entertained. I think maybe a spot of paintballing.'

'Don't you think that's a little bit insensitive, given the date?'

'Nonsense, utter nonsense. An inverted pyramid of piffle. Our countrymen died to protect our freedom to spend a Sunday afternoon paintballing. It'll toughen the boys up a bit. I'll see you after lunch by the minibus.'

So Norris Beaumont and I took the boys paintballing and shot ten degrees of hell out of them and each other. Norris captained one team; I took charge of the other. We both sent our troops over the top as fire-diverting decoys while we went for the flags ourselves. Field Marshal Haig would have been proud.

Leila called in the evening and I smothered the phone under the cushions. Felt much better.

Friday 18th November

I have thrown myself so completely into my work that I've demoted Leila from the forefront of my thoughts. Gone are the sleepless nights and the endlessly rehearsed internal dialogues. Of course, there is the complete frustration that I screwed everything up and embarrassed myself. But at least I now have the release that I've said something at last. I've promised myself that I will never again keep things to myself for so long. Farewell 'Jack the Bottler'. Hello Mr 'Open Man' Lancaster. From now on, I will sort things out quickly and move on.

There was a time when one word from her could have changed my life around completely. When I was a miserable banker, she was all the hope I had. Now that I have something else to focus my energies on, she has become an optional extra. It doesn't sound very romantic, but it's much more healthy. Perspective, I believe it's called (or maybe just denial?). It's almost as good as closure.

Tuesday 22nd November

The school is a hub of excitement as there are inspectors coming in on Thursday. It's the first inspection under Stuart Ackland's headship and he's as nervous as the rest of the staff. Bob Lowson has sent his only suit to the dry-cleaners to get the Bunsen burner stains off in time. Geoffrey Aitken has had his comb-over trimmed. Simon Reeve has started chewing Nicorette gum so that he can last an entire lesson without smoking his pipe. Amy Barbour has been told to put on a short skirt to distract them into thinking she's a good teacher. Even the cleaners are working overtime to make the whole place look like less of a bomb shelter.

Only Norris Beaumont remains unperturbed by the whole charade.

'It's my fifteenth inspection, Lanky. Did you know that?'

'I can't say I did.'

'Piffle, the ruddy lot of them. Every time, they tell me that I speak French like Colonel Blimp and that my methods are unconventional but effective. It's only so that this wretched government can pretend to keep an eye on the private sector. They only come here to moan about how much better our facilities are.'

'Is that so?'

'It is so. One word of advice, Lanky. Don't change anything in your teaching style. The children will smell a rat a mile off.'

'Teaching style? I don't believe I possess any such thing.'

Thursday 24th November

'Thsir, thsir, why are you giving us printed handouts? We don't normally have printed handouts.'

Blenkinsop, I'll murder you later.

'Thsir, thsir, can't we just watch a video like we normally do?'

Anson, remind me to tell your yummy mummy what a little pest you are.

'Thsir, thsir, you are our best, favouritest teacher. We've learned so much from you.'

'Very good Fereday, you little creep. Right, boys. Let's have none of that when the inspector comes in.'

And, sure enough, they were good as gold, and the inspector was charmed by my firm, but fun, teaching style.

I am an excellent pedagogue, a pillar of the community, a key worker.

Saturday 26th November

We're in the last two weeks of term and the school has switched from the football to the rugby season. Given that I am marginally less bad with the oval ball, I have been promoted to coach the under-11 B team.

We are on the bus for our first match, away at Cotcote House. I'm more nervous than the boys. They're stuffing their faces with iced doughnuts and crisps. I'm looking out of the window and trying to remember if the team going forwards in a maul gets the scrum at this age group, or whether it's given against the team which fails to recycle possession. Thank God I don't have to referee.

'Thsir, thsir. Blenkinsop's mooning out of the window to passing cars.'

'Fereday, you're a little sneak. And, Blenkinsop, pull your trousers up. We don't want to frighten the other motorists.'

Our bus pulls into the grounds of Cotcote House. It's a large, snobby school. Even their youngest boys are imbued with a sense of God-given arrogance that they are being groomed to run the Empire.

A wheezing Classics master comes out to greet me.

'Lancaster? You must be the new chap. I remember your father well. Terribly sorry. My name's Piggott. So, how are your crop?'

'Oh, you know. They're a fearsome and deadly fighting machine.'

Out of the corner of my eye, I can see Blenkinsop being travel-sick over Cotcote House's pristine lawns.

'Righty-ho. Should be quite a match, then. I'll get my boys to show your boys where to change. Why don't you come into the common room for a pot of tea? There are a couple of parents milling around already.'

We amble into the palatial entry hall.

'I say, Lancaster. I was wondering if you could be an absolute cove and referee for me this afternoon? I wouldn't normally ask, but I had triple bypass surgery last month and I can't keep up with these whippersnappers.'

'Of course, no problem. You might have to lend me some clothes and a rule book, though.'

I'm just heading off to the staff changing rooms when I hear a familiar voice behind me.

'Jeremy, *salve*. How are you? *Quo vadis* — not to mention how are you? I am not unaware of the fact that my boy hasn't made the A team.'

Oh. My. God. He hasn't noticed me yet. I hide behind one of the balustrades.

'Oh, Mr Cox,' replies Jeremy Piggott. 'How jolly nice to see you. Yes, we thought we'd try Frankie out in the B team for this week. See how he gets along. I have made him captain, though.'

Unbelievable. Even his son's teachers call him "Mr Cox".

'Francis, Jeremy. His name is Francis. And you appear not to be following. I don't think I pay *circa* twelve thousand pounds in school fees *per annum* for my son to play in the B team. Perhaps I don't have to remind you, open brackets, a lowly Latin teacher, close brackets, that I, open brackets, the successful managing director of a major city bank, close brackets, donated a considerable amount of money to the school sports hall.'

Jeremy Piggott draws himself up to his full height.

'Indeed you did, Mr Cox, open brackets, a parent, close brackets. I am currently *in loco parentis.* I alone will make decisions regarding your son's suitability for the under-11 B team. Perhaps if the little mite spent more time in your blasted sports hall, he'd make it into the A team.'

Jeremy Piggott — a scholar and a gentleman. I love the man already.

Ten minutes later, and I'm changed and heading out on to the pitch, where my team is warming up by throwing mud at each other.

'Thsir, what on earth are you wearing?'

'Shut up, Anson. There's nothing wrong with plus-fours and a cricket jumper.'

'Thsir, Blenkinsop is still feeling ill.'

I bet Sir Clive Woodward never had to put up with this kind of shit.

'Right, boys. Gather round and listen up. You have absolutely no idea how to play rugby. I am a useless coach and you have learned none of the basics from me. Fortunately for all of us, what you are about to play is not a game of rugby. Oh, no. You are at war. From now on, Cotcote House is your morbid enemy. Their fathers have slept with your mothers. Their brothers have stolen your PlayStations. And they themselves have kidnapped your black Labradors and tortured them to death.

I feel like Henry V before Agincourt.

'No, Fereday... Dry your eyes. It's just a metaphor... I'm sure Betsy is just fine... Look, if you try to play rugby against them, you will lose. Do not pass the ball except as a last option; you will only drop it. Do not kick it; it will probably go sideways. And, whatever you do, do not try to tackle anyone properly; you'll only get hurt. When you have the ball, run straight and hard. When they have it, try to trip them up. In the scrums, bite, scratch and gouge. In the mauls, pinch. In the rucks, stamp.

'And always remember this: they only have fifteen prepubescent boys on their team. Morley Park has fifteen prepubescent boys and a fully grown referee on their team. I can be very short-sighted at times. Win this for me, boys, and there will be an extra KitKat for every single one of you.'

I call the captains over for the toss.

'But thsir, we don't have a captain.'

'Oh, don't we? Right, Blenkinsop, it's you. Do up your shoelaces and come over here.'

Blenkinsop skips up to the halfway line and shakes hands with Francis Cox. Cox is a short, fat fellow and instantly dislikeable. He has a face that would market very well as a punchbag.

'Right, Cotcote House captain, which hand is my whistle in?'

'Your left hand, sir.'

'No, it's not. It's not in either hand. Bad luck. Right, Blenkinsop, I suggest you play with the wind and the sun behind you in the first half. Cotcote House, you can kick off, if you must.'

The thirty mini-men line up in their battle groups. I can see Mr Cox on the sideline attempting to reingratiate himself with Jeremy Piggott. He appears to be pointing at me.

I blow the whistle to start the match. I blow it again two seconds later.

'Sorry, Cotcote House. You weren't behind the kicker. Morley Park captain, do you want a penalty or a scrum in the centre?'

'What's a scrum?'

'Blenkinsop, do try and sound a little more intimidating.'

The match fizzes on. My little pep talk seems to be working. My boys are playing dirtier than an England vs. France encounter. But there's still no score. One of the Cotcote boys was clean through on our line when a dog ran on from the sidelines and tripped him up. A couple of minutes later, Anson broke through their ranks and did a spectacular dive over the line before looking up and realising that it was the twenty-two-metre line. Bowles also managed to cross their line, but then he ran over the dead ball line as well and ended up on the girls' hockey pitch.

And then Fereday hoists a kick high into the autumn sun. The Cotcote House full-back squints up and then sits down and starts crying.

197

'I can't see, I can't see,' he's yelling.

Blenkinsop can see. He picks up the loose ball and storms over their line.

'Put it down, put it down,' the entire team is shouting at him.

He does. 5—0. He's our hero.

'Boys, stop hugging each other. This isn't a game of football.'

Bowles dribbles the conversion along the ground and I blow the whistle for half-time. Twenty-five minutes have elapsed.

I'm too exhausted to say much to them in the half-time team talk. I haven't done this much exercise for years.

'Thsir, thsir, are you out of breath?'

'Not as out of breath as you should be, Drysdale. A little more effort from you in the second half, please.'

'And all of you, listen up. The wind and the sun have dropped. Keep on playing like you have been and there won't be any problems. I would give you some tactics, but I don't know any. Just go out there and beat them up.'

But the second half kicks off and it's disastrous from the start. I don't know what Jeremy Piggott put in their half-time oranges, but Cotcote House are playing like little devils. Perhaps Mr Cox has offered them all extra pocket money if they win.

Despite my best efforts, Francis Cox waddles over our line to score two tries in quick succession. The score is now 10—5.

But then they have a scrum on our five-metre line and I see him deliberately kick our front row's shins.

I blow up for a penalty.

'Cotcote House captain, over here, please.'

'What?'

'Don't "What?" me, young man. I saw you kicking our prop in the scrum. This is a warning. Next time, you'll be off.'

'*Canis filius,*' I hear him mutter under his breath.

'Right. That's it, early bath for you. I'm sending you off now.'

Cox Junior starts to trudge off the pitch only to pass Cox Senior trotting in the other direction. He ignores his son and makes straight towards me. He looks ridiculous with his Barbour over his suit jacket and his pinstripes tucked into green wellies.

'Ah, Mr Cox! What an incredible coincidence. What can I do for you?'

The boys are all huddled around in a group, watching.

'Lancaster, I thought I'd seen you on a playing field for the final time. Why did you send my son off?'

'Because I will not have a ten-year-old tell me in Latin that I am a son of a bitch. Now, am I going to have to send you off the pitch, as well? Is this to be a gala red-card day for the Cox family?'

Mr Cox eyeballs me. I hold his gaze. And then he looks away and makes an elegant attempt to leave the pitch with his dignity intact. Both teams of boys collapse into fits of laughter.

In a second half that only lasted fifteen minutes, we beat them 15—10. Jeremy Piggott congratulated me afterwards with a twinkle in his ageing eye.

as life is short, and time before the exam is even shorter, I suggest you concentrate on these words on the board.

'And no, Blenkinsop, this isn't cheating. I am merely preparing you for the exam to the best of my considerable abilities.'

Thursday 8th December

I had a day off school today — no lessons during exams — and a long-forgotten interview (I applied some time in March last year) with the civil service, which I'd been deliberating about whether to attend. I mean, who would want to be a servant? Especially a civil one? And even if you get to the top, you're still permanently under a secretary (although that does sound quite fun). But then I worried that maybe I'd become a little too mature and boring in the last month. So I made the informed and grown-up decision to go along and take the piss at the taxpayer's expense.

And the taxpayer should be very grateful that I did. The problem with these assessment centres — as I pointed out in my debriefing — is that they can never get close to simulating real-life office situations. Sure, the e-tray exercise might test your prioritising skills, but where are the round-robin joke emails from your friends interspersed with the request from Jens Jenger Jengerson at the Danish EU Commission for this year's fish quotas? Where is Buddy's lame electronic banter amidst the stern reminders from the Cabinet Office that the deadline for delivering your report, 'Delivering Target Deliveries', is overdue? And how can you decide which email to reply to first if you don't know how attractive any of the senders are?

If, as I continued in my debriefing, they really want to assess people's familiarity with computers at work, they should test some of the following: 1) How quickly can the candidate minimise undesirable internet windows when a superior appears? 2) How quickly can the candidate press alt and tab to flick between the test match score and the BBC news website? 3) Does the candidate know how to recall offensive emails sent in error to his boss? 4) Is the difference between 'reply' and 'reply all' indelibly embedded within the candidate's soul? And 5) Can the candidate fake an IT fault which will allow him to waste an entire day doing nothing?

'Thank you for that feedback, Mr Lancaster,' said my assessor, scribbling away furiously.

'It's not a problem,' I beamed graciously. 'Happy to share my expertise with you.'

The personality interview went well, too.

'When have you worked together in a successful team to secure a common goal?'

'When I was fifteen, I looked too young to buy alcohol, so I persuaded the local wino to purchase a bottle of vodka for me in return for a fifteen per cent commission. It was a mutually satisfying outcome for all stakeholders.'

'And when have you shown good communication skills?'

'The wino wanted a twenty per cent commission. I bartered him down to fifteen.'

'And when have you demonstrated proactivity?'

'I decanted the bottle of vodka, diluted it with water, kept half for myself, reapplied the seal and sold it on to a thirteen-year-old for twice the profit.'

'And leadership?'

'When I was caught by my headteacher for drinking the vodka in school, I blamed my best friend for forcing me to do it.'

'And integrity in an awkward moral situation?'

'I refer you to my earlier answer.'

They scribbled furiously.

But it was the group exercise that really gave me the chance to shine. I had to role-play a Treasury official attending a meeting with his colleagues to discuss proposals for a new national stadium. My brief was to resist any developments until the budgetary situation was clearer.

I decided to take control of the meeting.

'Robin, you can take the minutes. Sarah, you little fittie, you keep an eye on the time. Everyone else, you each have a ten-second pitch in which to convince me that I should fork out money on a bunch of spit-roasting footballers and their Neanderthal, revolting supporters.'

Almost no one else got a word in edgeways. I would definitely have scored top marks in the group.

Afterwards, we got the chance to provide feedback on the other participants' performances. 'Sarah,' I wrote, 'probably would. Susan, definitely wouldn't. Kevin, spotty and obnoxious. Robin, first-rate minute-taker. Took orders well.'

I can't wait to hear their feedback on me.

Friday 9th December

Back where I belong, at Morley Park, to invigilate in the main school hall.

Bob Lowson and I played 'Examiners' Chicken', which involves walking slowly down the aisle towards each other. The first one to flinch loses. I won 14—9, which boded well for my kids.

At one point I glanced over Anson's shoulder. Attempting to translate 'I left the house' into French, he'd put 'J'ai gauché la maison'.

One day that boy will be a Captain of Industry. I just hope it's somewhere in the English-speaking world.

Saturday 10th December

It's 7.30pm on a Saturday night in the run-up to Christmas and I am sitting by myself in a small room in the Home Counties, looking over ten-year-olds' French exams. I have down-sized at the age of twenty-six. It's still not *la vida loca*. But I'm happy. My dad would be proud of me.

And, apart from Anson's, the papers are surprisingly good. I can always blame the dodgier marks on Roddy Lewis's deviant pederast influence in the first half of the term.

I put my red pen down and think about London and what I would be doing if I were still there. No doubt I would just be gearing myself up for a night of stumbling, mumbling and fumbling that I wouldn't remember in the morning. I would probably be sharking an unsuitable woman. I would almost certainly be trolleyed.

And I think about Flatmate Fred and Jasper, Rick and Lucy, Buddy and Leila.

Like animals going two by two into the Ark — Rick 'n' Lucy. Flatmate Fred 'n' Jasper. Jack and sixteen-year-olds. Jack and Miss P. M. Gilmour… Jack and no one.

Leila, Leila, Leila.

I read back over this year's diary and there she is, idolised and idealised in vast streams of impotent prose. And I think: *Words are nothing. Nothing but post hoc justifications and poorly remembered trivialities. Semantics and pedantics. Bottled-up feelings, half-declarations, cowardly withdrawals at the last minute. The japes and scrapes of my reality and my imagination.* No wonder diarists are so unhappy.

Keeping a diary might have helped me to sort my life out: it's allowed me to think things through in a way that I wouldn't have done normally; it's shown me where I was going wrong with my career and my relationships. But it's now become an obstacle to my continuing happiness, a place of timid refuge where realities are blurred, real life is ignored and emotions are sullied by their tawdry articulation.

I remember what Claire (doctors 'n' nurses) led me to conclude in February: I am not a piece of flotsam at the mercy of fate. I can influence events around me. I can influence others. Nothing matters and everything matters. The time for thinking is over. Stop writing; start doing. Quit observing; participate.

Il faut cultiver le jardin, innit.

But how to put this Voltairean horticultural philosophy into practice? I reach for my mobile and scroll down to Leila's name. It's a month since I told her how much I liked her. And even then I left the issue hanging, even after she said that she liked me, too. I didn't try to argue it through. I just listened to her defence and beat a hasty and feeble exit.

Her phone rings once and I hang up in a sweat, tossing the phone away. *She's told me no. What am I thinking? She doesn't want to speak to me.* And I'm far too embarrassed to speak to her. It's a Saturday night. She's probably out with Buddy somewhere anyway.

But then my phone rings from under the sofa where it landed. It's a withheld number.

'Hello, Jack Lancaster speaking,' I say, expecting an intrusive sales pitch from Bangalore.

'Hello, "Jack Lancaster speaking". It's Leila Sid-day-bot-tome calling.'

I gulp.

'*Leila* Leila?'

'How many Leila Sid-day-bot-tomes do you know?'

'Er, one. But why are you calling me on a withheld number?'

'Because I tried to call you before and you ignored me on my own number.'

'And why do you think that is?'

'Because you have rubbish mobile reception in the sticks of Zone 7?'

'You horrible London snob. Maybe it's because I'm just a little bit embarrassed after my birthday confession.'

She snorts, not unattractively.

'The Jack Lancaster I know and... well, the Jack Lancaster I know and quite like doesn't get embarrassed by anything. Especially when he's swearing drunkenly at his boss or running naked across polo pitches.'

We laugh awkwardly.

'So,' I ask, after a pause, 'why is "Leila Sid-day-bot-tome calling", er, calling?'

'Well,' she says, suddenly turning serious, 'have you got any idea how boring Buddy is?'

I snort, very unattractively.

'And you've only just realised? I'd rather shave the skin off my bottom and sit in a tub of Tabasco sauce than spend half an hour alone in his company.'

She laughs.

'That's the problem, Jack. You're just so much more fun than anyone else.'

'And Buddy is a little dull in comparison?'

'Everyone is a little dull in comparison.'

'That's romantic,' I say, trying to sound indignant, but secretly leaping inside.

'Oh shuddup, you fat, balding French teacher,' she says. 'You know I've always liked you.'

'You have? You're not just on the rebound?'

'Well, that too.'

'Oh, thanks.'

'But I've sat there playing your birthday speech over and over again in my head,' she says with a hint of a choke in her voice, 'and I can't get rid of the niggly feeling that the only person I'm rebounding from is you.'

And that's the only bit of the conversation I can remember. We spoke for almost an hour. I told her everything. I cultivated my garden. I told her how I'd always liked her; how my dad's death had changed me; about how happy I was doing my new job. I told her about the Val d'Isère ski trip I was taking the boys on next week.

'Jack, I'd like to come, too.'

'Really, are you sure?'

'Yes, it sounds amazing.'

'Well, that would be great. Can you get holiday?'

'I don't care. If Mr Cox won't let me go, I'll take a leaf out of your book for once and tell him where to get off. I haven't had a day's leave since I started.'

'And what about Buddy? What are you going to do about him?'

'He'll live. I dumped him not long after your birthday.'

Went to bed a very happy man.

Sunday 11th December

I woke up this morning and my first thought was, *Yesssssssssssssssssssssssssssss.*

My second thought was, *Shit. I got that fit gap year teacher's number at the rugby match last month and now I won't be able to call her.*

My third thought was, *What am I thinking? Leila loves me (sort of).*

My fourth thought was, *Am I being used by Leila?*

My fifth thought was, *Sod it, I wouldn't mind being used by Leila.*

My last thought was, again, *Yesssssssssssssssssss.* If a couple of ignored phone calls works, then so be it. Perhaps an unwitting tactic of 'playing hard to get' is the way forward for us emasculated menfolk.

But then Leila rang in the afternoon and said that she wasn't coming skiing as my girlfriend. That would be too weird, she thought. She was coming as a single friend who was very fond of me. We'd just see how things went after that.

She's right, I suppose. We can't just meet up in the Departures lounge, kiss, and kick-start a relationship from there. But it doesn't half put me on edge. It's going to be like a week-long trial, with brownie points every time I carry her skis and minus points every time I sing karaoke in the chalet bar.

Not that I'm expectant or anything, but I'm going to do an hour of sit-ups and then pop down to the shops to buy some new boxer shorts. All of mine — even my lucky pair — have holes in them.

Tuesday 13th December

There's a lovely end-of-term atmosphere at Morley Park. A school is the best place to be in the run-up to Christmas. Offices have ghastly office parties where you end up spilling wine over Mrs Cox's shoes and talking to Rupert (bald). We have had carol concerts and school plays, feasts and staff pantomimes (in which Norris Beaumont dressed up as Santa Claus and Amy Barbour and Alice Price played his reindeer).

I've even enjoyed the report-writing. Most of the staff hate it. Bob Lowson habitually pulls a couple of sickies in order to finish them. I did mine in a single evening:

'When Harry is not tying his pencil case to the blinds, he is a pleasure to teach…'

'Last year George came eighteenth out of nineteen in the form. When Mr Lewis wrote, "There is only one way he can go from here", I do not think he expected him to come last…'

'David works well when under constant supervision and cornered like a small rat…'

And, for Bertie Anson and his yummy mummy:

'Bertie is a star pupil. Always generous and hard-working, he is a credit to his parents.'

I'm already looking forward to next term.

Friday 16th December

What do you get if you mix Norris Beaumont, Jack Lancaster, Leila Sidebottom and twenty small boys? Answer: a very good start to a skiing holiday.

'Norris,' I said after finishing my last school report, 'you're sure you don't mind me bringing my friend, too?'

'No, Lanky, of course not. Will be good for you to have some young company.'

'Why are you winking at me, Norris?'

'Oh, it's just my nervous twitch, dear boy. Ignore it. So, what's your friend called?'

'You're still winking. She's called Leila Sidebottom.'

'Oh dear. We can't tell the boys that; they'll murder her. Leila's a lovely name, but it's a little too informal. How about they call her "Miss Leila"?'

So 'Miss Leila' it was, and she became an instant hit with all the boys. Blenkinsop told her that he loved her just as the 'fasten seatbelt' sign went off over the Channel. Bowles started punching him because he loved her first. I patted her on the knee and lay back in my seat, smiling happily.

We've now been here for two days and the skiing has been beautiful. I can't exaggerate how much I love it. It's the perfect sport, the ideal combination of exercise and conversation — utterly pointless, endlessly enchanting.

But it's been so exhausting looking after twenty ankle-biters that we've passed out happily into bed every evening. My stud mission has not been helped by an overbooking in the chalet, which has seen Leila and me sharing a tiny three-bed room with Norris. He's been sweet about it. But it's hardly been conducive to nights of steamy passion in a Jacuzzi in front of an oak fire.

Still, there's a mountain of sexual tension between us, so I haven't given up hope. As she said, let's just see how things go.

Sunday 18th December

'I'll look after one group of kids this afternoon, and we'll dump the other half in ski school. You young things go off and enjoy yourselves.'

'Norris, you're twitching again.'

'Oh shut up, Lanky, and get on with it,' he said, throwing a slushy snowball in our direction.

So Leila and I had a beautiful afternoon skiing by ourselves. It was changeover day for most of the resort so it was very quiet. We played 'James Bond on the slopes', taking it in turns to be the villain and the spy as we chased each other down the mountain, yelling the theme tune at the top of our voices as we collapsed in happy exhaustion at the bottom.

Just before 5pm, we caught the final express chairlift up *La Face* and sat in the café at the summit, watching the pink-topped peaks in the distance, waiting for the slopes below us to clear.

I took a deep swig of my *gluhwein*. If I couldn't manage it here, with every atom of nature's glorious tapestry cheerleading me on, I couldn't manage it anywhere.

'Leila, there's something I've been meaning to say...'

'You don't need to say anything, Jack.'

She leaned in and kissed me on the lips. It was perfection. She cupped her gloved hand around my neck and kissed me deeper. We melted into each other. This was what I was born for. I lost connection with all the tangible nonsense beyond. Fireworks went off in my head. Angels played trumpets on distant sun-kissed peaks. Cherubim strung harps. Blenkinsop...

'Blenkinsop? What the bloody hell are you doing standing there?'

'Thsir, I got lost. I couldn't keep up with Mr Beaumont.'

He paused and grinned. 'Thsir, are you sexing Miss Leila?'

I looked at Leila, her hand still holding mine. She dissolved into charming giggles.

'Yes, young Thomas Blenkinsop. If Mr Lancaster doesn't take me back to the chalet and sex me immediately, he's going to be in a great deal of trouble.'

So I did what Miss Leila wanted. By the time we got ourselves and Blenkinsop back to the chalet, it was dark — it's not easy skiing with an erection when it's minus twenty degrees. Norris had left a note in our room saying that he'd found himself a bed in the hotel opposite.

Leila looked at me and smiled. It was like someone had turned up a wattage dial in her back. She glowed with happiness. I smiled back.

She walked over to my washbag.

'Jack, why is there a bumper pack of condoms in here?'

'Useful in alpine survival situations. They can hold a great deal of water.'

'Of course,' she said with a giggle, plucking one out of the bag. 'So, are you going down?'

'Only if you press the right buttons,' I replied.

We missed supper. By dawn, we had pressed every button known to man and woman.

Wednesday 21st December

'Jack, you haven't primed the kids to say nice things about you to me, have you?'

'No. Why?'

'I just wondered. They're all saying how great you are. Even if they think you teach a pointless subject.'

'Ha, well Val de Sloane Square isn't the best place to try out their learning. I'm probably the best French speaker in the whole resort, and I hardly know my *cul* from my *coude.'*

'Your arse from your elbow?'

'Very good, my little munchkin. You're more than just a pretty face and an utterly divine body.'

'Come here and ravish me again before the bus leaves, my big studdy stallion, and then we'll join the mile-high club on the way home.'

= A V. GOOD HOLIDAY

Friday 23rd December

Normally I hate Christmas. I think it's especially depressing for us twentysomethings — children no longer, but still childless ourselves, keeping up appearances in one big show of 'let's pretend' for the family. At around this time I usually start getting fidgety with angst at the sheer boredom of it all.

In the old days, I could predict exactly what would happen: my mum would cry, my dad would drink too much, turkeys would burn, cousins quarrel, elderly relatives tell the same batty old story five times between lunch and tea. We would make our annual midnight appearance at the village church, where people in suits would sit on one side and recite the old version of the Lord's Prayer, drowning out those in jeans on the other side, reading the official modern version from the script. Everyone would keep warm by singing the carols as quickly as possible, making no allowances for Mrs Tomalin on the organ, whose metronome was still set to British Summer Time.

The local retired GP would read John 1 in his 'I'm reading John 1 voice' and we would all remember to stand and pretend to be thinking about something more profound than lunch. The octogenarian vicar would tell a few charming little anecdotes and tactfully steer well clear of religion for fear of alienating the non-regulars (ninety-nine per cent). Occasionally he would pray for King George and, on realising his mistake, moderate it to Queen George. As we left, Mr Tomalin would call me by my brother's name and tell his wife that it's such a long time since he prayed for King George.

Distant cousins would send the same pack of highlighters that they'd sent every year since we were deemed old enough to want to highlight. The dog would vomit and we would watch *Carols from Kings* and the Queen's speech (just in case she abdicated). In three months' time, we would receive a typed thank-you letter from a godson that read, 'Dear [*name*], Thank you very much for the present. It was very kind of you. I look forward to using it. Lots of love, Blogs.'

'This year,' said Mummy, 'it's going to be different. I'm not going into the church where your father was buried to mumble prayers to a God that I don't believe in. I'm not going to slave over a stove for hours to cook a meal which makes us all feel guilty and fat.'

'You're right, of course. You're right,' soothed Ben, sounding alarmingly grown-up. 'This year Jack and I will treat you. You just put your feet up and relax.'

Sunday 25th December

Christmas Day.

Leila's parents were away for Christmas Day, so I asked Mummy if she could come and spend it with us.

'This is all very whirlwind. And what kind of people are away for Christmas?'

'Leila's dad's in the army. She has to work in London tomorrow. It's all very last-minute. Just be nice to her, please.'

And she was nice to her. Absolutely charmed and bowled over, in fact. Ben and I cooked while Leila fussed over Mummy, not even minding when she called her 'Lucy' by mistake.

'Leila,' she said, after she'd finally got the names sorted, 'you have my permission to dump Jack whenever you want. But if he ever tries to split up with you, there'll be hell to pay.'

Whoever said that blood was thicker than water?

We were just settling down after lunch to watch the Queen's speech when a text came through on my mobile from Rick.

'Lucy is in labour. Chelsea and Westminster. Can u cum?'

I decided to ignore the spelling. I desperately wanted to go. All of us did, but we had drunk too much. There was no way we were safe to get into a car.

'What about me?' said Mummy. 'I've barely touched a drop. I'll take the whole lot of you there.'

So we jumped into her car and hared up an empty M4 towards West London. My mum's face was alive with excitement behind the wheel.

'I haven't been to a birth for ages,' she beamed.

We left the car on a double-yellow line outside the hospital. Brother Ben scribbled a quick note of festive goodwill to any passing traffic warden.

We tore through the corridors of the hospital until we found the maternity ward. Rick was there, anxiously pacing up and down, while Flatmate Fred, Jasper and Katie tried to soothe him.

'Are we too late?' inquired my Mum anxiously.

'I'm not sure, innit,' said Rick, resorting to vernacular in his stress. 'She wouldn't let me in. Told me to get the beeping bloody sodding hell out, in fact.'

My mother laughed.

'I'm not surprised. I said far worse to Jack's father.'

A nurse popped her head round the corner.

'You can come in now.'

'What, all of us?'

She went back to check. I could hear her giving quick descriptions of us all. The head reappeared.

'Yes, all of you.'

We filed into a room where Lucy was cradling a tiny boy with flaming ginger hair. Rick ran over to kiss them both, dropping to his knees beside them. Katie went over, too, and kissed her nephew.

Lucy looked up and smiled.

'I'm going to call him Charles,' she said to my mum.

Thursday 29th December

I managed to persuade Leila to take time off between Christmas and New Year, which we've spent happily in the countryside — walking the dog, watching crap TV, having sex and playing Monopoly (a game she approaches with a vicious competitiveness... a bit like sex).

'You're a horrible little capitalist, aren't you?' I said this afternoon, as she repossessed my remaining houses.

'Yep,' she replied, grinning. 'Which is why we kind of complement each other. I'm the banker with the financial capital. You're the impoverished teacher who makes up my moral deficit.'

'Indeed,' I agreed. 'No one's perfect.'

In fact, nothing is ever perfect, I mused later when Leila fell asleep in front of the fire and I sat there staring at her, thinking that she combined the independent-minded elegance of a cat with the frivolous affection of a puppy.

Enough! I thought in horror. *No more of this slushy sentimentalism.*

I realised that, ever since I've known her, I've put Leila on a pedestal of obsession which had little to do with Leila and everything to do with the construct that I'd created around her.

The reality now is a little more prosaic, but no less exciting. She has her faults; just as we all do. Anything might happen tomorrow. We're twentysomethings. But, for now, I'm happy with today.

Friday 30th December

'What kind of tosspot plans on spending New Year's Eve with his girlfriend, his ex-girlfriend, his ex-girlfriend's one-week old son, his best mate who's married to his ex-girlfriend, his homosexual ex-flatmate and his homosexual ex-flatmate's current flatmate and boyfriend?'

'Ah, Brother Ben. So young and so naive. Enjoy whichever one of your forty-two parties you decide to go to.'

Saturday 31st December

It's ten minutes to midnight at Rick and Lucy's flat. Charles Fielding is happily asleep in his cot.

I go to the loo, take out my mobile and scroll idly through the phone book. This is my world, my external vital organ, my own little paradigm of names and numbers which lives its days next to me, and spends its nights, silenced, recharging its batteries on my bedside table while I recharge mine.

I count 209 names: 170 friends, 23 colleagues or former colleagues, 7 family members and 9 people I have no recollection of at all. There are 80 girls. I've pulled 30, slept with 7 and been out with 3.

'I love you.' I tap out the little phrase into my phone. Scarcely Byronic in its flowing loveliness. Just a '4056830968', then 'options', 'send'.

I send it. I 'send to many'. The whole lot, in fact. All 209 people who have ever touched my life sufficiently to make it into my mobile — including London Transport — have just been told that Jack loves them.

They'll dismiss it as drunken nonsense. Maybe it is. But maybe some things need to be said.

There's a knock on the door.

'What are you doing in there, Jack? You're not attempting a long-distance release, are you?' giggles Leila.

'No, I'm just having a think.'

I turn my phone off and walk out in to the corridor. She's standing there, smiling indulgently.

She leans forward and kisses me on the nose.

'You're a funny one,' she says sweetly, taking my hand.

They're beginning the countdown in the other room. Maybe I shouldn't have sent that text. But sod maybes. From now on, I only regret the things I haven't done. Never the things I do.

Six, five, four, three...

We kiss while Big Ben chimes. We dance, we drink, we laugh. We stay with the others until dawn and then walk back across an empty London to Leila's flat for breakfast. I write up my diary while Leila takes a shower. And then I close down the document for the final time.

'Accept all changes?' asks the computer.

Indeed, I think I do.

If you can predict the next twelve months on the basis of your New Year's Eve, it's going to be a very good year.

Acknowledgments

I would like to thank the following people:

My wonderful family of medics, for encouraging me not to become a doctor
Charlie Campbell, my excellent agent and friend at Ed Victor Ltd.
Ed Victor
Peter Mayer, for his fortunate choice of holiday reading
Everyone at Duckworth, and Caroline and Suzannah, in particular
Nikky Twyman, for her expert copy-editing
Matt, the first person to read every draft when he should have been working
Tom Wynne, my best buddy and the second person to read every draft
Lucan & Max, for playing poker with useful people
Carla & Josh, my favourite couple, for reading early drafts
Phil & Andrew, my tolerant flatmates
Simon, for his expert knowledge of credit derivatives
Dudley, for her one-person fan club in Otley
Frances, Jen, Tom, Sarah, Rick, Tim, Miranda, James, Sam, Janet & Frankie,
    for helpful suggestions
Ant, for suggesting I remove the sex scene (which was awful)
Ellie, for being as good with Photoshop as she is with a lens
All my friends, (and Charlie Anson, in particular), for their support ... and
    occasional inspiration in some of the scenes
The summer of 2002, for persuading me never to work in a bank again